Dedication

To Pam, David, and Leigh

Islanders in Mind and Spirit

and

The Loons.

Contents

PROLOGUE

Long before Europeans arrived to settle the Upper Great Lakes, the land was inhabited by the Odawa, the Ojibwa, and the Potawatomi. Together they were descendants of an ancient people called the Anishnabek, the Good People, or the Real People. The Anishnabek saw the universe as a great circle of life. All people who shared the circle found a special place in the natural plan of the universe. The Anishnabek conceived of life as consisting of three forms—the body, wiyo, the shadow, wdjibbon, and the spirit, wdji-tchog. Upon one's death the spirit migrated to the spirit land in the west or entered the body of another human being. Legend has it that Garden Island in the Beaver Island Archipelago of Lake Michigan was a spiritual center for the Anishnabek peoples. It was a sacred place, a place in the west where the dead were buried and spirits roamed free.

On June 27, 1844 Joseph Smith, the Mormon Apostle, was killed by a mob in Carthage, Illinois. In the ensuing crisis of the young church two men claimed to be his anointed successor, Brigham Young and James Jesse Strang. Strang claimed successorship through evidence of a letter written to him by Smith on June 19th in which he appointed Strang the one who "shall plant a stake of Zion. . [and] . . if evil befall me, thou shalt lead the flock to pleasant pastures."

Strang soon prophesized that he was visited by an angel who instructed him to remove his Saints to "a land amid wide waters . . . covered with large timber, with a deep bay on one side of it." The letter was thought to be a forgery. Brigham Young led his Saints to the deserts of Utah. By 1849 James Jesse Strang led his Saints to an island in the middle of Northern Lake Michigan named by the French voyagers, Isle du Castor, Beaver Island. Strang saw Beaver Island as the promised land, an isolated place to free his flock from the persecution of the Gentiles.

But Beaver Island was also the "promised land" for Irish refugees of the Great Famine of 1845-1850. Some had escaped the specter of starvation, typhus, and cholera to settle on the island and fish its rich surrounding waters. Their first homes had been the squalid tenements of New York and Chicago and the coal fields of Pennsylvania. Many had lived on either of two islands off the coast of County Donegal, Rutland and Arranmore. The virgin island reminded them of home. In letters sent back to Ireland the refugees extolled its beauty. Such stories took root and prompted an exodus from the barren native islands. Thus, two groups of oppressed people, each with strong cultural and religious traditions, made their way to the "promised land" in the wilderness of Lake Michigan.

Strang reported on his first visit to Beaver Island that he was met by Indians in canoes. He reported that they told him, "Thou art carried away in the spirit and brought to this land in the midst of waters in the North country, that the Lord might show thee what he will do hereafter." This divine blessing was not appreciated by the early Irish fishermen and traders who had settled the island. They thought the Mormons were a strange and difficult people, and they set about the task of sabotaging their immigration. Captains of lake boats were persuaded to break Mormon contracts for passage and deliver them to distant ports. The early residents spread rumors that Strang was a maniac who enslaved the ignorant by fraud and witchcraft. In turn Strang claimed that the center of Northern Great Lakes commerce, Mackinac Island, was suffering from moral and economic disease. It was a decadent settlement that lived off government subsidies and the whiskey trade. Churches had become saloons. Indian men submitted to corrupt temptations. Their wives were "intoxicated by compulsion and prostituted by violence". The rights of Indians were placed "below those of the dog" and thousands were murdered by "slow debasing processes of torture," caused by addiction to whiskey. Mackinac's decay could only be stemmed by the influence of the holy Mormon settlement at Beaver Island.

The residents of Mackinac responded to such pronouncements predictably. When Mormons laid over at Mackinac, mobs swept down upon them with threats of violence and recrimination if they continued on to Beaver Island. They spread a gospel of hate.

Such threats transformed Strang, a man of peace, into a man of iron. Knives began to glean in the belts of the pacifist Saints. Strang became a Joshua. In 1850 he announced before the Saints in the Tabernacle that God had commanded him to be King. His coronation date was set for July 8.

As news spread of Strang's coronation, a howl of derision went up from every saloon in the Mackinac area. The Gentiles planned a different kind of celebration. The fisherman and traders would drive his royal highness and his subjects into Lake Michigan on the Fourth of July. Armed fisherman rendezvoused at Peter Mc Kinley's store on Whiskey Point where they began drinking to celebrate the coming triumph. Mormon spies overheard them hatching a scheme to attend a Mormon service in the Tabernacle with concealed weapons and kill the Saints' leaders.

The fishermen at McKinley's saloon were awakened by the explosion of cannons the next morning. Strang threatened annihilation if the Gentiles returned fire. Within a few days the dejected Irish gave up hope of recovering the island. On July 8 Strang crowned himself king.

Few Irish remained on the island after the battle. They fled to the settlements along the mainland to bitterly denounce the Mormons. Nevertheless, the Mormon migration accelerated until almost twenty-five hundred Saints resided on the island. They cleared and cultivated the land, laid out orchards, and began the work of creating a Utopian society. They extended their influence throughout Northern Michigan with their newspapers. The preservation of natural resources was mandated by regulations governing the planting of trees and the stewardship of natural resources. Public parks were planned. Gambling, alcohol and narcotics were prohibited. With their voting strength they elected Strang to the Michigan legislature. But all was not perfect in paradise. Absolutism crept into Strang's leadership of the Saints. Taking the property of Gentiles and consecrating it to God was declared a right. Tithing was mandated. After taking a second wife, Strang conveniently endorsed polygamy. When an attempt to prosecute him for various crimes in Detroit failed, Strang ordered every Gentile to be baptized or leave the island. Several Saints were angered by Strang's brutal enforcement of Mormon law. They began to plan his assassination.

On June 16, 1856 disgruntled Saints shot Strang on the dock of Paradise Bay. The dying King was taken to Voree, Wisconsin.

Just as the expulsion of the Irish had begun on the Fourth of July, so too began the diaspora of the Mormons. A howling drunken mob descended upon the Mormons. They looted houses and stores, burned the Tabernacle, raped Mormon women, and drove the Mormons to the beaches where they loaded them into ships bound for cities across the lakes from Green Bay to Chicago. The diaspora scattered 2,600 men, women, and children to the four corners of the Great Lakes. King Strang died on the morning of July 9th, 1856, after celebrating the last King's Day. The utopian experiment died on Beaver Island with him.

The Irish fisherman and traders returned to their island. They moved into empty Mormon houses where the hearths were still warm and the cows still in the barn. Soon many more would follow from Arranmore.

Only the Chippewa people would remain to watch them arrive in their ships from the east. They watched silently, wondering if these new inhabitants would appreciate the manifest power of the spirit land which they would try to claim as their own.

History of Mormons on Beaver Island largely taken from:
O.W. Riegel's *Crown of Glory* (New Haven: Yale University Press, 1935)

Come away, O human child!
To the waters and the wild
With a faery, hand in hand,
For the world's more full of weeping than you can understand.

W. B. Yeats
The Stolen Child

Come away to the floods and the fields, the flower banks and the forest—out here, in open space and free air, where sea and earth and sky mingle in mutual embraces, like the greeting of youthful lovers! Listen to the pine-songs which are chants of praise, and the wind-warbles which are hymns of hallelujah! Look up yonder on the fire-dance of innumerable rolling worlds, and then answer me before the sun and all the stars—"Is there no God?"

James J. Strang
Gospel Herald

Part I
Journey
to
Na H-oileáin Áran

Aran Islands, County Galway, Ireland

North Carolina
1995

Chapter I
Boxes on Shelves

Sean Connaghan had grown up without his history. He had not cared. Life in the mountains of North Carolina allowed him everything a young boy needed—an eagle's view of mountains, streams, and valleys. From the stone cottage his father had built on a mountain bluff he could watch the seasons creep up and down the ridge line, autumn cascading color down to the valley, spring blossoming gradually up the mountain until stone precipices were awash in pink rhododendron. Such timeless change required no explanation of the past.

He remembered no other life than this one on the mountain. He sensed early that questions to his father about the past only caused a wave of distant remorse to sweep across his father's brow. His mother had died giving him birth, and Sean had grown to associate his father's pain with these questions. In time he came to an unspoken understanding that his birth was the source of his father's loss, a loss that could never be shared.

The loss represented one of the boxes which his father said had to be shelved in the closet. Whenever he began to fret about school or a lost friend or a disappointing sports loss, his father would tell him. "Just make believe that your disappointment can be neatly packaged in a small box. Imagine wrapping it up and tying it tightly with string, and then place it on that top shelf in your closet where you put your model planes. Then forget it. Every so often pull your boxes down and unwrap them. You'll discover that you can't remember what you packed away."

But Sean did remember them. Though he would never tell his father, he remembered every one. Over the years the closet filled with so many boxes that he avoided opening the door. What worked for his father did not work for him.

Sean's father was much older than other fathers. His sixty-nine years assured that Sean received his thoughtful attention. Most fathers were too busy in middle age to do more than shuttle their sons to baseball or scouts, but his father and he enjoyed a quiet comradeship that only the old can cultivate in the young.

What Sean knew of his father he liked. He liked him immensely. He liked his smell when he came into the cottage at night with earth and flowers under his fingernails. He liked him when he slit open a big brown trout to discover the best fly or nymph with which to bait his line. He liked him best on the porch when he gazed out over the mountain and recited the poetry of Yeats to the cadence of intermittent smoke puffs from his pipe. During one of these psalms in the heavy summer night in his seventeenth year he gathered up the courage to ask him about his past.

"Dad, do you remember when you took off the day and we visited Thomas Wolfe's house and the graveyard? You said under your breath, you can never go home. What did you mean?"

"You can never go home again. It was something Wolfe wrote, just a phrase, in a book."

"No, Dad," Sean probed plaintively. "It was the way you said it, over the grave. It was your tone. Your voice quivered."

John Connaghan tapped his pipe characteristically on the porch rail, scarred with soot from previous emptyings. He paused to gather his breath.

"Storm's coming. Can you smell it, Seanaghan? It's raining in the valley."

Sean could barely remember the last time his father had called him Seanaghan. He had stopped soon after Sean had scared an old black bear out of the garbage cans behind the cottage. The bear had skedaddled down the mountain as Sean banged two pots together. By the time his father had repeated the story to everybody in the county, it had gained epic Daniel Boone proportions. It embarrassed Sean when he heard it repeated by the old-timers in Tom Grayson's general store. The term of endearment, Seanaghan, had faded away with that story.

"Dad, the storm will pass. The question won't." Sean surprised himself with his boldness.

"I discovered Wolfe's *Look Homeward Angel* in the library of the big lovely." John never referred to the grand estate of William Vanderbilt as the Biltmore house. It had always been 'the big lovely'. "Read it in one sitting."

John launched into a recitation, a habit to which Sean was accustomed. The habit signaled engagement. He began tentatively, gaining momentum as his memory returned.

"In the haunting eternity of these mountains, rimmed in their enormous cup, he found sprawled out on its hundred hills and hollows a town of four thousand people. There were new lands. His heart lifted." He repeated the last sentence, hanging it out in the warm moist perfumed air for examination. "His heart lifted."

"You know. Seanaghan, when Oliver saw this land, he knew he could carve an angel's head. He knew he could carve the 'soft stone smile of an angel, a smile that was 'touched by the dark miracle of chance which makes new magic in a dusty world.' But he never learned, he never learned to carve that angel because he never knew it. His heart lifted with hope, but the hope didn't help because. . ." He stopped the last phrase in midair, like a smoke ring from his pipe.

"Because he never really found his home," Sean interjected in an attempt to direct the current back to the shore of the first question.

"Maybe. He *thought* he had. He dreamed of carving that angel anyway, he dreamed of creating something eternal. We all do."

"Dad," Sean paused to face his father's gaze, dreading the furrowing of his brow. "Dad, I want to go home. I want you to tell me about you and mother and home."

Lightning flashed in the distance. Thunder resounded in the valley, vibrating their bodies.

"You know what they say, home is where the heart is." He paused and then replied resolutely, "Let's leave it in the heart."

John Connaghan took the answer to Sean's question to his grave early one morning at the 'big lovely' as he cut the first roses of spring for a wedding in the mansion. He was found lying on his back with eyes open to the broad Carolina blue sky, a light red Rubaiyat rose clutched in his right hand. Sean brought the rose home that day and put it in a vase. The rose kept its petals for more than two weeks before they wilted and dropped off the stem.

The funeral had been a small affair with burial on the estate. John had few friends. Sean had grown up like a rare wildflower who had not yet been discovered. His father had not chosen to name him.

Chapter II
Inverary

With his father's passing Sean turned away from everything his father had built. When the attorney met with him in his Asheville office to read his father's Last Will and Testament, the dry legalistic prose conveyed the simple, distant image of a man without a history. Sean wanted more than memories of trout fishing. He escaped to the task of winding up his father's affairs and selling the only real asset of the family- the cottage. As he prepared it for sale, he boxed up the few remaining mementos of their life together. His mourning was punctuated by resentful anger which swept over him in waves that washed up on the shore of his conscience as guilt. He scoured the cottage for pieces of his past, but the search only prompted a realization that his father had lived only in the present. They had owned no camera. When Sean had asked to buy a Kodak Instamatic at Burdick's store, John had refused. "Vain to capture the past. Only kills what you need to sense and remember of the moment," he had said. "Besides, you think a piece of paper will capture the sense of what it's really like to live it, . . . feel it, . . . touch it. Memories are more powerful as you imagine them to have been. Photos change the spirit of it all."

There were no letters from distant friends or relatives. There was no box of little treasures from a past childhood, no metals or ribbons or rings to pass on. "Hell, there was no one to pass them on to," Sean sighed, "I might as well be looking for the bones of Peking man." It was during these moments that Sean despaired. How could a man have given so much to fill his life with joy and yet so little to which he could cling?

It was during one of these searching moments that he found one of his father's favorite books, *The Stolen Child* by William Butler Yeats. His father had loved Yeats. He had shared that love as they rocked together in their porch swing and inhaled the perfumed mist of Spring air. As he leafed through the book, he sensed his father's presence in the low, reverent tones which rolled off his tongue as he would recite the verse. Sean touched the page as if to pull the words from his father's voice. As he turned the page, one verse jumped to meet his gaze. It was circled. In the margin his father's scrawl rose from the page to meet his eyes.

"Rosie, I weep for your immortal spirit."

Sean froze, unable to read on. Was it really father's hand? Yes, there was the unmistakable upward sweep of the tail of the 'y'. Trembling, Sean read a verse that his father had never read to him, in a book that had put him to sleep many nights as a youngster.

Come away, O human child!
To the waters and the wild
With a faery, hand in hand,
For the world's more full of weeping than you can understand.

Sean read it again and again, as if he had discovered the Rosetta Stone. And then he wept uncontrollably. In this small verse Sean had found his only real legacy—a connection to his past and his father's,. . . Rosie. There was another whom he had loved. On this slim reed of verse he found a bewildering solace that would be his father's epitaph and his hope. Sean closed the book and cradled it in his arms. His father had ignored his own admonition. He had spoken of the past.

Sean didn't look back after the catharsis of that night. His despair had galvanized a resolve to find his own place in the world, as his father had done. As he drove down from the mountains on his way to college, he took pleasure in the strength which his father had given him.

John Connaghan had left his son a modest legacy with the wish that he pursue a degree in liberal arts at Wake Forest University in Winston-Salem. John had never gone to college, but he had been seduced by the beauty of Wake Forest on his occasional visits to study the Reynolda House gardens near campus. The gardener, Charlie Allen, was one of his father's few friends. Charlie's rose garden was, without question, one of the finest and most diverse collections west of Orton Plantation and East of Biltmore. On one visit Sean remembered staying in the gardener's cottage and dressing in a new white starched shirt to attend a Yeats poetry reading by John Montague, a well known Irish poet. It was one of those rare moments together. The reading was held in the great living room and presaged by the tickling of wine glasses to the strains of Mozart. His father had embarrassed him by mumbling verbatim each verse the poet read and clapping loudly after each reading. Still, it was a moment when all seemed right with the world. So it was natural that Wake Forest and the gardens would become his new home.

Old Charlie met him in the greenhouse upon his arrival. He looked older than Sean had remembered. He rushed to embrace him with a sprightly stride.

Charlie gazed at Sean in quiet contemplation of the young boy now grown tall and strong. Yes, he had John's sinewy build and his unmistakable broad shoulders. Running across mountains had made him fit and tanned. His thick, brown hair swept back from a wide, open face with large deep set brown eyes flanking a strong, equaline nose. He looked like a Greek relief of the young Achilles, stretching his bow. Yet, sorrow was etched in his face. He seemed a paradox – attractive, athletic, confident, but at the same, reticent, awkward. His face invited trust but was not trusting. His eyes took in everything, but revealed little. He walked with purpose, but gently. Charlie saw a young wounded lion who paced back and forth in his cage, searching for prey that was not to be found.

"Seanaghan, my boy," he bellowed, "Lord be praised, you look the spitting image of your father, bless his departed soul." He clutched him with a bear hug that Sean welcomed after the weeks of lonely introspection. "So are you ready for the halls of ivy, lad?"

"I guess so. I mean it's what father wished for me," Sean replied tentatively.

"More than you know, more than you know," Charlie replied. "Well, now. Let's retire to the cottage. I've got some tea brewing, and we can catch up".

They strolled through the gardens to the cottage where Charlie had prepared a delectable desert tray of scones, strawberries, and cream. Settling into an overstuffed chair, Charlie began.

"Well, young man, your father would have been proud to see you this fine day of your beginning college. You know he wanted it more than anything, not having had it himself. Ironic, isn't it? I've spent my life here next to the University and never really strayed much from this garden, and your father up there alone in that big garden in the mountains without the company of these bright people who stroll through every day. Sad. But now you're living it for him, Sean. "

"I'll live it for myself. Mr. Allen. It's not for him I'm here."

"So you will, lad. So you will. But you'll need some help and God knows I owe it to your father," Charlie replied as he refilled his teacup. "Sean, . . . I know you don't have the means to make it through four years here, and I'd like some company in my declining years. I'd consider it an honor for you to stay with me. Of course, you can think about it tonight. Your orientation doesn't begin for a few days."

Sean was overwhelmed with the offer. Even with careful husbanding of his modest legacy, he knew that there wouldn't be enough for room and board. Yet he hesitated more out of deference to Charlie's kindness than his own need.

"I don't know Mr. Allen, it's not that I don't want too, but . . . "

"Excellent then, it's done. We're mates. Just like your father and me were in the old days. Good show!"

Sean abruptly raised himself from the chair in astonishment. "Did you say mates? You mean you lived together. When? How? I mean, I didn't know you knew each other outside of gardening."

"He didn't tell you. Yes, of course . . . ," Charlie sighed contemplatively. "John never did confide much. Man of the moment, he was. Guess, I thought 'ole Charlie would be worth more than an honorable mention to his son. Well, it doesn't matter. You're here and that's all that counts."

"No, Charlie, I mean Mr. Allen, it does count." Sean added impulsively. "It counts a great deal. It's not just you who needs an honorable mention, its everyone that father knew from his past and shut away from me in that cottage. I can't reclaim my father, but I must know more about myself. Charlie, I'm desperate to know. I must be the only kid in the world who doesn't know for sure whether he came from a test tube or a womb. Do you know what it's like contriving a past to suit your teachers and friends? Why, I've said that I've descended from royalty, Indians, major league baseball players, and country music singers at one or another time in my life, and I'm tired of . . . "

Charlie raised his hands, waving them over each other. "Hold on, lad! Before you get your hopes tethered to this old mulch maker, I must tell you that I can't tell you all that much."

"What can you tell me?"

"Well, first, I can tell you that any past isn't worth knowing if it stops you from being yourself. And for many a man, his past is a heavy ball and chain that he drags through life because he doesn't have the tools or sense to cut it off." Charlie paused and looked deep into Sean's eyes. They were tired and sunken for a young man. He reached for his pipe, took a kitchen match and struck it on the side of the stone fireplace. "I guess you'll hear a lot of pontificating and moralizing if you stay here, and you might as well get used to it. But it'll not bring the cows home. I'll tell you all I know, and it's not much to chew. But I can see they'll be no rest until then."

Charlie began slowly at first, as if he were struggling to arrange a whole attic full of photos and letters in dusty disarray from years of neglect. His story emerged in bits and pieces. He had been a proud member of the Kings own 3rd Royal Fusiliers after a troubled childhood in Bermonsey where he had helped his father run a furniture antique shop. When the war erupted, he was detached to a Special Forces training unit that gathered together elite units from throughout Great Britain and Canada to train in Inverary, Scotland for secret operations in occupied France. It was there that he had met John Connaghan, a soldier of the Irish Guard. Charlie characterized John as one trying, like Charlie, to forget a troubled past. He offered that many young men found themselves in the same position. It was a time when the moment made one forget the past, especially if the past offered little.

"When your country is in a war for its very survival, only the future makes a difference. And if you know you might make that difference, you dedicate your life to it. You laugh harder. You work harder, and you play harder."

They had both loved Inverary. The great fjords of Scotland, and the mist rising from the surrounding mountains comforted them. It was a balm to their troubled spirits, and they avoided talking about the homefront. London seemed a world away, and they were out of the reach of German bombers. Their training was grueling, but the time came when they were told that they were to be the first unit to establish a beachhead on French soil. It was only later that a name was given to the place, Dieppe. Dieppe had been an abortive attempt, a horrendous ill-conceived plan executed out of an impatience on the part of Whitehall to strike back at the Germans and rally the homefront.

Charlie pulled himself slowly from his chair at this point in the story and stepped toward the fireplace. He continued as he stared at the stone. His voice cracked. "Had it not been for John, I'd be floating belly up in the Channel, Sean." Charlie tapped his pipe on the hearth and turned. His eyes were red and his cheeks tear soaked. "He . . . he rescued me from that black, oily sea and pulled me to shore. That's what your father was . . . nothing less than a hero. And I wasn't the only one who was pulled onto the shore that fateful night. A blessed angel he was to all of us. When our unit reassembled at Inverary, your father was awarded the St. George's Cross for bravery under fire in a ceremony led by Lord Anges Campbell, the Duke of Argyll. My injury separated us for the remainder of the war until I received a letter from John in Asheville. He asked me to come to work at Biltmore for him. Apparently, after the war the Duke had secured a position for him through one of his visits to Grandfather Mountain to host the highland games."

Charlie's voice rose now in a contented crescendo. "Soon after my arrival, this position came open, and here I am. And here you are, and that's it in a nutshell. Very simple. I owe your father my life and my work, and now I am grateful to owe you, his son, a fine bed and goose down comforter for the night in the most peaceful place to sleep on God's green planet. So what do you say, lad, its been a long day and an even longer story?"

Sean gazed into Charlie's clear blue eyes. He felt a kinship with his father through this old man. The story had given him a glimpse of his father that he had somehow known. A hero. St. George's Cross. If only he had known enough to tell all those school children who had taunted him so long ago. Why hadn't his father told him? It would have been so easy. Still, Sean's hunger would not allow a suggestion of sleep.

"There is more—isn't there, Charlie? What about my mother? Surely you must have known her. Surely, he must have told you about his love for her." Sean pressed for more.

"That's just it, Sean, he didn't tell me about where he grew up, or his family, or his love. Nor did I. It was a pain, an anguish that neither of us wanted to explore in that wonderful, dreadful time. Others took comfort in this sharing, but it was our capacity to forget that drew us to one another. I don't expect you to understand it. It was just our bond, our unspoken bond. I don't know about your mother, and I suspect that if I did, I never would have been pulled out of that black channel on that hideous night. Believe me, I so want to tell you more, but more I cannot. I'm sorry."

And with this last sentence Sean was struck by a certain finality to his journey from the mountains. It had been a long day. He had found his father and lost his mother again. He had gained a friend. Tomorrow he would begin another search. Yeat's verse rolled over and over in his mind as he pulled the down comforter over his chest.

Come away, O human child!
To the waters and the wild
With a faery, hand in hand,
For the world's more full of weeping than you can understand.

Chapter III
An Irish Press

Sean Connaghan approached his four years of college like a seasoned surfer, waiting patiently for the right wave, paddling quickly to catch it in the trough, and then riding it hard to shore until he exhausted its momentum. College offered an endless horizon of waves to experience, and Sean reveled in the exhilaration of mastering each new and different one. He also took pride in eschewing the party scene on weekends for the tranquillity of the library or an evening of readings at the Reynolda House. Charlie's teapot and willing conversation provided him with all he needed in social commerce. Retiring to the cottage at the end of the day, through the cool balmy air past the waterfall, renewed his spirit. Sean did choose to play club rugby, but only because it exhausted a seething anger that frequently overtook him. It also served to dissuade classmates from assuming that he was too much the eccentric nerd. Yet, he took arrogant pride in dismissing the bid he received from the only fraternity who expressed an interest in him. He often thought they had identified the wrong person.

In short, Sean played the part of the lonely surfer on the crest of the intellectual wave, and he liked it. Social relationships represented a complication that could not be mastered without superficial drinking or exposing himself as a vulnerable person. He had no interest in either. He hid himself behind outstanding grades and a concealed passion for learning. Yet, as he progressed in his studies, it became harder and harder to isolate his penchant for distant objectivity from his teachers. The better ones saw through his facade for what it was: a tortured, unrelenting chase to find himself.

Although Sean had chosen history as his major, he carefully stewarded his elective credits to take as many literature courses as possible. History was a way of understanding man's progress and folly. Literature revealed the soul. He gravitated toward Swift and Pope for insight, Emerson for reason, Thoreau for independence, Joyce for outrageous rebellion, and Frost for reflection. But each work offered only a glimpse of his longing for wholeness—a complete answer to what he perceived was a massive joke that God had played upon man. Shakespeare came closest to uncovering the riddle. Twain's wit put it into perspective. Tolstoy and Dostoevsky captured its unpredictable pathos. Dante and Goethe revealed its tortured soul. Still, it was as if each writer had been given only the gift to see the horizon from one earthbound perspective. They were caught in space, time and place, despite their valiant attempts to slip the bondage of viewpoint. Critical theory and commentary only fueled his frustration to find conclusions. He learned to disdain the endless critiques of symbolism, style, and motive, and syntax in an effort to construct, deconstruct, and reconstruct the meaning of *Billy Budd* or *Heart of Darkness* or *The Stranger.* Although he learned to master the art of analysis, he was left with the sense that he was participating in an author's gang rape. Whatever revealed truth an author had to offer could not withstand the modern scrutiny of the critical mind. So, he learned to avoid the trendy currents of campus thought.

Sean made the journey of doubt, questioning, and self examination which is called higher education—from the ecology of the stream to the metaphysics of Aristotle, from organic chemistry to Tocqueville, Freud to Sartre, St. Paul to Tilleck, Newton to Watson and Crick, . . . Da Vinci, Macheavelli, Jung, Einstein, DuBois, Ghandi, and Aristophenes. He added each book to the library of his room as a trophy of new thought. And with each addition, he longed for more. Sean Connaghan was becoming the personified fear of ideology and prejudice and inhumanity, the enlightened man. Ironically, he was also becoming intolerant, narrow and introverted. The distance he kept from his peers assured a splendid isolation. It helped his studies but drove him away from the risks of love and the loss of friendship. He was in danger of slipping over the edge of knowledge and into the abyss of intellectualism. He did not yet appreciate the chiriosuro of this educational paradox which eludes the conscious mind and can only be understood in the shadow of actual human experience.

Sean's emotionally distant relationship with his elderly father allowed him to perform well for his teachers, who quickly noticed his keen eye for critical insight and his persistent curiosity. He always joined the hunt in class and followed the teacher through each bramble bush of inquiry. It was not until his senior year that he encountered a professor who was more interested in him than the hunt.

Sean had waited anxiously to enroll in Professor Edwin Graves senior seminar in Irish Writers. It was to be the desert of the college supper, a completion of the circle that he had begun on that late summer day in the garden that became his home. It turned out to be considerably more.

Graves held his seminar near his office in the chapel steeple. Word around campus had it that he had been exiled there when a grievance by a trustee's daughter for sexual assault failed to produce a verifiable finding. Exasperated with a tenured professor who cast a cloud over the otherwise pristine campus moral landscape, the president had taken away his office, deprived him of the close company of his colleagues, and limited his course offerings to a few restricted seminars. Graves was to live out his days like some lonely hunchback. Of course, such rumors only enhanced his image among students. Faculty peers even relished the idea of being removed to the real ivory tower. One disgruntled colleague had lodged a discrimination claim against the college for disparate and preferential treatment in the assignment of course loads, using Graves as an example of how academic crime pays. The old president had miscalculated. After the winds of campus gossip subsided, Graves had become one of the most popular figures on campus, sublimely nested in a lofty perch above the petty din of campus politics.

Graves' classes were held in a large storage room so near the carillon that the room vibrated when the bells rang. The room was bare and sparsely furnished, unlike every other nook of the movie-set campus. One long table with twelve leather chairs, castoffs from a defrocked fraternity, were scattered about the room. Exposed beams and two-by-fours had not been walled over, so the room conveyed the impression of an old attic garage where discarded baby carriages and bicycles might be tossed. Various boxes of books and black instrument cases of assorted sizes were stacked in each corner. A portable blackboard, scratched with age, listed on one rickety leg without a wheel.

Almost forty years after construction the room still smelled sweet with sawdust produced the previous year. Above, the carillon chamber had been renovated to accommodate the newly donated upper register bells, cast in France with the donors' names inscribed ornately on each. The class ended at 5:00 p.m. when the chimes began. The bell schedule guaranteed a quick departure for the students. It was into this cloistered perch that Sean and his classmates arrived to await the entry of the elusive "hunchback of Wait Chapel."

What they saw step gingerly into the room was a middle-aged balding bachelor with a starched white shirt rolled up to his elbow, baggy brown trousers, and a Swiss polka-dot tie. He was hardly the rake of ravishment so popular in campus lore. But from the moment he spoke in his low dulcet tones, students felt a rush of warmth, a rapture that was inexplicably Irish. Everyone felt it, that is, but Sean Connaghan, who distrusted such impressions.

Graves classes followed no orthodox approach discernible by the students. Each day he simply scribbled the assignment for the next day on the rickety blackboard. He began each class with a reading, a short excerpt from the day's assignment. One day it might be Joyce, another Yeats. There was no pattern, except one perhaps divined by the teacher. It frustrated some, intrigued others, but by in large prompted much discussion of the possible connections offered by a seemingly chaotic approach to study.

It was the second week of class. Graves had just completed reading a selection from *Portrait of an Artist as a Young Man*, when he turned to Sean.

"Connaghan, tell me," he queried, "a young man is sitting in a boat in the Irish Sea on a foggy night. He is poor, lonely, drunk, and Irish. He thinks he sees a lighthouse in the distance. What is the purpose of the lighthouse to this young man.?"

"I guess I'd need to know why he was there in the first place, Dr. Graves," Sean replied cautiously. He resented being used as a learning foil.

"Why must we know more, Connaghan? A lighthouse seems uncomplicated enough. Why not accept it for what it is?"

"Because you asked what the purpose of the lighthouse was through the eyes of the young man, his perception?" Sean replied adroitly, proud of his response.

"So what does he see, from his perspective?" Graves persisted.

"That depends on who he is, and where he's going?"

"Which gets us back to your first response. Mr. Connaghan, it seems that our Irishman's boat is traveling in a circle." The class laughed. Sean stiffened his resolve. If this was a game, he would win it.

"Let's get our boat moving. What perspectives might one have on the purpose of the lighthouse, considering where our man might be?"

"But where he might be depends on who he is . . . if he is an existentialist, atheist, communist, capitalist, taoist, or whatever. The response depends on the man. The purpose of the lighthouse is unknown because the man is unknown."

"Very well, Mr. Connaghan, then our young man must drift until he finds his purpose."

"Yes, if his purpose is to die from grief as a poor, lonely spirit, the lighthouse has no purpose. It is merely one object of many on the horizon. But if he wants to come out of the fog and safely return home, then it is a beacon. It just all depends on your perspective."

The pace of the interchange quickened. Sean felt that he was onto the professor's scent.

"So, our young man can see the lighthouse as a beacon to guide or as an object of passing regard."

"Yes, it just depends."

"What if he thinks that the purpose of the lighthouse is to stop the fog from coming in or to dissipate the fog when the beacon hits it—like a giant vacuum cleaner sucking up dirt in its way."

"Then I would think the young man had way too much to drink." Sean dismissed the hypothesis curtly. Several students chuckled.

"But, you just told me that it depended on the young man's perspective. Does not that perspective include the whimsical, the outrageous, or the imaginative, or is it limited always to the subjective, relative situation of the actor in the situation- in this case our young man on the boat?"

"I guess I would have to concede that in order to be consistent."

"You would indeed, if consistency of theory were important to our young man. But it is unimportant. Even those who embrace all perspectives, frequently forget that which is hidden by logic. That which is psychological, . . . beyond logic. The artist, especially the Irish artist, drawing from his or her Celtic roots, can experience the lighthouse as a means of guidance which engulfs the fog, clarifying his view of reality through the supernatural rather than the logical. Thus, what you may perceive as Joyce's madness may be a completely new and different dimension of reality which is slightly beyond our reach. Illusion is only illusion because we cannot find the right perspective, or there are too many holes to plug without the aid of science, and so we dismiss imagining another reality." Graves paused and gazed out the window. "The view of our young man may not encompass his perspective but a different reality of the lighthouse itself. It is only in this way that you will begin to understand that Joyce as artist, or any artist, breaks new ground by inviting your spirit to step barefoot into a new dimension, a new reality apart from rhetoric or orthodox ways of thinking. Remember the lighthouse, Mr. Connaghan, you may need it to dispel the fog that you have just experienced. Now, class, can you provide any examples of Joyce's unorthodox approach to reality which is informed by his Irish roots?"

Sean was exasperated by the class. New dimension. Unorthodox reality. Joyce was a product of his times. All authors were. History defined their reality. The idea that they could push the envelop of time, place, and space to create a new reality apart from the culture in which they were raised was sheer nonsense. It was this thought that hardened his resolve to prove Graves out to be an academic charlatan. The battle was joined, and in each class he seized every opportunity to challenge Graves' anti-intellectual view of the Celtic artist. It became a mission. We are trapped by our culture. Reality is a function of every experience in morals, events, and relationships which define the culture. Catholicism, oppression, poverty, the land, the sea, climate, all conspire to make a person's thought inextricably bound to his or her way of thinking reality. Sean had the proof in reams of commentary, and he would prove it. And so the seminar room became a war zone of repartee which some in the class resented. *Connaghan vs. Graves*, it was renamed by some. Or, *The Revenge of Connaghan*. Others, more sympathetic to Graves' position, called it simply *Connaghan's Wake*.

Graves, on the other hand, treated the ongoing debate with deference, even kindness, as he queried Sean with passage after passage to explain. He never lost his patience but instead seemed to enjoy every parry. Yet, each attempt at explanation, no matter how insightfully reasoned, rarely provided Sean with the feeling that he had won. Graves' command of the literature seemed too great. There was always a paradox or contradiction to be exploited, another unanswered question. Graves even conceded much to Sean but still seemed to prevail in mesmerizing the class with his transcendental view of the Irish artist. To Sean, Graves seemed the campus Pied Piper instead of the "hunchback of Wait Chapel." By the end of the semester, Sean was exhausted and angry. He could not fight something so soft as Graves' art. It stood apart from everything he had learned about the pursuit of knowledge.

But he didn't give up. In fact the class just convinced him that the study and teaching of history was to be his life's work. He had accepted a Danforth fellowship in graduate work at Yale. In history, he thought, there was at least fact, patterns, trends, and inferences to support a view of cultural cause and effect. Literature was, as he suspected, just desert, not the main intellectual course of the meal.

By the time final exams rolled around he had resolved that the class had been a mistake. He wrote his exam true to form, not giving an inch to Grave's approach. Yet, when he handed in his bluebook, he felt a tinge of sadness at departing the chapel attic. The feeling quickly dissipated when Graves asked him to join him for tea in his office.

"Oh, shit," Sean thought to himself, "A final, last ditch attempt at redemption from my errant ways."

As Graves poured the tea, his guard seemed to drop. "Sean," he said, "You have served a valuable purpose in my class, and I am grateful. You stimulated learning for all of us, and that is the greatest gift a teacher can receive from his students. For whatever motive you may have challenged my words and thought, I believe you have learned a great deal from this experience. It can only begin to make you a fine teacher." With these words he reached across the table with an extended hand.

Sean was dumb struck. "Well, I...I enjoyed it too," Sean replied, nervously, shaking his hand.

"Sean, there are few students who I trust strongly enough to ask to join me in a scholarly pursuit, but I would like you to consider traveling with me as my assistant to Ireland this summer. Our library has just purchased the complete works of one of the few indigenous Irish presses, the Dolman Press. I have been selected to examine and catalogue the collection before arranging for its transportation home. The collection has not been surveyed, and some manuscripts have never been published. You never know what we may find, . . . maybe, . . . the lost link to the new dimension, eh?" Graves paused and looked directly at Sean. "Sean, I took the liberty of chatting with Mr. Allen and learning a little about you. Hope you don't think it was presumptuous, but I think you might find this trip rewarding in many ways. Well, I hope you'll give it careful thought. And if you decide to come along, well . . . , maybe we can see that lighthouse. It's off the coast of County Clare, and the natives say it's been preventing the fog from coming in for years."

The bells began their daily chatter, ringing out the Alma Mater as Sean descended the stairway from Graves' perch. The words of the last refrain echoed in his ear, "Thine is a noble place, Mother so dear." As he walked alone down the path to the gardens and across the bridge to the waterfall, his heart welled up in his throat. The University already seemed so far away. He was going home. Home to Ireland, his father's home.

Ireland
2000

Chapter IV
Strumpet City

The high voice of Loreena McKenitt on the radio muffled the road noise as the taxi traveled down the shadowed expanse of O'Connell Street. Through the rain spattered window Sean caught glimpses of statues of famous Irish statesmen and bards. Yeats must be among them, he thought. Dublin. City of Yeats. If only his father could be with him. A poignant sadness momentarily overcame him. The statues streamed past him in the Irish mist, haloed by the lights of oncoming cars. The words of Yeats "September 1913" streamed into his mind and mixed strangely with the McKenitt strains.

Yet they were of a different kind,
The names that stilled your childish play,
They have gone about the world like wind,
But little time had they to pray
For whom the hangman's rope was spun,
And what, God help us, could they save?
Romantic Ireland's dead and gone,
It's with O'Leary in the grave.

The taxi stopped abruptly at the curb. The driver jerked the meter box arm back into place.

"Mulligan's of Poolbeg Street," he muttered, turning toward the back seat, "Say, wake up lad, we're here."

Sean sat upright to pay the driver, then stumbled onto the rain soaked street with his duffel bag in tow. "Mulligan's," he thought as plunged through the door, "just like Graves to choose an Irish pub for their rendezvous. Pubs, that noisy center of two major Irish passions, conversation and drink, places where one could chase the bygone Dublin ghosts that Graves loved so well."

Sean tossed his dufflebag next to the end of the bar and ordered a Guinness. As the stout pint was plopped on a cardboard coaster, a voice bellowed behind him.

"So you really think Romantic Ireland's dead and gone Seanaghan! Good God, man, its all around you!"

Sean turned with a start to see Graves, ruddy-cheeked, hair tousled, bedecked in baggy brown tweeds and wobbling from side to side. At least he looked like Graves. But this Graves was yelling like a drunken dock worker.

"How did you know, Dr. Graves, that I was just thinking about . . . "

"You're an open book, Connaghan, it's in your blood whether you believe it or not!" His voice grew louder as he swayed toward the bar, "Yeats' ghost has already grabbed you, and he'll hold on like a banshee delivering the dead to hell. Yeah, like a banshee from Hades. Just like me, you haven't got a chance now. Erin go bragh!" Graves laughed in a high whistling scream. "Com'on over to my table, we've got a lot to catch up on, like a thousand years. Holy Jesus, like ten thousand years!"

Graves draped his arm over Sean's shoulder as he stumbled over to a booth in the corner and sat down. Empty pints littered the table.

"Dr. Graves, I'm kind of tired from the trip. Couldn't we just talk tomorrow? All I need now is a good bed."

"Bed! Jesus, you can't squander your first night in Dublin. Unless you're talking of Molly Bloom's bed, eh? Yeah, there's a plenty of Mollys here. No?" Graves' voice lowered as he moved his face into Sean's and whispered. "This town is best savored through the bottom of a pint. Drink up, Seanaghan. The night is yet a pup!"

A sense of miscalculation and disappointment swept over Sean. If the summer was to be spent in pubs with a bleary eyed professor, it held little promise. He should have trusted his original instincts about Graves. The campus gossip had been confirmed. He was just a bullshitter. He tentatively toyed with catching the next plane out tomorrow.

"So you're the latest American sacrifice to the mighty Graves." A slim young woman with close cut black hair slipped onto the bench next to Graves, who had fallen into a stupor against the back of the booth. "Name's Lily, Lily Garrett. You must be Sean. Surprised, huh?

They all are. Every summer he brings a new one here. Maybe you'll stay. Some don't, you know. Guess I can't blame them, but they're the losers. You a loser, Sean?"

"I feel like one. I could have had a job in New York this summer that would have paid my expenses for the year. Now I'm beginning to wonder if I'll be chasing banshees across the Irish moors with a demented asshole."

"He's not demented, Sean. Possessed maybe, but not demented. He's just seen too much of life here."

"Yeah, from the back of a pub!" Sean's voice rose in frustration. "I'm beginning to doubt if there is really a Dolman Press, or if it is just a figment of the "DTs!"

"Don't worry about that. That's one thing he's possessed by, that and his students. You'll see." Lily gazed intently into his eyes. "Just be patient."

"So how did you get hooked up with the 'great Graves'," Sean intoned satirically. "You one of his Molly Blooms?"

"Piss on you, you little shit!" Lily's eyes flashed. "I don't fuck him, if that's what you mean."

"Sorry, sorry!" Sean held his hands up. "It's been a long day, and all I really want is a bed to crash in. Let's start over. How did you meet this character?"

"Trinity. I'm a graduate student. He taught there three summers ago. Yes, a Joyce seminar, as you might have guessed. Hell, he was Joyce in that seminar—irreverent, wild, sensuous, and crazy with wordsmithing. How could you not love a teacher who loved his subject like a new born baby."

"I could, believe me, I could. Look, the guy's a charlatan."

"Maybe. But that's the magical part of him. You have to be a charlatan to understand the Irish. In fact, it's indispensable. You've got to be half mad to understand the madness of being too close to God."

"God? Graves only god is some plot of Celtic earth that he can worship."

"That's part of it, but it's not all. He knows more than you think. You just have to open yourself up to him. Besides he's onto something in his Dolman papers. Stick around. You'll see. It will take you places you've never been."

"Pretense. That's what he's up to. Pretense! If I'm going to stay, I'll need more evidence than that, Lily."

"You'll get it, Sean. It's an Irish thing, no need for evidence. You'll just have to experience it. Look, it's clearing outside. Let's get this son of Joyce home, and we'll talk about it tomorrow. I'll be working with you. Besides, you'll enjoy the sunset over Dublin. Best in the world. Joyce called it the 'strumpet city in the sunset, dear, dirty Dublin.' Com'on. I'll help with your luggage."

The two students propped up the mumbling, slumping Graves, draped his arms around their shoulders, and stumbled into the rosy colors of a Dublin sunset. Brilliant hues of color reflected off brightly painted Georgian doors as they walked a few blocks to a guest house. Sean was too deep in thought to enjoy the view. Maybe this journey would take him somewhere he had never gone before. He was too tired and disappointed to think of it now.

Chapter V
Tara Hill

The work near the Long Room of the Trinity College library wore on Sean. His boredom was relieved only when Lily would appear periodically to deliver an ever growing stack of boxes filled with manuscripts, letters, and assorted withering and aged newspaper clippings. The routine of sorting and cataloguing on his Macintosh computer began to breed a simmering resentment. Even the clicking of the keyboard seemed like Chinese water torture.

Graves rarely appeared, and when he did, the odor of stale scotch and beer permeated the room. He would briefly inspect the computer printouts of the index, mutter a few instructions and disappear. He did not even harass him in his characteristic thought provoking manner. The summer would end, Sean thought, as mistakenly as it began. He resolved to confront Graves. Graves had brought him to this bibliographic hell hole, and he expected more from the experience. What was so significant in this work, anyway? What did Graves hope that his precious archive would reveal?

Sean lifted the next sheaf of letters onto his table. Habitually, he began typing the entry. Letter from Eliza Cropper to James Cropper, dated 1826. Sean stopped. 1826? Eliza Cropper? Must be misplaced, Sean thought. No author by that name in the catalogue. Besides, the date was much too early for the Press. He leaned back in his chair and began reading.

My loving Father,
You must not worry about me. The work I am about comes from our gentle Lord who protects us with His almighty grace. Although I cannot reveal my location, rest assured that I am safe in His loving arms.
The soldiers have not yet discovered our location, and we have been able to protect several hundred from their slaughter. If only there had been time to save more. No one would believe that such evil deeds

could be accomplished by a civilized people. Great care has been given to remove and bury the dead at sea and blame it on the plague, but some day we shall reveal this horror as the insidious crime it is.
I await news that you will dispatch ships soon to relieve us. The messenger of this letter will carry your reply to me. I shall await it with great anticipation.

I remain your adoring daughter,
Eliza Cropper

The ornate script was smudged by ink and brown with age. He typed it on the screen and read it again. Slaughter. Rescue by ship. Now here was an interesting little historic vignette worthy of investigation. It would be an interesting interlude from the days boredom. He left the screen and strolled into the Long Room to consult the Dictionary of National Biography. Sean's thoughts raced faster than his eyes across the entry.

James Cropper, devout Quaker, devotee of Adam Smith, wealthy Liverpool merchant who joined forces with London abolitionists to advocate market solutions to the problem of slavery in the West Indies. Financed hundreds of provincial antislavery societies. Became the unofficial philosopher and strategist for the Anti-Slavery Society. Advanced plan to eliminate Irish poverty and West Indian Slavery. Textile mills would be built on Ireland's rivers to process unlimited supplies of cotton from the West Indies which would eventually destroy West Indian slavery by flooding the market with cheaper textiles from Ireland. Monopoly and special privilege would thus die at the invisible hand of a enlightened political economy.

Jesus, Sean thought as he returned to his research nook, this guy was a Quaker Karl Marx. No, he was one better. He was a Quaker Adam Smith intent upon breaking the backbone of slavery with shrewd economic tactics, thrusting the sword of capitalism deep into the back of the power elite. As he closed the door, he observed Lily at the screen, one hand clutching the letter, another pressing the delete key.

"Hey, what are you doing?" Sean's voice pierced the silence.

"Nothing. It's a worthless piece. We find these scraps occasionally. Incidental garbage. So, how's it going? Ready for a tea break?" Lily stuffed the letter in her jeans pocket.

"If it's so incidental, why are you keeping it, Lily?" Sean moved closer.

"Oh, Graves likes to keep a record of this stuff himself. Kind of a hobby. Wants to know what the authors kept, you know. Just a hobby."

"Won't fly, Lily. I've been keying worthless junk for days, from laundry slips to grocery notes. This piece is no different. All part of the collection. It is my solemn duty to input it." Sean intoned this last phrase in mocking ridicule. "So indulge me, Lily. You're treading on my professional dignity as an archival artist." He reached for the letter.

"Sorry, champ, it's for Graves," Lily replied as she began a purposeful stride toward the door.

Sean grabbed Lily's arm and swung her around into a neck lock. He reached into her tight jeans to retrieve the crumpled paper. It slipped out in several pieces as Lily sunk her teeth into his hand.

"Owww . . . you bitch!" Sean screeched as they both dove for the floor in a panicked struggle for the pieces.

"Sexual harassment! Beast! Let me have it, or I'll ruin you," Lily screamed.

Sean rolled over, laughing uncontrollably with two shredded pieces in his hand. "Sexual harassment? Sexual harassment?," he repeated derisively, "What happened to 'Rape'? My, aren't we politically correct! And you a student of Joyce. Can't you do better than that, Lily? Besides, who got bit here. At least you could pay for the rabies shot."

Both had struggled to their feet and were circling each other, exchanging epithets.

"Okay. You win! What do you want for your two pieces?" Lily waved her piece of the letter as she backed toward the door.

"Well . . . ," Sean mused playfully, "Since you brought up the subject, I guess I'd exchange my piece for your piece."

"Son of a bitch, you will!" Lily whispered under her breath.

"What did you say?" Sean inquired in a controlling voice.

"I said . . . ," Lily paused. "I said . . . meet me at Tara Hill tonight at ten o'clock. We'll talk about it then. I'll send a taxi. 'Till then, go . . . go play with yourself, you fool!"

The slamming of the door broke the interminable rustling of books and papers in the Long Room. Sean imagined Lily striding through the great room, ruffled hair on end, as readers lifted their eyes from their books in disgust. The pace of summer life had picked up. How could James and Eliza Cropper produce such an emotional outburst? Sean smiled. Dull, dry, moribund Adam Smith was at the root of a charge of sexual harassment. Yes, things were picking up indeed.

The taxi drove out of the Dublin suburbs in a dense fog drifting off the bay through Blanchards Town on the road to Boyne. Occasionally, the road would straighten and the last glow of the late summer sun revealed undulating shadows of green, black hills punctuated by white farm houses with their lights aglow. Sean heard the squealing play of children in a holiday camp as he rolled down the window to smell the clean country air. Why Tara Hill? Sean thought. A tea house, set next to an affectionately attended garden of picture perfect flowers, heralded the entrance to the hill. Sean remembered Thomas Moore's poem:

The harp, that once thro' Tara's Halls,
The soul of music shed,
Now hangs as mute on Tara's walls
As if that soul were fled.
So sleeps the pride of former days,
So glory's thrill is o'er....

A storm rumbled off shore. "So sleeps the pride of former days." Sean repeated the phrase softly aloud against the sound of the distant thunder. Tara Hill, he thought, seat of the inauguration of Irish kings for centuries, and one woman, Macha, who had disguised herself as a leper and lured her royal opponents into the woods, one at a time to be lashed up and enslaved. Could Lily be a twentieth century Macha? The thunder moved closer.

The car grinded to an abrupt stop, its diesel engine chugging an erratic beat. "That's the end of that, lad. Park's closed. You still want to go up there. Rain's a'comon, you know."

"Yeah. Can you wait?" Sean replied.

"Till the cows come home, if ya please. It's your quid. But mind your step. Them college diggers been chopping holes all over this place. Nothin's sacred anymore. They'll be making movies here someday, I suspect." The driver turned the ignition off and settled down in his seat, pulling his tam over his eyes.

Sean started the climb up the hill, stumbling through the dark past a small church with a smashed stained glass window and finally coming upon a stone edifice. It was a deserted, unassuming place, this Tara. "Tara of the green mounds," Edna O'Brien had called it. "Tara with its stone of destiny and inherent hallowedness, where the kings learned their many taboos and the prescriptions that would bring them good luck—the fish of the Boyne, the deer of Luibneck, the bilberries of Brileith, the cress of Bossnach, water from a well and hares of Naas. Tara, the site of conventions and synods of warriors who had sat down with opponents' slain heads under their belts and guts falling about their feet." The thunder was now echoing in the valley as lightning was beginning to flash like lasers through the mist, illuminating briefly the stone edifice of ancient kings.

Where the hell is she? Sean thought. A rabbit dashed from behind a bush, causing Sean to trip in startled flight against a large stone. As he looked up, a beam of light struck his eyes, blinding him momentarily. The voice he heard was not Lily's, but Graves!

"So you've finally kissed the Blarney stone, Seanaghan. Except this Blarney stone launched kings to glory and death. Gaze closely upon it, man; it harbors the hopes of all Irish for a country free of tyranny and oppression from all its invaders—Vikings, Saxons, and English, especially the English." Graves spoke with a sure, confidant air. The words emanated with sober articulation as firmly as they did in the chapel bell tower.

Sean struggled to his feet to see Graves in a new tan trench coat and brimmed Burberry hat. He was surrounded by a group of seriously intent young men and women.

"Where's Lily? She was supposed to . . . ," his words trailed off into the darkness. The purpose of the rendezvous had obviously changed.

"Sean, it wasn't supposed to happen this way," Graves responded in a ominous voice. "But you've come upon a piece of information that requires you to make a decision—a decision I had hoped, we all hoped you wouldn't have to make."

"Let me guess. I can't say, 'Frankly, Scarlet, I don't give a damn'. One of those decisions, huh?"

"It's no time for your sophomoric wit, Sean. Although you probably don't appreciate the significance of what you read today, we can't take any chances. You see, I took a risk when I invited you here. You're too sharp and too damn independent. And you're a budding historian who is probably already itching to find material for his dissertation. It was my miscalculation. Most of the others were content to catalogue, tour, and get soused every weekend in the pubs, but you're too curious. Yes, I should have known it."

"I'm surprised, Professor. You seemed infallible to me." Sean's courage welled up. "You're talking like a poor read of a class B movie script. Shit, you even look like Errol Flynn in that get up. You can have your precious letter, or what's left of it, and I'll be winging my way home tomorrow."

"The only script that went awry was the one that was written for you to spend a quiet Irish summer cataloguing manuscripts. We're ad-libbing now, Sean, and I don't like to ad lib." Graves' voice was muffled by the rising thunder which was now reverberating in the valleys. "The decision is simple. You are an honorable man. I am an honorable man. And you will take an oath, an oath on the stone of Tara, if you wish, that nothing you have found, or which will become known to you, will be revealed to a soul outside this circle of friends."

"And if I don't?"

"Then you shall suffer an unfortunate accident. Tomorrow's newspaper will report that one Sean Connaghan, visiting graduate student and lover of Yeats, stumbled and fell, striking his head on a rock near Tara Hill. His companion, Lily Garrett, told *The Times* that they had a lover's quarrel in the library of Trinity College just hours before, a quarrel which many in the reading room will verify. Remorseful and a romantic by heart, according to his close mentor, Dr. Edwin Graves, Mr. Connaghan chose to ascend Tara Hill on a stormy night to consider his fate. He is survived by no known relatives."

"Convenient. Real convenient. Never thought you'd take advantage of an orphan, Graves. And what about the taxi driver?"

"No problem, he's one of ours. So what's your decision, Connaghan, *The Times* tomorrow or an interesting summer, more interesting than you could imagine . . . and a trip to Yale in the Fall?"

"And what's to prevent me from disclosing this little meeting and what I know, which is precious little, later when all is quiet on the Western front."

"I will be blunt. The IRA. And when you least suspect it, as they say."

"Great. I can see my epitaph now, 'He came to catalogue but joined the IRA'."

"We're not IRA, Sean, but they do protect our work. You would never be asked nor would I ask anyone to make that commitment. Our work, unfortunately, requires protection."

"I guess there is no choice. Looks like you have a convert . . . to what, I have no idea."

"You will. Now, get down the hill, and remember that your word was given on holy soil. See you at the library tomorrow."

The lights went off and the small group, like one giant mystical beast, descended down the opposite side of the stone. Sean was left in the dark. It had begun to rain. The black clouds overhead seemed to assume the shapes of Viking warriors racing to pillage the Celtic villages below. The early morning singing of the keyboard seemed so welcome now. Sean longed for it. So much had changed. Graves. Lily. The earth seemed to move under him, under the dead shapes of fallen Celtic kings.

Chapter VI
St. John's Eve

The deck of the *Naomh Eanna* was packed to the gills with the assorted necessities of island life as she churned through Galway Bay on her daily summer passage to the Arran Islands. Bicycles were wedged against stacks of lumber and packaged appliances. The sweet odor of cow manure mixed with the fresh fragrance of oranges and cantaloupe. The *Naomh Eanna* was a working boat, her long wake stretched like an umbilical cord from Galway to Kilronon harbor on Inishmore. The cord had not always supplied the food of modern life to the islands. Only those desperate hide skin boats called curraghs had connected the islands for centuries in times when men prayerfully gazed at the horizon for signs that the sea would not envelope them in a seething maelstrom. But these days few men braved the seas beyond Galway Bay in their long slim caskets. One damaged curragh even rested on its side on the ferry's deck, content to leave its crew engaged in a spirited game of chess. They puffed on their pipes and watched the quickening waves smash the bow and wash along the sides of the lumbering old scow. *Naomh Eanna* mocked the foolish ancient curragh ritual. It would eventually subvert the engrained rowing skills of this generation of "riders to the sea."

Sean felt buoyed by the rising sea and fresh air. His eyes settled on the chess game below. The men were suspended in a critical engagement. One false move and checkmate would climax the game, but neither seemed to recognize the scenario. Sean was tempted to shout out the next move, but hesitated. Something whispered to him through the Galway mist which made intervention unseemly. Even such small things must be allowed to ride the fortunes of the waves, pulled inevitably toward an unseen destiny. Graves may have been right after all, Sean thought. That Irish lighthouse was out there pulling him to Arran as strongly and surely as the *Naomh Eanna* drove her course to Kilronnan.

"Looks like you be seeing the Hy Brasil, Seanaghan." Lily gently touched his shoulder.

"Hy Brasil? You are an enigma Lily! Two days ago you were accusing me of sexual harassment on the basis of manuscript abduction. Now you're going to convince me, I suppose, that I'm demented enough to think that Brazil lies off the coast of County Clare." Sean sighed the breath of a trapped man. "If the next move in your little perverse drama is to convince me of my insanity, you need go no further, I'm well on the way to the funny farm."

"And you the historian, a product of the great American system of higher education! I'm surprised." Lily taunted unmercifully. "I meant a compliment, Sean. You must never assume in the Irish that defensive edge which characterizes the American mind. Saint Brendan saw it out there and captured the imagination of the 10th Century mind with it. Hy Brasil was a vision, some say. Others believed it. Arran folk did for sure. So did thousands of monks who made their desolate homes on the rocky cliffs of Skillig Michael." Lily pointed to the South. "Hy Brasil may have been a vision, but Skillig Michael wasn't. It's out there—that islet where monks retired and huddled in exile to watch the battle between the angelic hosts of Heaven and the powers of evil. Evil was hurled into the abyss of the great ocean, they wrote. People around here believe in an evil that can reach up out of the depths and grab their fragile curraghs." She gazed down at the chess players below. "I'm thinking those men down there with their hole gapped hide-skin believe it enough to ride the ferry back today. Hy Brasil. You might call it Atlantis. With the right mixture of light and cloud, you can see it. Saint Brendan did. John Synge wrote to Yeats about a sighting. But if your rationalist mind needs evidence, as I suspect it might, then take the word of one of your trained historians, T.J. Westropp, who observed it as having two mountains, one wooded, in the central tract: between rose buildings, towers with curls of smoke, rising against a golden sky at sunset. 1944, Sean. *Irish Times*. Want the bloody citation?"

"Sweet Jesus, Lily. You really have submitted to Graves' gibberish. Saint Brendan, angelic hosts, mythical islands. You'll be telling me next that the great Irish Saint landed on Plymouth Rock." Sean turned toward the stern, stretching his arms to the sky. "Please, God, deliver me from these damnable saints of yours!"

"Actually, Sean, he probably did." Lily replied tentatively, anticipating Sean's bombastic reaction. She calculated right.

"Let me get this straight now, Lily," Sean interjected. "The Irish discovered America, but it was really Atlantis, and they couldn't find it again because they lost there subway map and were hopelessly trapped in Greenwich Village where they developed a curious taste for bagels and lox, all except Saint Brendan, of course, who caught Leif Erickson's boat back to the Old World, only to forget the coordinates of his passage until Christopher Columbus journeyed to Skillig Michael to find them documented by a dying monk who told him with his last breath." Sean drew a deep breath. He was on a roll. "You know, Lily, people like you didn't kiss the blarney stone, they fucked it." Sean abruptly stopped his stride with this last statement as an old women in a red shawl seated next to him gathered up her knitting and moved inside the cabin. Sean slumped against the deck rail and ran his fingers through his hair.

"Oh, for fooks sake, Sean, calm down. I meant nothing by it. Just a legend. Take it or leave it. But Dante did, you know. Some say that Saint Brendan's *Navigatio* inspired *The Divine Comedy*, and others . . . ."

"Ah . . . divine comedy. Now we're talking. Divine comedy, that's just what this journey is. We can agree on that!" Sean grabbed Lily by the shoulders and looked sullenly into her blue eyes. "Yes, let's understand each other. I may be Graves' puppet in this silly goddamn farce, but you're pulling the strings, and I want to know just where this 'divine comedy' is leading us. No shit, Lily, I'm at the end of the line here."

The *Naomh Eanna* was passing the lighthouse at Straw Island near the entrance to Killeany Bay. The view of the lighthouse captured Sean's attention momentarily and drew his thoughts back toward Wait Chapel. Lighthouses and chapel steeples, towering guides in high seas of emotion. He remembered so clearly that first question from Graves and his response.

"A young man is sitting in a boat in the Irish Sea on a foggy night. He is poor, lonely, drunk, and Irish. He thinks he sees a lighthouse in the distance. What is the purpose of the lighthouse to this young man?"

Sean whispered the dialogue under his breath.

"I guess I'd need to know why he was there in the first place,"

"What was that you said?" Lily whispered in return, taken by Sean's sudden change of mood.

"I guess I'd need to know why he was there in the first place," Sean repeated the phrase in a prayerful trance. He was trying to make a distant connection between past recollection and present events.

Lily gazed into his blank eyes. Sean was pale. "You Okay? Sea turned your stomach, maybe? " Lily waited patiently for the reply. "Sean, can you hear me?" She gently touched his cheek.

"Not the sea, Lily, it's that infernal lighthouse. He was right."

"Who? You're making no sense, man!"

"Nothing. Lily, do you believe in fate. You know, destiny?"

Lily smiled. "It's a great wonder you'd be askin' that, Sean Connaghan. And you with Irish flowing through your blood. "

"Irish in my blood? How do you know? Hell, how do I know?"

"Name, I'd guess. I just always thought that . . . ," Lily looked down as if she had something to conceal. The *Naomh Eanna* was now approaching the pier at Kilronnan, and Lily chose the moment to switch gears. "Now will you look at that pier! Who would have thought that one could arrive in such modern luxury when just a few decades ago, one had to be ferried by curragh. Synge thought it one of the singular joys of arriving on Inishmore, crashing through the wave crests and descending into deep troughs. Wonder what it was like for Eliza Cropper? Must have been quite an ordeal."

Lily had not uttered the Cropper name since that day in the library, and its mention pulled Sean back to reality.

"Cropper? Oh yeah . . . our *raison d'être* for this trek to the goddamn Celtic fringe," Sean intoned sarcastically, "Liza, the savior of a free Ireland, Liza. How could I forget our archival quest for the Irish Grail. Oh boy, I just know that Liza holds the promise of a great Irish future. Free, free! Thank God we're free at last! Let me see, we'll just make a stop at the local church, find her diary in the attic and bingo, centuries of oppressive history will be exposed for world view. And since we all know that history will free us, the British will immediately respond by removing troops from the North and settling the whole problem. And we should win the Nobel Peace Prize." Sean lifted his arms in mock beseeching. "Liza, deliver us! Deliver us from the snares of our history!"

"Glad to see you're back in form, Sean," Lily mumbled plaintively. "But I still like the Celtic version better."

The ferry listed to the starboard as wooden palates of lumber were rolled onto the wharf. Horses and cattle followed in a compliant row. Eager passengers waved to friends below. The crowd at the wharf surged forward as the gates opened to anticipate the embraces of family and friends. Lily waved at an older man in baggy woolen trousers tied loosely with a bright red and yellow belt, a criosanna. He appeared so typically local in his tight woolen fisherman's knit sweater and matching tam. Catching her wave, the man raised his hand furtively in quiet acknowledgment as he tapped ashes from his pipe against a pier pylon.

"Who's the local talent, Lily, . . . another archival warrior?"

"Asshole! His name is Michael Robartes, and he knows these islands by the back of his hand. Lived here his whole life. He's our contact. So try, if you will, to dispense with the American cynicism in favor of a little Irish charm."

"Our contact. How deliciously Ian Fleming. I can't wait to meet Goldfinger."

"Sean, for Gods sake!"

"Okay, okay," Sean bowed and swept his hand in a graceful semicircle. "Of course, Miss Manners, when in Rome . . . ."

As Sean and Lily disembarked, the man in the red and yellow criossanna disappeared into the crowd and emerged at the end of the wharf where he turned abruptly and walked toward a dilapidated fish house. Sean and Lily followed his purposeful stride until he disappeared into the house.

"Wait here," Lily instructed.

"Yessir, boss lady," Sean replied with a crisp salute. "I shall guard the baggage with my life."

Lily gave him a quick kiss on the cheek. "That's the spirit, Seanaghan, you're catching on. We'll make an Aran man out of you yet."

Dumbstruck by this gentle gesture, Sean stood in shock as Lily rushed with her bag into the fish house. Lily was a good person, Sean thought, a bit demented with Celtic nonsense, but a good person. This wasn't that bad after all. It was a sunny day. He was in Ireland. It was certainly better than Wall Street in the sweltering summer heat. The simple beauty of white washed cottages on the hills against the clear blue sky calmed his nerves.

Sean waited nearly an hour before the man in the red and yellow belt emerged and approached him. The *Naomh Eanna's* horn tooted two short blasts as its engines churned the ferry slowly away from the wharf.

"Failte mialte, Sean Connaghan!" The man greeted Sean with outstretched hand. "Name's Robartes, Michael Robartes. Welcome to Inishmore. Well, I'm sure you've had a long voyage and you're tired. We best be getting along".

The man picked up his luggage and began to stride toward the village.

"Whoa, partner. Where's Lily? I thought she was . . . " Sean grabbed the handle of his bag, bringing Robartes to an abrupt stop. "She didn't tell you. Well, son, take a look at the bow of the ferry out there," he said pointing to the departing *Naomh Eanna*.

Sean saw Lily at the bow waving. Cursed bitch, he thought, as he raced down the wharf toward the ferry.

"Traitor!" he yelled through his cupped hands. "You . . . you . . . Macha!"

"Hy Brazil, Sean, remember to look for it. Hy Brazil!," Lily smiled and shouted back as the ferry churned a broad arc in the bay and sped forward into the cold open sea.

"Lovely woman, that Lily," Robartes whispered across Sean's shoulder, "Wise beyond her years. Well, how about a good bowl of hot soup, my friend?"

Sean nodded in futile acceptance as he watched the ferry disappear around Straw Island. Macha had tricked him again. He resolved that it would not happen again.

Evening was falling as Sean and Robartes began their journey out of Kilronan on the road to Kilmurvey. The sounds of singing and dancing emanated from the last pub they passed and faded into the distance. The high melancholy pitch of the uilleann pipes drifted above the din of laughter and conversation. Sean felt strangely content and reconciled to this new place. A hearty meal and draft had helped. The road widened to reveal open vistas to the sea across bare rock. The setting sun illuminated the white thatched cottages on the hills, turning them shades of pink and purple. In the distance along the road great fires were being lit as the night darkened. The two men strode together in silence at a steady pace through the intoxicating air of sea and wildflower. As they passed a cottage, boys ran around them with burning turf to light a bonfire carefully built on a small rough platform of loose stones.

"Do they light fires every night here?" Sean inquired.

"Heavens no," Robartes replied, "Wood is much too precious on the islands. Why, don't you know, 'tis the Eve of St. John's. Aye, it's a special welcome for you, to arrive on St. John's Eve with a path lit from Kilronan to Kilmurvey. A grand time, it is , to travel on St. John's Eve."

"And so what are we celebrating on this grand eve, Michael?"

"Now I'd guess that depends, Sean. I suspect no one really knows for sure. It's the longest day of the year, and for some it's probably just that and no more. But if you have a mind to worship, it's Saint John the Baptist that we be rememberin'. Of course, some say it's a leaving from the distant past when Druids feasted and made fire offerings to Baal. The Druids would drive cattle between two fires to cleanse them. Now the boys will carry a wisp of fire to the hearth to protect the household from harm for another year."

"And you, Michael, what do you believe?"

"It's a bright path home on an otherwise dark road. And a beautiful sight to behold, it is indeed. Aran stars to light up a starry night. It's our little gift to the universe."

Sean gazed forward at the next rise, and it did seem like the distant scattering bonfires blended into the starry horizon. The glimmering flames leaped to touch the stars. The island seemed to float in a sea of twinkling lights that danced with the heavens. Sean did not know whether he was walking among the fires or the stars. For a brief moment he felt he knew the answer to Graves' question.

"So how did you get roped into the Graves group, Michael?" Sean probed cautiously.

"Graves? Never met the man. Heard Lily talk about him. Must be quite a character from what I hear." Robartes quickened the pace.

"Then you don't know about Liza Cropper and why I'm here?"

"I know Lily, and that's enough for me. Lily's an island girl. Known her since she danced as a young nipper about these fires."

"So what did she tell you, I mean, about me."

"Just said you wanted to research a little island history, and you needed a guide."

"Marooned," Sean muttered under his breath.

"Oh, she did say that I was to introduce you to old Rose Malloy. Said she'd be about helping you too."

"Rose Malloy. Who is Rose Malloy?"

"It's tomorrow you'll be meetin' Rose, and I'd guess that she could tell you anything you need to know about these old sea rocks and their people. But Lily told me something else about you."

"What's that?"

"You'd be asking too many questions, too quickly. It's St. John's Eve, Sean, and if you listen hard, you'll hear the fairies in the wind. I suspect you'll find what you need, but I'd take a little time to get accustomed to this place so you can understand the answers when they come." Michael turned left down a lane toward an inviting cottage with light streaming from its windows. Pausing at a bonfire he scooped some fiery turf on a flat stone and cupped it against the wind. "St. John's fire for the hearth and another year on this blessed land."

"Do you really believe in fairies, Michael?" Sean shuttered as he asked the question. As soon as it was out of his mouth, he felt like he was four years old on his father's bed after the close of a bedtime story. Yet, strangely, it felt like the right question to ask here on a brilliant starry night.

Robartes stopped and turned toward him. The glow of the coals cupped in his hand sparked and flamed up, illuminating a craggy, weather worn face with a broad smile.

"Sean, we Aran folk are simple people. Fairies come naturally here. It's an explanation for many things we'd rather not face, or cannot. Now, if I didn't believe, where would I be? But for now, no more questions. It's been a long walk, and tomorrow will break before we know it. Come. There's a soft down bed waiting for your weary soul. The fairies can wait."

Sean liked Michael. He seemed without the intrigue that had plagued him since his arrival in Ireland. Despite the questions ahead, he felt surrounded by the simplicity of life. It felt good.

Chapter VII
Hy Brazil

If Sean thought that the mystery of Liza Cropper would unfold the next day, he soon realized that everything on the island unfolded at its own pace. Robartes' promise of introducing him to the sage Rose Malloy proved elusive. Robartes was a fisherman who plied the coastal Atlantic waters several days at a time. Depending on where and when the halibut were running, he could be gone on his trawler for days. At first Sean's frustration consumed his thoughts. He tried in vain to locate the elusive Rose, but the islanders would usually plead polite ignorance. He was beginning to think that his eviction from Dublin had been a convenient ruse to isolate his knowledge of the Cropper letter.

When Sean pleaded for help, Robartes remained a fortress of silence. His reply was always the same. "When the time is ripe and you are ready, she will find you." Or he would say with a wink, "Of course, I'd be thinking the fairies could deliver her to you one night." Then he might add in Gaelic, "Bedad, is mor an truagh'e," which Sean later learned meant, "It's a big pity." Still, it was hard to blame Michael. He too seemed an unwitting pawn in Graves' chess game.

Why did life have to be so complicated in such a simple place? As time passed, his dilemma languished in the face of the hard facts of island life. His quandary was such a small stone on the rocky landscape.

Lily must have anticipated the long wait, for she had secretly packed a book in his bag by J.M. Synge, the famous Irish poet and playwright, along with a note that read:

> Connaghan,
> When Yeats met Synge in Paris, Synge had resolved to become a critic and interpreter of French literature. Yeats told him to give up Paris. He told him harshly that his poems and essays did not come out of life, but out of literature, images reflected from mirror to mirror. He urged him to go to the Aran Islands where he

would find his 'Irishness' in hearing Gaelic and seeing first hand the harshness of the Irish experience. I enclose Synge's Guide to the Aran Islands. If you seek answers, you'll find them here. Enjoy! It's better than looking at a
computer screen! Lily.

Sean had opened the book for the first time, as he often did, with eyes closed; his finger searching the page for serendipitous guidance. The ritual revealed Synge's mystical muse about island life.

Some dreams I have had in this cottage seem to give strength to the opinion that there is a psychic memory attached to some neighborhoods.

Lily would have beamed with self-satisfaction at the revelation, he thought.

As each successive day slipped into another night, Synge's book became his constant companion. Soon he began to search out the churches and ancient forts of the island, tracing Synge's steps and marveling at the accuracy of his narratives. His descriptions of the people seemed as relevant as they were in 1898.

The complete absence of shyness or self-consciousness in most of these people gives them a peculiar charm . . . their way of life has never been acted on by anything much more artificial than the nests and burrows of the creatures that live around them.

The guide was a strange mix of lilting romantic charm and harsh stories of death at sea, women keening at funerals, and oppressive evictions by the local constabulary. Fairies mixed impudent trickery with child snatching. There seemed a curious logic to these interventions into the natural order of things on the island. One could experience them only by living in the current of music, language, and work which always flowed out to the sea and beyond. Paradox ruled the islet. Charm and laughter coexisted with the feeling of eminent disaster. The sea dashed at the rock, but the rock was still inhabited by fairies.

One day a little girl told him while pointing at a sheer cliff overhanging the ocean, "Do you see that straight wall of cliff? It is the fairies that play ball in the night, and you can see the marks of their heels when you come in the morning, and three stones they have to mark the line, and another big stone they hop the ball on." Sean liked the children. They were like him, free to explore the island, with all the time in the world for fairies.

It was on one of his Synge inspired treks that he ventured out to explore the largest of the pagan forts on the island, Dun Aengus. As he strolled down the 'high road' west of Kilronan, winding past the highest point of Aran, Oghill, he was met by the little girl who proudly had told him about the cliff fairies. She skipped alongside him on her light hide-skin pampooties, a blithe little spirit filled with the happiness that only children on a desolate island can find in the organic perfume of wildflowers and sea spray.

"So Katy, what manner of fairy mischief have you discovered today?" Sean playfully asked.

"Oh, the fairies be sleepin' now, Mr. Sean, just waitin' for night to come out and play. Why sure you must jesting with me not to know that. And where is it you'd be walkin' today?"

"Dun Aengus, Katy. Are there any fairies there?"

"For sure, there'd be a plenty there, sleeping in all those rocks. But it's not much to see, Dun Aengus. Just a place for boys to play capture the Vikings. I be takin' you to a better place, if you wish?"

Sean kicked a stone down the road. "Oh? And where might that be, my pretty young guide of Aran?"

Katy blushed, and ran ahead of him. "Come see for yourself!"

The young girl raced down a lane to the right, bright red hair streaming behind her. Occasionally, she would leap and spin as gracefully as a ballerina executing a *tour je te*. Sean followed the enchanted merriment. He knew her destination, the little fifteenth-century Church of the Four Beauties. How appropriate that a beautiful young sprite would lead him there. He also guessed from Synge's account that he would find her at the Well of the Saints, a well prominently featured in one of his plays. Its water was said to be a curative for all kinds of ailments. But when he arrived, there was no Katy to be seen. Only the clear water of the well reflected his image. He heard a beckoning cry from over the rise in the distance.

"Here, Mr. Sean, come see the old monks beehive," Katy called.

As Sean strolled over the rise, the rude beehive shape of an ancient stone clochan appeared a short distance away. Clochans were a common sight on the mainland, shelter for lonely Christian hermits of the past. Sean often imagined them to be a place for wrestling with the soul. But he had not encountered one on the island. Katy's voice echoed within the clochan, creating an eerie semblance of a banshee cry. Sean approached the low doorway and crouched to enter.

"Stop that yelling. Its hurting my . . . ," Sean's words were caught in mid-air as his eyes settled, not on Katy, but an old women sitting cross-legged on the earthen floor. Instinctively, he backed into the stone wall, breathless. The woman was staring intently into his eyes in a way that discerned more than he cared to reveal. A chill overtook him.

"I take it you've been looking for me, Sean Connaghan." The old woman spoke in a deliberate tone.

"Rose? Rose Malloy?"

"The very same. Won't you sit with me?"

The shaft of light from the doorway spotlighted the old woman's hands. They were the hands of a working woman, callused and twisted with arthritis. She clasped them in a prayerful tangle, like the roots of a tree which had been confined to a small plot of fertile ground surrounded by rock. The soil had allowed growth, but the surrounding rocks had forced the roots to turn within.

"You . . . you startled me. I'm sorry, I . . . Where's Katy?" Sean gasped, recovering his breath.

"Never you mind. I'd be thinking she's playing at the well."

The two sat in silence for several minutes in the dark quiet chamber. The wind was picking up outside. Finally, the woman spoke.

"I've been told you study history. What have you learned from it?"

"That's a very sweeping question. I really don't think we have time for . . . ," Sean hesitated.

"We have an eternity for a question that important, Sean. It is what you study . . . no? It seems only fair that two wanderers share answers with one another. You did want some answers?" Rose challenged him with a measured voice. Sean sensed a command that he must obey.

"Well, I never thought about history that way...you know...as answers . . . only as a flow of events and people in time."

"A flow controlled by what?"

"I don't really know. Politics, economics, governments, ideas . . . nothing. Good God, what does it matter?" Sean's voice revealed exasperation.

"It matters a great deal indeed."

"Yeah, and I suppose you're going to troop out that old saw about how we are doomed to repeat the mistakes of history if we don't understand them."

"No, I wasn't. But as long as you be bringin' it up, are you sure that there were mistakes, . . . or that if we knew them, we could avoid them again?"

"If I didn't believe that, I wouldn't be sitting here on this island in the middle of nowhere." He paused, gathering resolve. "Yes, goddamn it, I believe we are set on this earth to improve our little wretched condition, if not for any reason than to show that we are not doomed by our wretchedness. Knowledge is power and that power can transform people . . . and people can transform nations."

"Knowledge . . . ah yes . . . but what about truth? What about the power of truth? How is truth revealed by your powerful knowledge, if the truth be hidin' in history? Who really cares about a past that people accept as regretful happenings? Don't we just excuse it or explain it away as some force beyond our control? The ancients said it was the gods. The monks who prayed about it in these stone huts said it was original sin. Your modern historians attribute it to oppression. On the island we might say it was the fairies. What does anyone care about rectifyin' the injustices of the past? Do you Sean . . . do you?"

Rose had leaned forward into the light with this last statement. Her eyes were white, translucent, without color . . . blind. Blind, yet filled with tears. She could not see Sean's finger as he moved it from left to right in front of her. Thick white hair covered most of her brown face, a face rippled with deep set wrinkled crevices. She looked more like a Native American than Irish. But her voice was strong and clear. Her language only occasionally lapsed into Gaelic dialect. She waited intensely, almost frozen, for a reply. Her image demanded truth and sincerity.

"Yes, Rose Malloy, I care . . . ," he repeated emphatically, "I care about the truth!"

"No matter where it may take you? No matter how incredulous?"

"Yes."

Rose settled back into the shadows, untangled her hands. She reached out to touch Sean's forehead where she traced the sign of the cross. She spoke softly, deliberately, in tones dispassionately objective.

"I am the last descendent of Eliza Cropper. Liza bore my grandmother out of wedlock, the product of rape by an English soldier whom time has long since forgot. I tell you what I know from stories around the hearth and a diary which was given to me on my Grandmother's death—Liza's diary. The stories are most surely part legend, but the diary is real. It speaks of the brutal genocide of people in the village named after the legendary Hy Brazil of Saint Brendan, a village in a remote area near Connemara which was constructed in less than one year to process and weave cotton from the West Indies. British regulars along with Irish constabulary destroyed the entire village of more than five hundred men, women, and children, leaving only a remnant to make it to this island in curraghs. Most were eventually hunted down by the constabulary. Some migrated to other islands. Some are said to have escaped to the West Indies and then on to the American frontier." Rose paused.

"And Liza? What happened to her?" Sean inquired.

"What I'd be tellin' you now, you may not be ready to hear."

"I feel I must know. Something in this place tells me I need to know. Beyond Liza, there's something else, isn't there...isn't there Rose?"

Rose lapsed into island brogue as she answered.

"Yes, say it's the fairies or the fates, but there is more for you than just history here. And if you be a feelin' it in your heart, you should hear it."

Rose sighed and continued in a somber and reflective voice.

"After her rape and imprisonment, she went mad, taking no comfort in the solace and ministrations offered by the local priest. On the eve of her journey to the mainland for trial, an escape was arranged by currugh to Arranmore, an island, off the coast of County Donegal. This secret was known to only a few families who took it with them to their graves. It was their revenge, the island folks revenge for the many injustices done to them and done to the Quaker Friends who later sent foodstuffs to them during the famines, courtesy of James Cropper. The constabulary of course attempted to conceal knowledge of the escape by reporting that mad Liza had leaped off a cliff in despair. The appropriate mournful notification was sent to her father. Liza was indeed mad and lived a tortured life on Arranmore until my Grandmother's birth. She disappeared shortly thereafter, never contacting her father. Rumor had it she caught a steamer to America, but more likely she walked into the sea one night in frightened and lonely desperation."

"But there's more. Isn't there?" Sean leaned into the shadows toward Rose.

"Yes, after her birth, my Grandmother was raised by an Arranmore fishing family, and had a relatively uneventful life. She gave birth to my mother, Bridget, who married a local boy, Paddy Malloy. Paddy perished at sea. Grieved by her loss, my mother sent me to Inishmore to live with friends. She could not bear the reminder of her first love, I was told. She married again after my leaving. I was born a Malloy, but your mother . . . ."

Sean recoiled in shock—his mother? Rose cupped her hands around Sean's face, as he trembled. "Yes, Sean, your mother, also named Rose, was born in 1936 in Arranmore of Bridget and Seamus Gallagher. She was an artistic woman, who I have been told, was the darling of the island, a dancer, a singer, . . . a buoyant woman who drew a smile from every young man in the community. That smile settled on one, James Bonner. But their love was short lived. In 1955 Bonner and others were returning from the annual potato hoeing on the mainland when their curraghs were dashed upon rocks in a terrible storm. Seventeen Arranmore youth perished at sea that day. Your mother lost the lilt in her step and the perpetual smile on her face. Some say she too descended into madness . . . the madness of Liza's misfortune. It was five years later that she enlisted in the service. She married your father in 1962 and left with him for America. We never met him. I give you her last letter to my mother, which tells of her marriage to your father. It is all we have left."

Sean trembled as the letter was pulled from the old woman's skirt along with Liza's diary, Rose gently placed it in his hand. He caressed it slowly and began to cry and rock back and forth. Years of longing and motherless anguish poured out and echoed in the clochan of hermits. Rose embraced him and whispered softly in his ear.

"Sean, we are a troubled race who have always tried to be Saints. It is our destiny on these rocks to live a troubled life between sea and heaven. You have lived the burdens of the Irish without the spirit that sustains us. Our ecstasy of living in this place, on these islands, has been paid for by the keening of woman for generations. I give you history, it is you that must find the truth in it."

In his anguish Sean failed to see Rose leave through the shaft of light in the doorway. When he emerged into the quickening west wind, she was gone. The sea spray lifting from the bluffs blanketed him in a diaphanous mist as it softly descended through the setting sun of another ever changing island day. Slipping the diary and letter into his breast pocket, he headed down the lane past the Well of the Saints. Tomorrow he would find a lofty perch on the northern cliffs and search for Hy Brazil on the horizon. He believed he might see it. After all, he was Irish.

Chapter VIII
Alchemical Rose

Sean burst through the low doorway of the cottage to see Robartes engaged in solemn conversation with a fellow fisherman. He had seen him on the Kilronan wharf. A book lay on the table. The man was patting it and speaking in low tones with a clipped Gaelic cadence. He stopped abruptly upon observing Sean.

"Saints be praised, I thought I had lost you Sean! There's a wicked storm brewing in the west, and it's no time to be tramping about the island." Robartes rose from the table and patted the man on the shoulder. "Matthew was just leaving."

The man removed his heavy weather oilskin jacket from the hook near the door, nodded to Sean, and pulled the door closed as he left.

Sean's tongue raced ahead of his thoughts. There was so much to tell.

"Michael, you were right. I met Rose Malloy, or I should say, she met me. Just as you said. And she revealed the story. Liza Cropper. Sweet Jesus, the whole shooting match, and much more . . . .much more. Try this on for size. I'm Irish. Yes, by God, I'm as Irish as . . . as you, you old cod jigger."

Sean paused to stroke his forehead, running his fingers through his hair. He turned the table chair around, striding it like a horse and gazing directly into Robartes' eyes.

"Yes, this American cynic heard it all today. Such revelations, like a dream it was. I still can't quite believe it, but it answered so many things. Did you know that my mother is descended from . . . ."

"Lily's comin' tomorrow," Robartes interrupted casually, nonplused. "Care for some tea? I'll put some on."

Sean rose from his chair and tossed it against the wall.

"Hell man, didn't you hear me! I hit the mother load. Liza Cropper, Arranmore, Inverary, my father, me . . . it's all related. It's strange! It's wonderful! It's my answer to so many things."

Robartes had taken a box of salt from the cupboard and was pouring it on the table, three lines in equal measures. Sean was perplexed.

"What the hell? Look here, Michael, I'm telling you about a miracle. My miracle . . . and you're playing fuckin' games! Haven't you heard anything I'm saying!"

"Yes, I'd be hearing it all, but right now you must do exactly what I say. If there's any Irish runnin' through those veins, you'll be absolutely still . . . and quiet." Robartes repeated the command slowly in a loud voice. "Silence! Sit down!"

Robartes encircled the rows of salt with his right arm, inclining his head down over them.

"Our Father who art in heaven, hallowed be thy name . . . ," Robartes intoned the words solemnly, as if he were in a trance. "Thy kingdom come. Thy will be done."

Three times he repeated the prayer. Each time with a stronger voice. Then he took Sean's hand across the table and raised his eyes to the ceiling.

"By the power of the Father, and of the Son, and of the Holy Spirit, let this disease depart, and the spell of the evil spirits be broken! I adjure, I command you to leave this man, Sean Connaghan! In the name of God I pray. In the name of Christ I adjure. In the name of the Spirit of God I command and compel you to go back and leave this man free! AMEN! AMEN!"

Sean was stunned as the two men sat across each other silent for several moments. Sean finally spoke first.

"And what, pray tell, was that little sermon about?"

"Sean, me boy, Rose is dead. She passed on three days ago. She was buried today."

"You're crazy! I saw her. Must be a different woman. Yes, that's it. I know. We can verify. Yes, that's it." Sean paced the floor nervously. "This woman was blind, . . . and her hands were twisted with arthritis. Was Rose . . . ?"

"Yes, Sean, she was blind and crippled." Robartes replied with a sigh, brushing the salt from the table into his hand.

"Dead, you say."

"Rigid as a field post, bless her departed soul."

Sean stopped pacing and cupped his hand over his mouth. He was going to vomit.

"Hold on there lad," Robartes said moving to his side and propping him up by the waist. "You'll be fine. I've been about breaking the curse. You'll feel fit as ever tomorrow."

Sean broke away from Robartes' embrace.

"I don't want to be fine tomorrow. I was fine today. I'm always just fine, dammit! Today, I was different. Real for once, with a home and a family and a heritage with cousins and aunts and uncles and a . . . " Sean settled into the chair, sobbing quietly. "Wait! The little girl, Katy, she can tell you. She can prove that Rose was there. Let's find her. Let's go and find her now."

Sean started for the door. Robartes met him, grasping the door knob.

"She'll not be found . . . not tonight or any other night," Robartes answered ominously.

"What do you mean? There can't be that many little girls living here with the name Katy." Sean observed Robartes eyes rise in exasperation toward the ceiling. "Okay, so maybe you're right. There probably are a lot of Kates here, but she must live close by."

Robartes lifted his hand from the door knob and walked over to the table where he picked up his pipe.

"Let me describe her to you. I'd be thinking she was a very beautiful girl about ten years old. She had long red-gold hair that streamed about her as she danced as lightly as the air itself. And she'd be wearing' a green kirtle and scarlet mantle brooched with gold, after the old Irish fashion."

Sean's shoulders slumped. "So? There are a lot of girls that could dress like that here . . . you know . . . for a dance at the pub with the family. And half the girls on this island are strawberry blondes."

"But this one took you to the Well of the Saints and then disappeared. Right?" Robartes lit his pipe and puffed heavily, as if he were stoking a fire with bellows.

"Okay. Checkmate, you wise old Irish fox! How did you know? Let's go. Time's a wasting!" Sean again moved toward the door.

"If you'll be a wantin' to go to Hell, I'll not be journeying with you. Your Katy will be a banshee, Seanaghan, and I'll not be chasing banshees on a stormy night, nor any other night for that matter. I was describing the common form that a banshee, that fairy spirit of doom, takes when she appears to young men in the day. But at night she rides the mist like the most terrible dream you've ever had . . . keening for another young person to take her place at death's door so that she might enter heaven at last. You saw a banshee Sean, the banshee that delivered Rose, God bless her spirit, to her reward."

"Banshees, fairies, monks that see mythical islands! You people are nuts. If you haven't read the newspapers lately, it's almost the 21st century. Banshees just aren't what they used to be, Michael. We've split the atom. Hell, we've found quarks, unlocked the secret of DNA, and can predict the course of hurricanes. Superstition went out with the middle ages. Despite how much you may want to avoid the fact, even this island is slowly moving into the 20th century. Michael you don't fish in a curragh anymore. Wake up and get with the program."

"On this island, Sean, banshees <u>are</u> part of the program. I'd be thinkin' you know that. Otherwise, you wouldn't have believed everything you heard and saw today. Maybe it was Rose, or Rose's spirit. I'll not deny such a happening. If what you heard is true, in time it will prove itself."

"Wait. I can prove it. If I was just imagining things . . . ," Sean quickly walked over to the coat rack and reached into the side pocket of his coat. "How do you explain this?" He pushed the diary at him.

Robartes examined the book and read the title. *Guide to the Aran Islands* by J.M. Synge.

"I never read it myself, but I'm sure its enlightening. The tourist folk sure like it. Sells pretty good these days."

Sean grabbed the volume from him. How did his guide get in his pocket. He searched his other pockets furiously.

"That's not it. I mean, how in hell . . . I had it here . . . the diary with a letter in it . . . Jesus, I <u>am</u> demented."

"No. Just a little bewildered. You've been on this island alone too long. I should have been more attentive to your needs. I should have sought out Rose earlier. But she's been a hermit for years, and I feared that if you approached her too early, she'd slam the door in your face. She's never liked strangers . . . bit on the peculiar side."

"You mean, you knew where she was all this time, and you didn't tell me! Michael, you're a shit head!"

"I guess I deserve that. But there is something I can do to make it up to you. That man who was here is a relative of Rose's and a fellow fisherman. Several days ago I told him about the purpose of your visit and asked him to tell Rose of your need to see her. Well, . . . " Michael reached for a book on the cupboard shelf. It had been laid on its back, concealing the title. *The Alchemical Rose and Other Essays* by William Butler Yeats. "Rose said she wanted you to have this."

"Great! A woman I never met, . . . but conversed with today when she was dead . . . leaves me a book of Yeats. Wonderful!" Sean slammed the book on the table. "I had the answers to my life in a diary and a letter, and it's exchanged for Yeats. Isn't that sweet irony? My life for Yeats."

"Chin up, Seanaghan, it's not everybody that'll be seeing a banshee and live to tell 'bout it. Besides, maybe it holds some kind of message for you. Who knows?" Robartes comforted Sean as he handed him the book.

"Believe me, Michael, I've read these messages before. They don't agree with me. It's Professor Graves stock and trade. He loves dead end questions. No answers, just questions."

"I'd be thinkin' its time to retire. And as me dear departed mother would tell you, 'falling is easier than rising.' So, let's to bed, Seanaghan. She'd also say, 'if the day is long, night comes at last'."

Robartes turned out the lights and stoked the dying embers as Sean climbed the narrow steps to the loft.

Before switching off the light, Sean opened the book. Inscribed in the front were these words, written in feminine script, "I believe in one God, the Father, the Almighty, maker of heaven and earth, of all that is seen and unseen." The word unseen was underlined.

Chapter IX
Borders and Time

Before Sean awoke, Michael Robartes had slipped out of the cottage and caught a ride to Kilronan to meet the early ferry from Galway. He left some tea and scones on the table with a note to meet him in Kilronan to welcome Lily. He had planned to rendezvous with her at the Sruffaun, a pub that catered to the local fishermen. The ferry was earlier than expected that day, and Lily had already tucked herself into a corner table with a cup of tea, reading the *Irish Times*. She rose to embrace him in a fond sisterly greeting.

"I didn't expect you back this soon, Lily."

"I know, but when I received your message, Graves insisted that I come at once. Sure he's a hardy taskmaster, that one," Lily opined. "So, do you have them?"

"Tricky business it was. Without the help of Katy and Matthew all may have been lost. That Matthew is an artist." Robartes said with a broad smile.

"They don't call him 'the soft fingers of Shannon' for nothing," Lily replied with a wink. "But how was Rose lured out of her lair? Good grief, she's been a recluse for years. She would have protected that diary with her life, or burn it before anyone took it from her."

"That's the curiosity of it, Lily. When Katy told her of the American from North Carolina, she didn't hesitate to follow her to Teampall an Cheathrair Aluinn. I suspected it would take a much more elaborate ruse to lure her away from that secluded hovel in Onaght. But when Katy returned to tell us that Rose had given him a book and letter . . . well, we had to do some fast thinking. Thank God Matthew could pull the switch, or we would have had a time trying to subdue him. He was wired." Robartes motioned the pub-keeper for coffee, exchanging brief pleasantries.

"So how did you keep him from pursuing Rose and Katy?"

"You know the young lad well, Lily." The pub-keeper delivered the coffee, and Robartes filled the cup to the brim with cream. He stared into the cup. "I told him that Rose had died and that Katy was a banshee."

"Michael, you didn't?" Lily pursed her lips and shook her head in mock disappointment. "Shame on you! And he bought that line?"

Robartes continued to stare into the cup. "I don't say that I was proud of it, Lily. Especially now."

"What do you mean? You've never hesitated for 'the cause' before. Your father would have been proud."

"He's a good lad, Lily," Robartes replied quietly, "Like one of my own before the sea ate them . . . damn the day. He's a searcher, and he's taken to our place like an island hare. He's a bit touched by it . . . not a tourist, this one."

"Sean?" Lily exclaimed, "Not the Sean I know!"

"He's changed, Lily. Rose told him some story about being related to Liza Cropper. He took the bait . . . hook, line, and sinker. And that's not all. When Matthew picked me up this morning . . . " Robartes paused shaking as he lifted the coffee to his lips, " Matthew told me that Rose died last night. Apparently she took refuge in a church on the way home during the storm. She must have gotten disoriented. As blind as she was, I'm surprised she didn't wait for Katy. But I had told Katy to report anything unusual as soon as she heard it. And she was true to her word. When she couldn't find her at home, the Constable sent out a search party. They found her at Oghill near the old abandoned lighthouse . . . " Robartes spoke in a trembling voice, ". . . curled up in her shawl, clutching her rosary. Saints above, forgive me! I may have killed her!"

Lily reached across the table to comfort him. She clasped his hand tightly in hers and whispered, "Michael . . . you listen here . . . Rose was an old woman. She lived a full life, and had she known . . . had we ever had the opportunity to reason with her, she would have understood. It was God's will, Michael, as sure as I'm sittin' here."

"It's not that easy, Lily. They'll be talk. You know this island, and Katy can't be trusted for long. Little girls will eventually share their secrets."

Lily pondered this last statement. They stared at each other, knowing what had to be done. Lily spoke it first.

"Sean must leave on the next ferry."

"Yes, he must. Kilronan will be buzzing with the news," Robartes replied. "For his own good, it'll be. He should be comin' soon. I'll be goin' to the wharf to book a passage. I'll send Matthew for his belongings. But how shall we tell him?"

"It'll be no lark," Lily sighed as Robartes raised from his chair. "You be off, I'll take care of it. Oh, Michael, the diary?"

Michael removed a brown paper bag from his jacket, put it to his lips and kissed it. "Rose's legacy. Take good care of it, Lily. It will be a poor ransom for my soul if it brings nothing for the trouble."

Lily took the package, stuffed it gingerly into her back pack and hugged him. "It will, Michael. Saint Brendan will meet you at the pearly gates himself. God be with you!"

"And with you, my island beauty!" Robartes took a few steps before he stopped and turned about.

"What is it?"

"One more thing. Katy brought a book that had been given to her. In my contrivance I gave it to Sean. She said it was from Rose."

"Was it?"

"I'm not sure now. I guess we'll not be knowin' that".

"What was the title?"

"*The Alchemical Rose*. Yeats, I believe."

Lily ordered another cup of tea and waited for Sean. She turned over one explanation after another in her mind. She regretted not asking Robartes for more information about their conversation the night before. Sean was an artist when it came to ferreting out insincerity. The task would require her to muster every Machiavellian skill she had learned from Graves. She wondered whether it was all worth it. Her vow to Robartes had resounded like a clear trumpet, but in truth she had doubted Graves' methods for some time now. He had too much faith in the power of revealed injustice. She was beginning to cast aside the innocent fascination she had with the old professor and the confidence he had once inspired. Having lived on the island, she knew all to well how rumor would grow to legendary proportions overnight. The mystery would dominate island conversation until it either was solved or a wild fable took its place. Such stories did not pass quickly like a hurricane and blow out to sea. They could swirl and swirl until they became an obsession.

As she mulled over several possible scenarios for deception, Sean suddenly appeared at the table.

"So, the old man finally let you out of his cage." Sean spoke with his characteristic sardonic edge. It put Lily at ease. Perhaps, he hadn't changed that much. Dealing with the old Sean would be manageable, Lily thought.

"The caged bird sings more beautifully than the freed one, Sean," Lily replied coyly.

Sean smiled. It was working.

"Not here, Lily. And you an island girl . . . tisk, tisk . . . you ought to know better. So you missed flying about the cliffs, and they've sent you to push me off one, no doubt."

"Sean, you haven't changed a bit. Did you see Hy Brasil?" Lily replied tentatively, fearing that she might show her hand.

"You could say that. In a way I experienced it. But It faded when I thought I had landed on it."

"That's a new one. Nobody's ever landed on Hy Brasil. Thought you didn't believe in that 'gibberish', as you put it."

"Did I say that? No, it's real. More real than you'll know."

Sean was different, changed, Lily thought. Was he humoring her?

"So Lily, you've come to retrieve me, eh?" Sean stared deep into her eyes.

Lily was taken off guard. "Well, how did you know? Did Graves wire you?" she replied, recovering her balance.

"In a way he did. I discovered the answer to the riddle of the lighthouse, and I was right . . . right as rain, Lily."

"Oh?" Lily stirred her tea. Jesus, she thought, he's fishing. He must know something. If she only had queried Robartes longer.

"Yeah."

"So spare me, island sage. What is the answer?" Lily spoke playfully, placing her chin in her hands and breaking into a broad grin as she batted her eyes.

"This is a role reversal, Lily," Sean parried artfully, "Finally, I'm the true believer and you're the skeptic. Come on, Diogennes, humor me. I think I've earned it."

Lily felt the balance return.

"Okay. Shoot!"

"My answer was right. Graves' drunken, lonely Irishman looks to himself to find his position in his crazy, tragic sea-tossed world. He was not in just any boat. He rides the waves on a curragh. And despite his great skill, the sea may take him anyway. I said that our Irish friend, an Aran man if you will, must know why he is there in the first place. I intuited correctly, Lily. But to know the 'why' of the answer, one has to live here until the sea drowns your voice, until you hear the thrushes in the grass, and see the ponies dance across meadows at sunset, and begin to hear the monks chant at night in the howling wind. Then you know why you're here. You know where you are . . . nowhere . . . the place we all are. And when you learn that, you learn that you're at the mercy of the fates. That lighthouse out there on Illaunatee doesn't call the islander, it warns the wanderer. To our lonely rider on the sea in the curragh, he knows where it is. He doesn't have to see its light. He knows where home is Lily, despite what Michael may have told you, I have found something of myself here. Verifiable or not, I've felt it. I could find this island, if I had to, in a darkened sea, drunk or sober." Sean paused and motioned toward the door. "So when do we leave?"

"How did you know that we're going?"

"It's played itself out. You know that Rose is dead. There's nothing more to be done here. I also believe that you have the diary and the letter, and there's nothing I can do to get it from you. Graves has what he wants, and I have my freedom, if I don't ask anymore questions. The historian in me wants to read that diary, but the islander tells me that I know all there is to know."

"Sean, I don't know what you're talking about . . .I . . . ." Lily's reply was transparent and hollow.

"Aran man to Aran woman, . . . Lily you're full of shit! But it doesn't matter. You see, I've got what I want and you've got what you want. For whatever reason, I'll never know. It'll do you no good. It's tainted by Rose's death. You'll never be able to prove what's in it. The

Sein Fein has no credibility, and the only one that can verify it is dead. She took the story with her to the grave. In fact I don't know why you left this enchanted place to begin with."

Sean stood abruptly. "Let's go, Lily. I'm anxious to get on with my life. This farce is over. Com'on, I'll pay for the tea."

Lily and Sean were well beyond Straw Island on the ferry before Lily ventured a response to Sean's remarks. They had struck a deep nerve in her. Michael was right, he had changed.

"Sean, someday I'll send it to you. I promise. When it's used. After we use it, I'll be sure."

"That would be good of you, Lily. I'd like that."

The lighthouse was fading into the mist, its beacon still visible.

"Sean?"

"Yes, Lily?"

"There really are fairies on the island you know."

Sean smiled and kissed her on the cheek. A tear rolled off her eyelid.

"Yes, my sweet island lass, and they play ball on the cliffs every night."

Part II

Journey
to
Isle du Castor

Beaver Island, Charlevoix County, Michigan

New Haven
2003

Chapter X
A Forgotten Peace

Time and distance makes a young man forget the face of fear. Sean settled into life at Yale with a resolute conviction that he was no longer alone. He had found a forgotten peace in Ireland.

Life as a graduate student offered a steady pace of work that drowned out the feelings of anxiety and loss that had threatened to wash over him in the past. Sean descended deep into the bowels of Western historical consciousness, but he was not prepared for the intellectual rending that was ahead. He had thought that the study of history would steer him away from the internal struggles of the soul. Instead, he found himself challenged by the stories of the tortuous human condition.

For four years he immersed himself, as only a graduate student can, in the arcane myriad of thought and historiography of Western cultural history, specializing in American culture. Sean was contented with the sublime isolation of the academy. In a habitual daze of thought he moved from seminar, to library, to his small apartment, interrupted only by bicycle rides around New Haven. Friendships did not develop easily for him. They required the risk of exposed vulnerability which he simply pushed aside. The exploration of history offered enough stimulation. He became a cloistered monk, at prayer with ideas. He liked it that way. The life of the student offered comfort and safety. Sean followed current events only with an eye to connecting them with a greater historical theme or pattern. Even his interest in Ireland waned as the years passed. He read with only half-hearted interest of the resolution of the Irish troubles and the political settlement with Sinn Fein and only occasionally wondered what Graves would do now that he was out of the work – whatever the nature of his work was. Only on a few occasions would Sean indulge a memory of Lily. It was better to forget. Even the tragedy of 9/11 and the "war on terror" seemed distant to him. He was a lonely hunter on a vast plain,

But classes hardly presented the same safe refuge. The university in the late 20th century had become a battleground in the "cultural wars" of society. Post-modern thought sought to deconstruct the safe moral conventions of canonical thought. History was being reinterpreted by a generation of scholars who questioned the substrata of assumptions upon which history had been written. Nothing was sacred anymore—immune from question. History had always been written through the eyes of the victors – not by the defeated, oppressed, or disenfranchised. In the 19th century history was viewed as a progression toward greater human enlightenment. That perspective collapsed under the weight of new voices who wrote from the standpoint of women and African-Americans. Western thought had failed to deliver upon its promises of justice and equality. It was a fraud. Cultural history had to be deconstructed to reveal the patterns of the dominant culture, cultures of resistance, and the cultural hegemony that oppressed minority voices. History could not be properly appreciated or understood without exploration of the undercurrents which informed them: nationalism, consumption, empire, class formation and labor, radicalism, gender arrangements, cultural production, and genre. The purpose of the university had always been to prick the conventional balloons of society. Increasingly social commentators saw these challenges as reflecting the "closing of the American mind" rather than its opening.

Sean's mind was opening. It was opening wide as the beak of a hungry chick. He identified with the disenchanted. Sean had never had much in the way of material possessions, and his young life had experienced loss more than most. Of course, he soon would be disabused of that perception.

The reckoning came in his seminar in "Methods and Practices in U.S. Cultural History." This particular class focused upon an examination of the history of American religious movements from the perspective of Antonio Gramsci. Gramsci was an Italian Marxist who, having become disenchanted with Stalinist Russia, was imprisoned by Mussolini upon his return to Italy. Gramsci's nine volumes of observations on history, sociology, and Marxist thought, known as the *Prison Notebooks,* were calculated to transform the Christian worldview of society to a Marxist one. To Gramsci, Christianity's influence on cultural morals and manners formed the primary barrier to realizing the Marxist dream. Christianity's control over the masses had blinded them to the reality of their oppression. Only a broad alliance of the Left, together with a capture of the organs of culture – education, churches, and the media, would transform the old Christian culture through "cultural hegemony" into one free of exploitation and oppression of the deluded masses.

Angela was a Gramsci devotee, but she hardly seemed the type to advance Marxist interpretations. An attractive Hispanic woman from a traditional Catholic family in California, Angela dressed stylishly in tight jeans and a pashmina shawl. She sported Marc Jacobs shades. Sean was intrigued by her passionate mastery of Gramsci's writings but found her enthusiasm unsettling. In fact he viewed the course as more ideological discourse than historical examination. Theories about historical interpretation were necessary, he supposed, as a frame of reference, but they seemed all too simplistic. He admired Angela, but he was unprepared for what would soon transpire in a classroom encounter with her...

Professor Turkle began the class with an observation of the theologian Harold O. J. Brown concerning the uses of history: "Should history be used as a means for destroying ideals...and presenting the young not with heroic examples but with deliberately and aggressively degenerate ones?"

Angela almost leaped from her seat. "That question is absurd and normative!" she responded. "It assumes that historians should create heroes, when our job is to reveal them as flawed human beings caught in a web of historical context!"

The class was silent. No one would object to the role of the good historian. Angela paused; waiting for a reaction, then took an unexpected turn.

"And when the context is flawed, it is the duty of the historian to reveal the cultural flaws as well. That is what Gramsci accomplishes so aptly. His goal is to free humankind from the bondage of the religious shibboleths which have enslaved our progress to some myth of eternal salvation or reward. There is no reward except what we make here on earth in the improvement of the human condition!" Brushing her long black hair from her eyes, Angela rolled on relentlessly. "Religion ultimately fosters only division, violence, terror, and war. All countries go to war with God or the gods on their side. Only by the destruction of religion will we free ourselves from the bondage of thought slavery and build a humane society. Our duty is to expose all religions as the thought poisons of our culture."

Sean knew full well the power of religion to foster violence, but he also understood the dangers of meddling with history. It seemed a razor's edge.

As Sean's thoughts drifted, Angela's eyes leveled a cool gaze at him. She seemed to read his thoughts.

"So, Sean. Does that make you feel uncomfortable?"

"Not really." Sean answered uncomfortably, preferring non-engagement.

"So you're okay with your bourgeois Eurocentric, white male, power!" Angela derided. "Secure that you don't have to engage because people like you will continue to control the culture."

"Now, you're getting a little too personal, aren't you Angie?"

Her voice took an edge as she leaned forward. "It is personal!" She shouted. "History is written by people like you – the privileged class. What kind of history will you write?"

Sean looked toward Professor Turkle in the vain hope that he might intervene or at least raise a caution flag. Turkle crossed his arms and shrugged. There was no foul. He obviously enjoyed the engagement.

"I'll write it fairly, objectively."

"Yeah, like Bill O'Reilly!" Angela replied, and the class howled. "You missed the point. You can't. You are the product of white power!

You were raised to revere or at least acknowledge the traditional perspective and power structures of our age."

Aroused and suddenly angered, Sean laid siege. "And what perspective do you represent? The oppressed masses? You'll distort history with a liberation ideology that discards the rule of law. Where will we be then?" He paused and then demanded. "Tell me! Anarchy and then greater repression by a government that will restore order? No,

I'll take the passive repression by free institutions, even flawed, rather than give more authority to government by provoking anarchy. I prefer the Glorious Revolution to the French Revolution. I prefer evolution to revolution."

Angela interrupted Sean's outburst. "You just don't get it! Gramsci is advocating a change in human consciousness as his revolution. He hated the violence of the Bolsheviks as much as the fascists. He's talking about winning hegemony over the minds of the people. Only by dispensing with the evil of organized religion can we truly be free to contemplate our future. Look at what religion has wrought, Sean. O'sama Bin Laden's critique of Western decadence is religiously inspired and only fueled war in Iraq, to say nothing of the perpetual conflict between Israel and Palestine! And what about your precious Ireland – the source of modern terrorism? Do you forget the little fact that the Provisional IRA made league with Libya to acquire arms and bombs for their ruthless campaigns against civilians? They invented modern terrorism! American interests supported them! Hell, the CIA even supported O'sama! It's a story as old as the Crusades – as old as religion itself. How sad!" Angela paused for breath. "Now, it's our turn to tell the real stories and evoke the coming of the new consciousness."

Sean couldn't help reeling in laughter. The class was rapt.

Professor Turkle had retreated to the corner of the classroom, arms crossed, a wry smile on his face.

"God, you sound foolish," Sean interjected. "So how do you explain Bishop Tutu's reconciliation commission? And how were the Irish Troubles resolved? I'll tell you—because of the intervention of Father Alec Reid, with the blessing of the papacy, as a go-between between Sinn Fein's Gerry Adams and the British government. And as for the Crusades, none other than Saint Francis of Assisi may have had a role in bringing it to an end. And how do you explain Detrich Bonhoeffer's involvement in the plot to kill Hitler? It seems to me that religion has prompted more good than evil in this bereft world!"

"Incidental pabulum, Sean," Angela shouted, "You don't get it.

Religion started this nonsense in the first place. People feeling impelled to act upon their emotions according to what they were told to believe by the Church. Oh yes, the Church really doesn't like violence,"

Angela intoned sarcastically. "But religion is the originating force in the whole of Western history. We assassinate the voices who speak up! Consider King and Gandhi, just to mention a few. No, Sean, I'm talking about the historical power structure that has supported racism and sexism for centuries, not the occasional critic or martyr to the cause of social justice. You're speaking impressionistically, not systemically. If we don't begin to expose the truth about religious cultural power and its subversion of freedom, we are doomed by a million more Osamas!" Angela punctuated her last remark with a sharp, stiletto look at Sean.

Sean did not get a chance to reply. Professor Turkle finally intervened to move the conversation in a different direction, and Sean was secretly relieved. Angela prided herself in having the last word. He decided to avoid her after class. Convincing Angela that religion was merely one dynamic in the swirl of human history was a hopeless endeavor.

Sean hustled purposefully across the quadrangle. He breathed deeply of the crisp spring air, shedding his anxiety with each long stride. He hated confrontations. He preferred to be left alone with his thoughts.

Angela had a different idea. Sean was too engaging to let go. She had long been attracted by his aloof indifference but to see his passion in full intellectual flight, aroused her. She was enraptured when his sleepy brown eyes flashed, his nostrils flaired, and his chiseled chest heaved in exasperation. She had long admired his solitary quest. He trained endlessly on the track and free weights between classes. Every woman in the class knew he was "hot," and yet inaccessible. But he didn't know of such opinion and would not have cared. Sean was the lonely hunter on the Serengeti, and she wanted to chase him, or he to chase her. She was a huntress, and she loved it.

"Wait up, Sean," the familiar voice sounded from behind him.

He quickened his pace. It was Angela.

"For Christ's sake, will you stop!"

Sean halted abruptly, turning on his heel as Angela ran smack into him in full tilt. Her book bag swung around him. It became entangled with his bag and swirled them to the ground in a heap of knowledge.

"You said 'for Christ's sake'," Sean intoned sarcastically. "I thought you were in the business of shedding religion for the new consciousness! You're a pitiful pedantic, Angie!"

He tried to jerk his bag to his shoulder, as he rose, but it was caught, and he tumbled back unto her. Angela quickly wrapped her pashmina around him and gave him a kiss on the cheek.

"Don't you love the spirit of the fight? Got you now in my cerebral clutches. You're a goner, Sean."

Sean jumped to his feet, leaving Angela in the heap. She was laughing uproariously.

"Why can't you mind your own business?" Sean screamed.

"Oh, but you are my business," Angela replied, "a student in sore need of an education!"

"Me? Seems that you are the one that has forgotten why we are here. Remember? We are here to **study** history, not to play games with it – to socially engineer society! Hell, most of the people going to work in the factories and shops could care less about your tripe. Society is not your playground. Our intellectual bantering doesn't amount to a hill of beans when people are trying to make ends meet."

"That's just the point," Angela muttered as she rose. She dusted off her jeans and wrapped the pashmina gracefully around her neck. "They are the point. They just don't know it. Slaves of their own social conventions – religion, national pride, and conformity."

"No. I'm not going there again," Sean replied, picking up his bag and striding down the walkway.

Angela followed step for step at his side. "But it's our duty to show the young a better way. That's what we are here for. Remember? We will be teachers some day."

"Yeah," Sean sputtered. "That's a scary thought. Our duty is to break down the culture – destroy the old icons – de-mythologize the hero – foment rebellion – destabilize the church, family, and the rule of law. Good grief, Angela, that's no game. It's anarchistic nihilism!"

"Wake up from your ambivalent slumber, Sean! Get your head out of the books and read the *New York Times*. The threat to your "civilization" lies in its ignorance of the simple roots of our existence. The "war on terror" is an old story of religious conflict. Globalization is just another word for capitalistic hegemony to line the pockets of the rich and impoverish the poor. And it's ruining our environment. Global warming is a fact, not a theory. Ecologies are changing worldwide. The North Pole is melting; the world is exhausting its precious resources, while televangelists are convincing people that all they have to worry about is eternal salvation!"

"So, what's that got to do with history, Angela? Tell me that."

"Just about everything. History teaches us to be suspicious about the agendas of our institutions. Now, that's really an American tradition. Even you could agree with that! But we need to forge a new commons – a new way of thinking about saving humankind in **this** world, not the next."

Sean stopped his stride and looked directly into Angela's eyes. She blinked and smiled. He did admire her naïve spirit, even though he could not share it. "You're an impossible dreamer, you know. Humans just can't move on to a higher order of thinking. Historians are not supposed to unravel the mysteries of the human condition. We just report them."

"How 'bout report them with a perspective toward liberation of the mind?"

"So who could disagree with that, Angie?"

"There's the spirit, Sean. So invite me to your apartment this evening for dinner, and we can figure it out?"

Sean was flabbergasted. His apartment was his private cloister. He rebelled at the thought. Such entanglements were to be avoided. But the loneliness of years of solo study suddenly and unexpectedly swept over him. He relented.

"Seven, sharp! At my place. But only for dinner. I've got to study."

"Okay. See you then. I'll bring the food and cook Mexican," She waved and strode purposefully across the Quad."

Sean wandered home thinking about the lost time he would spend cleaning up his apartment. He regretted the impetuous invitation already. "Damn, Gramsci" he thought, "It had been so peaceful."

Chapter XI
The Visitor

Sean lacked social graces, and he knew it. He tried to repress the thought. His father had taught him about nature and not etiquette. He was habitually uncomfortable at the dinners hosted by professors or at university banquets. He was out of his element, and he despised the wine and cheese chatter of an obligatory cocktail hour.

He straightened up his rooms as best he could, frustrated by the absence of enough bookshelves. Books multiplied like rabbits in his apartment. He stuffed clothes into already packed closets and drawers. "Why does it matter anyhow?" he thought. "After all, his objective was to get rid of Angela as soon possible."

Angela arrived dressed to the nines, tight True Religion jeans tucked into Gucci high lizard-skin boots. A diaphanous purple blouse swirled around her hips. A turquoise stone the size of a quarter gleamed at her throat. A green pashimina laced slim shoulders. She clutched a grocery bag in one hand, and in the other she held a bottle of wine.

"A Pinot Grigio to soothe the troubled mind?" she lilted.

"I don't drink," Sean replied bluntly.

"A graduate student that doesn't drink. You're a rare bird indeed Sean Connaghan. Maybe tonight will be a first! Where's the kitchen?"

Sean showed her the curtained alcove where he prepared his Spartan meals, and she began to unload the groceries, pausing to open the wine and pour herself a glass. There was an awkward silence. Sean felt uncomfortable with Angela's abrupt take-over of his apartment, and the ensuing silence was awkward. Fortunately, she began to chatter about the exploitation of Wal-Mart employees and how she refused to buy there. A knock on the door interrupted her happy digression.

"Who could that be?" Sean muttered. "Not a visitor for months and now two!"

Striding across the floor he swung the door wide to see a young woman framed in the afternoon light. Sean stiffened, and his mind raced. It was Lily.

"So, Seanaghan! Surprised to see me? Like a blithe fairy floatin' in, I am."

She embraced Sean's taut frame and studied his face before quickly kissing him on the cheek. "Why you're blushing! Whatever for?"

Sean felt as if he had been struck by summer lightning. He was speechless for a moment before his wits returned.

"Lily, I…I…don't.."

"I know," she said lightly touching his lips with one forefinger, "You don't have to say anything. Nice digs," she noted, casting one look around the cramped apartment, "but you need some more bookshelves."

Suddenly, Angela emerged from the kitchen alcove, wiping her hands with a dishtowel.

"You **do** live a secret life, Sean Connaghan. Just as my friends said, "Angela extended her hand toward Lily. Name's Angela. I'm one of Sean's colleagues in historical crime. Nice to meet you, Lily. It's good to know that Sean is actually a social creature, after all."

"I wouldn't go that far in my estimation," Lily replied smiling as she shook her hand, "but he does have his own charm hidden within that serious demeanor."

"Well," Angela paused, sensing the awkward moment, "I'll just put on another plate for dinner. I'll let you two catch up."

Sean slouched into his worn couch, rubbing his forehead, as Lily pulled a chair up to him. He tried to recover his composure.

"It's really good to see you Lily."

"Mean it?" She whispered, "I hope that I'm not disturbing anything…I mean…you know."

"Oh, her? No…no. Just an acquaintance from school. Nothing like that. But how did you get here? I mean, why did you decide to…"

"Well, Graves is lecturing at Columbia, and I thought I'd catch a train up from New York to see if you were still alive. You ought to be ashamed for not writing me," she chided.

"How is the venerable bastard, anyway? Still chasing ghosts for the Provisional IRA?" Sean said, avoiding the issue of no letters.

"Well, that's another reason for my trip...I..."

Sean interrupted, "I should have guessed. This is not a social visit."

"That's not true. I've missed you so much. You can't imagine."

"Yeah...imagination is not my strong point, especially when it comes to you."

"Okay, I'll give you that. But I am concerned about Graves. Ever since the Good Friday Agreement of 1998 and after the decommissioning of the IRA Army Council in 2001, Graves has not been himself. More drinking and now he has gotten himself involved in the Oglaigh nah Eireann, a group christened by the Irish media as 'the real IRA.' It plans to resurrect the conflict and believes that no political settlement, short of union with the Republic will suffice. And in the present climate, I'm surprised that customs agents didn't arrest him at Kennedy when we arrived. But then, he has always been deep under cover." She paused for Sean's reaction.

"Why are you telling me all this, Lily? I mean, all that mystery surrounding our work and the implied threats. Spiriting me off to the Aran Islands. Christ, that's all in the past. Forgotten. Done. Got it!"

Lily leaned forward and implored. "Sean. Please listen. You may be the only one that can reach him now. He thinks of you as a son."

"Now there's a revelation! The great and mighty Oz thinks of me as a son?"

"Please trust me, Sean. I know him well."

"I bet you do," he intoned, "Maybe in his bed?"

Lily slapped him hard across the face. Then, placing her face in her hands, she wept. He realized he had gone too far.

"He's my father, Sean," she whispered through her sobs.

Sean shuttered. It all made sense to him now. Lily's sobs took him back to the loss of his own father. He understood her fears. He wanted to help, but it was not in him. Distrust and isolation had hardened him. Sean searched for a soft tenderness in his reply, but it would not come.

"I'm sorry, Lily, I can't"

"You mean, you won't," she replied.

"No, I mean I can't. It's not in me. And I really don't believe that it would make a difference. I'm simply headed in another direction."

"And you can't be bothered, right?"

Lily rose and walked to the door. As she opened it, she turned toward Sean. Her eyes glistened with tears.

"There really are fairies on the island, you know. I thought you would remember. I thought that you finally had seen that lighthouse through the mist. I thought you had changed. Guess I was wrong." And with this last remark, she shut the door behind her.

Regret swept over Sean as he rushed out to the landing and yelled down the stairs at Lily's retreating figure.

"Lily, come back! You don't understand…I want to help you, but.."

Angela had emerged from the kitchen and stood in the entryway. She solemnly took his hand and led him back to the couch. She sat down beside him and tenderly brushed his long hair from his forehead.

"You're more promising than I had thought, after all. 'Seanaghan,'" she rolled the name out, attempting to humor him in a poor Irish brogue, "I like it!"

"What do you mean?"

"Well, I've been listening. Anyone who served in the IRA has got to understand the need for a new consciousness. I should have known. That's why you've been so secretive."

Sean jumped to his feet.

"No, Lily…I mean Angela…you're mistaken. You've got it all wrong! Oh, I'm so confused."

He slumped back into the couch.

"Known that for years. Now I understand why. No need to explain. Well, you are truly a candidate for Gramsci, after all. You have given up the IRA, but you, my friend, need a replacement for your feelings of aggression against the imperialist foe. And I've got just the medicine for you. You need to change society's consciousness from within – not by force and violence from without. Gramsci learned that lesson in Russia. You learned it in Ireland. Boy, you are a find for me! My first convert."

Sean moaned in disbelief and rolled over flat on the couch, stuffing a worn pillow in his face.

"You could not be more wrong...wrong...wrong," he muttered over and over.

"Sure. I understand your need to conceal all of this. In these times one can't be too cautious. Don't worry. Mums the word. You can depend on me. Wouldn't want you to lose your fellowship for a comrade in arms...or rather thought. Sorry. But just in case, it's probably time that you exited New Haven for awhile. I suspect the FBI may have been following Lily. One can't tell these days. I have an idea."

Sean rose from his turmoil and sat on the edge of the couch, threading his fingers through his hair nervously.

"There's no convincing a person like you, with all those conspiracy theories running loose in that fertile mind. I give up! I'm no match for insanity. What's another crazy idea when you are in an asylum?"

"Well, I know that you have been struggling for a dissertation topic, and you've come up short and frustrated each time."

"How did you know that, busybody?"

"Common knowledge. Librarians talk. Students listen. It's our business. Besides, rumors provide what little fun we have in our cloistered existence. Of course, that's beyond your kin. You're the chief monk in the cloister. Just hear me out."

"Proceed, oh great nun of the convent."

"Sean, I don't appreciate that illusion."

"Okay...sorry. Get on with it!"

"Well, as you may have guessed, I have been researching American religious movements, and Mormonism has intrigued me the most. You know, the idea that an indigenous religion could develop, combining the myth of manifest destiny with divine inspiration. Just the stuff that would prove Gramsci's thinking. Well, I came across all of these manuscripts and letters by a guy called James Strang who settled an island in Northern Lake Michigan as a branch of the Mormon faith. He even claimed that he was the real prophet of the Church of the Latter Day Saints, anointed by Joseph Smith."

"You mean Brigham Young was a usurper?"

"Yes. And I believe that the letter of Strang's appointment from Joseph Smith is to be found at Beaver Island. That and more. I believe that you might also find evidence that Strang was really a fraud, along with Joseph Smith, and that a conspiracy existed among the elders of the Church to create a religion solely as a corporation to enrich themselves and perpetuate a paternalistic sexist and racist society free from government control."

"You know, Angela, that I would not necessarily buy into the conspiracy thing."

"Hey, let it lead you where it will. I'm confident you might get there. You were IRA!"

"No..wasn't"

"Oh..forgot. Of course," she whispered. "Look, you need a topic and you need it quick. Plus, you have to get a chapter on your advisors desk before next fall. So, I'll give you my notes and you're off."

Her last remark prompted her to look down at her watch.

"Oh…I'm late for a meeting. Got to run. See you tomorrow. What a productive evening! And more excitement than I've had in years. Delicious. You're in my web, Seanaghan. Can't escape me and Gramsci now!"

Sean slumped into the couch as Angela kissed him on the cheek. He had experienced more kisses that evening than he had in years. That was the only gift of the evening. They had dredged up memories that would be difficult to shelve. But he would turn to work to forget. Angie was right. He was desperate for a dissertation topic. And he did like islands.

Chapter XII
Passage

The frothy wake of the twin engine Cummins diesels slapped the channel breakwaters and rebounded into a choppy chaos of on-coming surf. Sean Connaghan gazed backward at the closing drawbridge. He could barely make out the form of the bridge-master, alone in his glassy perch. He envied the simplicity and power of his work. Very few people could stop time and movement for five minutes without engendering wrath.

The wait at the bridge was accepted as an inevitable inconvenience of traveling down Bridge Street at the height of the summer season. To most it was a quaint interlude, a reminder of the purpose of the vacation respite. As the clanging of the bridge's warning bells abruptly stopped, and the traffic streamed forward, Sean felt a distance with the mainland. The turbulent teal green inland sea lay ahead, with its choirs of whitecaps stretched to the horizon. The song of wind and wave soon drowned the plaintive noise of modern recreation. The Cummins revved and sent the aged trawler surging forward.

Sean lost his footing briefly, dropping to his knees, and almost sliding overboard. Struggling to grab the gunwale, he felt a taunt forearm pull him upright.

"Lock your knees and lose your ass, baby Prof," the voice bellowed above the Cummins, "you're not in the main reading room of the Library of Congress. This card catalog floats!"

"Hey, I've been on boats before," Sean shouted over the engine noise, "and most of them had captains who didn't try to wash the fishermen off the pier in their wake."

"This ain't no boat, baby Prof," the captain shouted back as he coiled the bow mooring line. "It's a Great Lakes trawler, and fishermen who fish piers need a little spray in the face. Makes them feel like they're out in the big lake, fighting to pull in a giant salmon. Anyway, you got balls! If you'd booked a passage early, I wouldn't have had the pleasure of preventing your academic high-ass from falling into the drink." The captain dropped the coiled mass on the deck. "And now if you'll excuse me, I'll adjourn to the galley to prepare scones and cream for high tea."

Sean began to regret his decision to hitch a ride with this vagabond fisherman. It was foolish of him not to plan ahead to book passage on the ferry at the height of the summer tourist season. The ferries were packed to the gills for two straight weeks. But how could he ever have anticipated this journey? Just a few years ago, he was culling through antiquarian book stores in Dublin. And now he was bounding across Lake Michigan toward a remote island in a fishing trawler run by a swarthy Indian with hair down to his shoulders who thought he knew more about the Library of Congress than he did.

He had met John "White Fox" Whitesides at the Parkside restaurant near the municipal docks. The restaurant owner, Leo Markle, bought the restaurant's specialty, whitefish, in bulk from the Indian. The business had suffered of late because of the settlement of an ancient treaty dispute over fishing rights on the Great Lakes. Commercial fishing was now under the exclusive control of the Odawa Nation. Leo, a patient man with sparkling blue eyes, now depended on Native American fishermen to supply his daily needs. The hoards of summer yachters and tourists had made his restaurant one of the most famous watering holes on the lakes. The supply was spotty at best, but Whitesides seemed the most reliable and experienced of the Little Traverse Band of Odawa. Most were still re-learning the art of gill netting which had long ago disappeared from the lower Great Lakes culture.

Leo had listened to Sean's predicament as he waited for Whitesides trawler, *Amikwa*. Its rusty hull had slipped past the long line of glistening glass, stainless steel, and white fiberglass yachts moored in cocktail chatter at the docks. The pungent odor of dead fish wafted through the air in defiance of the pristine world of elegant recreation. Sunbathers on deck rose from their ritual baking to grimace at the odious intrusion. Even the quaint quality of a working vessel in the harbor no longer seemed appropriate for a starched scene of bright sails and polished brass. The playground of the present only tolerated the past in museums.

After a brief chat Leo persuaded the skipper to take the young graduate student to Beaver Island. It was a small favor. The student planned to research Island history. Whitesides knew he was late—too late for the lunch crowd again, but he also knew that Leo was slow to anger. How could he not accommodate this small request? It was in keeping with the Chippewa custom of reciprocal generosity. Whitesides swallowed his resentment momentarily and acceded to the ancient pull of custom. So the passage was booked, and a detour to the island arranged. Sean thanked Leo for his kindness. When the fish were unloaded, he threw his baggage on board. It was an impulsive act for Sean to venture onto the big lake in what looked like a vessel that could have auditioned for the part of the African Queen. That passing thought now weighed heavy on Sean's mind.

The swells grew deeper as the dunes faded into the summer haze. On the forward horizon storm clouds formed in the distance. Afternoon thunderheads rising to forty thousand feet cast roving shadows across the water, turning it a dark purple. Shafts of sunlight christened the whitecaps with an iridescent glow. Sean felt a kind of exhilaration he had rarely experienced since childhood. The same feeling had swept over him the first time his radio flyer wagon had careened down a riverbank into a rushing mountain rapids. It was one of the last times in a cautious childhood when he chose to chance fate on the whim of the moment. His gashed lip and a broken nose had convinced him that such momentary impulses were too costly to risk repeating. As the waves began to break and wash over the bow of the trawler, he wondered if this experience too had a similar price tag. To Sean, every good feeling always required payment at some later time in the currency of pain and grief.

"Hey, Jack London. You better get your ass in the wheelhouse before that front hits!"

Sean wobbled toward the wheelhouse and shut the small entry door, muting the wind and waves. The Indian was lifting a fifth of Johnny Walker Black Label to his lips.

"Pretty rich brew for a . . .," Sean stopped his speech abruptly.

"For an Indian," the skipper rejoined. "Yeah, I clean ran out of cheap firewater."

"I meant for a fisherman," Sean said awkwardly, recovering from his near foipa. "What is it with you anyway? I thought the captain was supposed to extend every courtesy to his passengers. How about a truce until we reach the island?"

"Okay. Truce." Whitesides extended his hand and Sean shook it. "Name's *Payzhikwaywedong*, but Anglos call me Whitesides, or White Fox, if you want. From Thunder Clan. Beaver Island Chippewa of Little Traverse Band of Ottawa & Chippewa. So we're stuck with each other. Besides, the lake's angry, and we must not tempt its fury, . . . could raise a bad manitou."

"Manitou? I suppose you're going to tell me that the lake is infested by some prehistoric Nessie."

"You're the professor. You tell me."

"Somehow I get the impression that you must have been an abused student who harbors visions of lashing his high school history teacher to the mast and torturing him with oblique questions about Native American history, like how Tecumseh perished at Tippecanoe."

"He didn't perish. He was killed. And it wasn't at Tippecanoe. It was Moraviantown. But I give you some credit for knowing more than my history teacher."

"Then I wasn't far from the mark after all. Now that you've answered a question, perhaps you would be kind enough to tell me about your 'manitou.' Are we about to be engulfed by some Jonahian beast?"

Whitesides paused before he answered. "A manitou is a spirit of a living thing which reveals itself as good or bad only to those who respect the power of its being. Look inside yourself. Look at the lake and you will sense its direction. Ignore it, and you ignore your connection with all that surrounds you . . . your manitou and all others."

"Thanks anyway, I think I prefer Nessie. Facts are easier to digest for a historian than fiction."

"Fiction!" Whitesides bellowed. "Just what I would expect from a *chemokmon*. People like you have fictionalized our facts into oblivion. It is your facts, *chemokmon*, that have become the reality of this ruined planet—your science, your philosophy, your history!"

Sean started to laugh uncontrollably. "My God, I thought I had left the university behind. And now I'm being lectured on the tyranny of Western Civilization's devastation of the noble savage. Well, Mr. John White Fox, it's a damn good thing in this storm that the learning of Western Civilization gave us that radar screen to get through that raging storm up ahead."

Whitesides glanced at the blank radar screen.

"Doesn't work. Not since I bought the boat from 'ole Jonas Martin on the island. No, baby Prof, it's just the manitous and us. Fiction, baby, fiction!"

"Great. Just great! In manitou we trust! When do we inscribe it on the coins?"

The Indian was now sprinkling loose tobacco from a Sir Walter Raleigh pouch over the side of the vessel. He chanted in low moans, occasionally interspersed with a sharp staccato invocation.

"*Missipeshu*!"

He's gone native on me, Sean thought, drunk and native.

"Missy piss on you!" Sean yelled against the rising wind. "This is no time to make a statement about the effects of passive smoking on the nation's health."

Whitesides raised his hands skyward without replying and continued the chant.

"*Missipeshu, Missipeshu*!"

"Hey, is this thing on automatic pilot or . . . "

Whitesides burst through the pilot house door and grasped the wheel, glowering. "You think this is just a sport, hey baby Prof? Your irreverence is what I would expect from one who studies but does not learn. *Missipeshu* may now give us both the lesson of our life. Maybe you're one of those who think any body of water surrounded by a continent can't eat men and ships, but your Rudyard Kipling saw this lake as a nightmare—a hideous thing to find in the heart of a continent." He pointed at the dark sea ahead, now tossed with huge white breakers, casting foam a fathom into the angry air. "That's your nightmare, baby Prof, that's *Missipeshu*!" Even your explorers had the good sense to say *Te Deum's* for safe passage. I suggest that you do the same if you hope to weather this passage."

Whiteside's sober soliloquy started Sean's heart pounding. Whitesides was drunk, and they were both at the mercy of the coming nightmare.

"Okay, what do I do?," Sean contritely asked.

The Indian mariner stared dead ahead.

"Hang on, were coming about North Northwest and heading into its teeth. If we're lucky we'll miss the rocks at Iron Ore point and pass to the South of Beaver. You can watch for the South Head beacon. If we see it, I'll make a course correction. That should do it!"

"South Head beacon?"

"Yeah, it's the old lighthouse on the South end of the island, and let's hope its not on the fritz. The Iron Ore Bay property owners restored it for effect. Sometimes it works, sometimes not. Tourism just might be our redemption after all."

"It's bad, isn't it?"

"*Missipeshu*, baby Prof, *Missipeshu*!"

The storm front surged to meet the boat's bow. The first huge wave crashed and swept over the deck, drowning their voices and causing *Amikwa's* twin propellers to spin in midair at each wave crest. The wind screamed at them, as it smashed against the vessel's sides erratically, first pushing it at the crest to the starboard, then to the leeward as Whitesides spun the wheel to control the forward slide down the surfy sea mountains. For the next two hours they plunged through the darkness to the South Head, unable to hear each other over the roar of wind and sea. For the first time in his life Sean repeated what he remembered of the Twenty-third Psalm over and over, but the stories of his childhood, of banshees screaming down to lift him into the sky intruded. Whitesides was right. It was a nightmare. *Missipeshu* and banshees and Kipling's hideous thing all charging at him at once, until he glimpsed a flicker in the distance. Whitesides saw it too.

"Time it, Sean," Whitesides yelled, "Time it!"

"What?"

"Time the flash. How many seconds between flashes?"

Sean tried to keep his eyes on his cheap Timex. But the second hand had stopped

"Take mine," Whitesides offered.

Sean tried to focus on the dial. One, two, three, four. He timed it again.

"Four," he burst. "I think its four!"

"Shit! Those assholes ought to be reported to the Coast Guard! It's supposed to be three. Summer jackasses playing yachting games. Toys! We'll just have to hope it's South Head."

Sean remembered little after this last tirade. He remembered a lunge of the boat downward and a whirling and crash that sent him through glass and water and into a deep sleep. He saw a long boat open with many passengers, a family at the oars, talking in merriment of going home. The boat had scarcely gone out of sight when a terrifying darkness enveloped it. It was a strange, foreboding darkness; a strange emptiness in the sky and a spine-chilling blackness on the sea. It was like an evening on which hundreds were being hanged.

Chapter XIII
Awakening

Sean felt the warmth of evening sunlight through the sheets spread across his torso. His eyes flickered open to a blinding white Northern light, only to close tightly again in burning repose. As he tried to lift his hand to shade the glare, a piercing pain shot up his arm to his shoulder and neck. He felt his moan before he heard it. Squinting, he slowly opened one eye, then another, to a blurred haze of light and mottled shades of black and white. When his eyes finally focused, the ceiling danced with a vibrato of shaded images. Birch trees! The shadows of birch trees, just like he had seen every morning flicker across his bedroom wall as a boy. The vision comforted him. He could imagine the leaves tremble in a quickening breeze, the kind of August mountain breeze which foreshadowed an afternoon thunderstorm.

"Storm, storm," he suddenly shouted out. "Jump . . . swim . . . grab it! Help me grab it! It's gone. Grab it! Reach, reach! Harder! Swim!"

"Hold on, sailor. Relax. You've got it. You reached it. You're safe. Lie back down." The voice spoke as firmly as the hands which gently pressed his shoulders back onto the sheets. "You're safe. There's no storm. You're here on the island. Out of the water. Out of danger. You going to be fine, just fine. Now go back to sleep."

Sean slipped back into sleep's arms as the voice softly sung a lullaby. "Shlaf, meine freude, shlaf in himlisher ruh."

Sean awakened to the sounds of whispers.

"He's overdo, Leah, you know as well as I do that he should have arrived months ago."

"Yes, yes...but he's here now and . . . well, it will just take a little longer than usual," the lullaby voice responded.

"Usual. Usual. There is no usual in this business," the first voice rose in frustration. "Wait until I get my hands on Whitesides. Every time he hits the bottle, it's trouble."

"Now, you know that there was no other way. Only a native could deliver him here. Any other way would be too risky."

"No more risky than losing him at sea."

"Quiet! Remember now, Our Father Protar was almost lost at sea too upon his first visitation, and consider what he accomplished,

. . . sainthood, island sainthood no less."

The whispers drifted down the hall as footsteps on the pine floor tapped toward the room. As Sean struggled to raise himself on the bed to hear more, the door pushed open to reveal a dark-haired, stocky middle-aged woman in khaki fatigue shorts and a green work shirt rolled up to the elbow. Her hiking boots clomped across the room as she rushed around the bed to spread the curtains. The open window revealed the stunning brilliance of sand dune, wildflowers, and tall grass cascading down to a sandy beach and into a wash of lake teals and blue reaching to the horizon.

"Well, mashugena, you're up!"

"I have some doubt about that. In fact I have some doubt about whether I'm alive or just been thrust onto the set of a Robinson Crusoe movie."

The lullaby voice laughed heartily as the woman removed the pillow from under his head and vigorously ruffled it to fullness. As she lifted his head to replace the pillow, her long, glistening black hair swept across his face revealing her large, deep-set brown eyes . . warm poignant eyes.

"We should be so lucky. There hasn't been a film made of this island since Jimmy and Mary Gallagher's 50th wedding anniversary two years ago, unless you count the Chamber of Commerce tourism video. No, Sean, I'm afraid you've washed up in the remote equivalent of the Wayne's World garage. Everything here is either homemade, broken, or imported from the mainland Sears."

"How did you know my name?"

"Oh, well . . . , " she hesitated, "It's not everyday that someone arrives on driftwood. Has a romantic touch. I've already had to fight off the staff of the *Beaver Beacon* for an interview. Had you not awakened today, you would have been caught by them at the 'hareport' for an interview on the way to the Petoskey hospital. You're famous, Sean

Connaghan! Not since the first mate from the *Milwaukee Belle* was found dead stiff in the surf of Iron Ore Bay has there been this much excitement around here. That is, unless you count the Colombian drug runner that landed at the 'hareport' last May, or the time . . . ."

"Anyone tell you that you speak in stories instead of sentences. Good God, I feel like I just survived the wreak of the *Mary Deare* to become the subject of tabloid curiosity for summer tourists and Northern hilljacks. Could you kindly just tell me who the hell you are, where I am, and why my back feels like Jaws had me for lunch?"

"Sorry, left my manners on the mainland. It's the loons you know. You live with them long enough, and you start warbling in fragments like a mad woman, they say . . . ."

"Whatever they say, they're right on target. You are loony."

"Yup, how did you know? Of course I didn't coin the name, but it does have a ring to it—the loon ranger—it's me.!"

"Okay, I've got it. I've slipped through the looking glass and you're the mad hatter, and we're going to have a tea party." Sean settled into the bed and pulled the sheet over his head.

"Silly me. I do have some tea but . . . okay. Look, it gets a little lonely here, and I do ramble. Let me concentrate on giving you the *Reader's Digest* version, . . . if you'll come out from underneath there."

Her lullaby voice returned with this last entreaty. Sean allowed one eye to peer over the sheet.

"Promise?"

"Scout's honor." She raised two fingers in the V sign. "You know I was a . . . no. My name is Leah Greenbach, resident biologist of the university biological station in which you presently reside. Sand Bay, Beaver Island, formerly of Woods Hole before University of Miami, before Queens, New York. Daughter of George Gershwin of Broadway where I played child vaudeville shows, before I was enslaved as a strip tease artist on 42nd street, where I learned to love and admire the haunting cry of the loon from audience reaction, which of course in turn stimulated a love for distant marshes in Lake Michigan. Nice ring to it, huh?"

Leah's story rolled from her tongue as quickly as an island hare scooting into the bushes.

"Stop, please! Don't say anymore. I think I've got enough to work with for the moment. How about that tea? I might as well enjoy this reverie. They won't believe it in New Haven."

Leah brought a tray with an ornate teapot and cups to the bedside table. "Whiffenpoofs. Yaley right? Should have known. Stiff upper lip, short cropped hair, and that look of arrogant indifference. Whiffenpoofs. I always loved that name. Should be the name of a bird, but only thing close is "whinchat," small European saxicoline bird, *saxicola rubetra*, brown and buff in color, frequents grassy meadows, known for its incessant whine."

"I can relate to the whine part. How about the chat?" Sean sighed.

"A punster, heh? You may have some potential for island conversation after all. So tell me, how does a Yaley find himself on the Isle du Castor?" Leah daintily lifted her cup to her lips in mocking sophistication, batted her eyes playfully, and paused for a reply.

"Mormons, Leah. I came to study the Strangite Mormons. It's the subject of my dissertation. I've exhausted the Coe Collection at the Yale Library. In particular I'm searching for evidence that a letter, purported to have been written by Joseph Smith to James Strang, which appointed him ruler of the Church of Latter Day Saints, is authentic. Such a letter would prove Brigham Young to be a usurper and . . . "

Leah interrupted, "Now whose telling stories?"

"Occupational hazard for an aspiring historian, I guess," Sean replied, "But for an American historian, the Mormon experience seems to capture the essence of American manifest destiny."

"But how is it that Native Americans didn't believe in this destiny. Weren't the American Indians the descendants of the Lost Ten Tribes of Israel according to Mormon faith?"

"Not bad for a biologist, Leah. How did you become a student of Mormonism?"

"Easy, slick. Three reasons. First, if you live on this island you can't avoid it. Part of the lore of place. Second, the stuff is as loony as the birds I study. Third, one of those lost tribes happens to be my own, except we believe that we're the chosen people. Not that there's room for more, but I happen to place more credence in the Ark of the Covenant and the dead sea scrolls than engraved plates dug up in somebody's back yard in New York. Holy matza balls, if anyone was going to be led to holy tablets by heavenly messengers in New York, it would have been my people. Hey, not that I don't believe in angels. They're all over this island. But think about it, Mormons in the heart of Irish Virgin Mary country? Only manifest destiny here was disaster. Indians, Mormons, and Irish Catholics don't mix...different manitous, angels, spirits, whatever. Just too much unholy competition for holiness."

"And I wonder how I got here," Sean interjected.

"I suspect the manitous didn't expect your arrival either. Just another example of manifest destiny in action, the myth of the melting pot is alive and well on Beaver Island!"

With this exchange they both laughed at the strangeness of their exceptional encounter.

"Speaking of manitous, what happened to Whitesides?" The memory of the crash surfaced, and Sean felt overwhelmed with embarrassment for not asking earlier. "Is he all right? Was he injured? Where is he?" Sean sat up.

"Hold on champ! He's fine, just fine. In fact he's probably at the Shamrock saloon in Saint James retelling the story for the umpteenth time. By the time he's done, the great manitou himself will have lifted you up out of the sea and deposited you gently on shore for a marshmallow roast. You know he dropped you off here. Guess he knew Doc Murphy was on vacation. Didn't have a scrape on him. He seemed more worried about calling his insurance agent to make a claim on that old scow, *Amikwa*. Anyway, nobody ever did worry about Whitesides. That tough Ojibway has weathered more storms on this lake than the French explorers."

"Leah, did he pull me in?" Sean queried seriously.

"Yeah, Sean, he did indeed, and I assure you that the next issue of the *Beacon* will enshrine his heroism in its pages with hyperbole the likes of which you shall never read again. The Irish love a good sea story, although they prefer a few dead bodies to convey a sense of unsolved mystery for the tourists. Yep, Sean, your destiny is island legend."

"I'm not here to be grist for legend. I'm here to find a few facts at the Mormon Print Shop. Then I'm outta here . . . on the biggest damn ferry I can find."

"That's tomorrow, Sean. There's always a tomorrow here on the island. You know, they creep at an endless pace from day to day. I'll give you a good breakfast and the address of a friend's "bed and breakfast," far from the limelight of the prying curiosity of the *Beacon*." She laughed. "Then I'll be off to study my loons and you to the Mormons. Both species are on the edge of extinction here. Until then, Seanaghan, sleep well."

Sean froze. "How did you know that name?"

"What name? Oh, . . . Seanaghan?" Leah recovered quickly. "It's Irish, right? The Irish are fond of mixing first and last names. Guess I heard it on the Island. Go to bed. It's late."

Leah picked up the tray, walked to the door and switched off the lights. "Sweet dreams, Seanaghan," she whispered under her breath in her lullaby voice. "Welcome to your awakening."

Sean gazed out the window at the night sky. The Northern Lights illuminated it with pulsating curtains of color. It was the first time he had seen them since that first lonely night on Inishmore in Robartes cottage. Perhaps, Graves was right. The mystical had a life of its own. Too much had happened. He was drifting without oars, wondering if the lighthouse's beacon was strangely pulling him to another distant shore.

Chapter XIV
Saints & Sinners

Sean awoke to find a note from Leah on the bedside table. It read:

> *Off looning to Barney's Lake. Left clothes and sundries in suitcase in closet. Hope they fit. I've telephoned Harvey Burdick down the road to give you a ride into St. James. Since we have students arriving today, I've taken the liberty of arranging boarding at Kate Fox's B & B. It's called The Dove. Kate works with Harvey at the Shamrock Saloon. You'll like it. Blueberry muffins and coffee in the kitchen. Help yourself.*
> *See you around. Happy hunting! Leah.*

The message ended with one of those smiley faces which Sean despised. At least she hadn't written, "Have a Nice Day!" below it. He turned the note over. "Have a Nice Day!" Leah was an incurable optimist, he thought, a little crazy, but full of buoyant passion for life. He owed her.

By the time Sean had finished breakfast, an old Land Rover pulled up in the driveway. A tall, angular man with graying temples emerged and walked toward the station. Sean met him at the door.

"Harvey Burdick. You must be Sean Connaghan. Welcome to the island! Leah said you needed a ride into town. If you don't mind, I'm running behind and have an errand to run on the way. Could we . . . ?"

"Sure, I'm ready. Let's go."

The Land Rover bounded down the driveway in a cloud of dust and onto a broad gravel road lined with towering northern pine and spruce. Sean grabbed the dash handle to avoid being tossed into Burdick's lap. His bruised back wrenched in pain.

"Could you slow down a bit, Harvey? I'm still recovering from my accident, and . . . "

"Sorry, I forget. We're accustomed to these corduroy roads. Damn county road commission on the mainland could care less about the island. We've been trying to get the King's Highway repaved for years." Harvey slowed and veered to avoid a large pothole. "Leah didn't tell me about an accident. What happened, fall into the marsh looking for loons?"

Sean was perplexed. Didn't the whole island know?

"She didn't tell you about the wreck of the *Amikwa*?" Sean sensed a need for caution.

"*Amikwa*? No. I just assumed that you were one of those visiting lecturers Leah brings in from time to time. Aren't you from Yale?"

"Ahh . . . , yes, I'm working on my dissertation."

Sean saw no need to draw anymore attention to his situation. Maybe, Leah had exaggerated in the interest of conversation, and he could avoid a diversion from his primary task on the island. She was prone to exaggeration. It was all a nightmare anyway which he preferred not to relive with endless questions.

"So, Harvey, you lived on the island long?" Sean asked him just as the Land Rover nearly careened off the road to avoid a scampering raccoon.

"Love those little guys! Masked robbers. You got to respect a creature who can raid the recycling station time and time again after those mainland bureaucrats forced the closing of the dump." Harvey returned to the question. "Me? An islander? Sean, me boy," he lapsed into a mock Irish accent. "You gotta' be born on this island to be an islander. No matter how wealthy, influential, or even blood related to island kin, you ain't an islander unless you've been born here. They're like that raccoon. They've survived on less than you and I probably had when we arrived in this world. They've seen the Mormons try to steal their island. Almost starved themselves trying to help family in Ireland survive the potato famine. They've seen the lumbering industry founder when coal and oil replaced the old wood-fired steamers at the turn of the century. They've watched the fishing industry come and go. When the lake was fished out in the 70's and fishing rights given back to the Indians, they lost their historic right to survive. Now they depend on the largess of the yachters and tourists and turn to selling old homesteads and farms to investment groups and developers to sustain them. They have to be ingenious to survive. Oh, they'll charm you with their blarney, but you'll not get close to their legacy. Its guarded like a lephrochan's treasure."

"Legacy, what do you mean by legacy?" Sean inquired.

"Why their history of course. Their secrets, their religion, their knowledge of every inch of this island, their feuds, their folklore, their music . . . everything that's left after survival. It's what they have left, and you'll never be a part of it."

Sean could tell he had struck a dissonant chord in Harvey. "Sounds like you're envious to me, Harvey," he risked.

"I guess I am Sean. They're a proud, close family. I guess I envy that."

Harvey's admission touched Sean. He spoke in poetic strains, with a bold honesty that inspired trust.

The Land Rover pulled into a grassy driveway on a windswept knoll before a modest, but well maintained, log cabin, worn with age. Ancient apple trees with small maturing fruit swayed in the breeze off the lake. A large garden of wildflowers near the back of the house softened its rustic features in an impressionistic blur of color. The cabin seemed pulled away from the rest of the island, an antique island of its own . . . a museum without life, yet possessing a life of its own in another time.

"Com'on, let me show you the home of the one person who became an islander without being born here. I've got to open it up for the daily hoard of tourists."

As Sean approached the leaning porch braced by four huge square-cut Mormon hewn logs, his vision blurred momentarily. The cabin seemed to change in a flash of bright light. It suddenly appeared new. He could smell the sweetness of freshly cut cedar. Flowers surrounded the sides of the house. A rain barrel appeared below the roof. Sean turned back toward the Rover to rub his eyes. The Rover was not there. A horse bayed in the barn. A rooster ran across the yard in front of him. A fence encircled the front yard. Sean's body quivered as he yelled, "Harvey, look!"

Sean turned his eyes toward the stone stoop upon which he stood, shaking his head. Harvey turned around from the door and cast his eyes toward Sean's feet. Sean removed his right foot from the large threshold lake rock which centered the stoop.

"Well . . . will you look at that, that stone is broken, split right down the center. Now how do you suppose that happened? Old Protar set that center stone in 1895, over a hundred years ago. I bet those Oliver boys have been vandalizing again! Summer residents. No respect for island! Last year the historical association had to install a burglar alarm system to deal with them, and now they've taken to the outside. Boy, I wish I could nail them, just once."

"No, Harvey, I think I did it. I felt it crack when I . . . "

"Nonsense. That center stone is almost a foot deep. I know. I helped reset it five years ago when the Association restored it. It would take a sledge hammer, at least, or a pickax to crack that stone. No. It's those Oliver boys. Probably still angry from being questioned by the deputy last month."

But Sean knew that something else had happened. His interest in Protar suddenly grew.

"So Harvey, this Protar fellow, how did he get to this island?"

"I never thought you'd ask. The guy fascinates me. Maybe it's because I'm an outsider myself," Harvey replied, engaged by the opportunity to tell the story.

Harvey took an old rusty key from his pocket and opened the old three planked door of the cabin to reveal a sparsely furnished but spotless room with low beams and a cast iron stove. Tucked away in a corner was a small hand-hewn wood bed. Under the window stood a large wooden chest with a wash bowl on top. A hand woven rug bordered with flowers provided the only color in the room. A narrow kitchen contained only a few cupboards, a cutting table, and dining table set with metal dishes for one person.

"Welcome to the home of Feodor Protar, physician, actor, newspaperman, recluse, Barron, and beloved island saint. Thoreau of the island! Here was a man who knew the secrets of the island and the secret of life itself."

"And what was the secret, Harvey? Wait, let me guess . . . indoor plumbing!"

"Smart ass! Protar became the island saint because he sacrificed everything he owned to help others. He was one of those few people who made the transformation from tourist to islander. The son of German scientists of aristocratic lineage, he was exiled to Siberia for freeing the serfs on his estate . . . and escaped. Educated at the University of Dresden as a chemist, he immigrated to Chicago as the manager of an opera diva with whom he eventually acted on the stage. Wrote and eventually owned and edited, *Die Neue Volks-Zeitung,* in which he advanced the ideals of democracy and decried the exploitation of immigrant laborers in the meat packing industry well before Sinclair Lewis thought of writing *The Jungle*."

As Harvey droned on, Sean stepped over to the washing bowl on the chest. It was full of clear water as if it had just been set out for morning use. Sean touched the water with his index finger and shook it. Circular ripples waved to the edges of the bowl. Sean's eyes blurred once again as he gazed at his reflection—a reflection that suddenly revealed not his clean shaven face but the face of an old man with bushy eyebrows, wide-set brown eyes, and a long white beard. Sean turned quickly away, shaking. It was the accident he thought. Did he have a concussion? Yes, that was it. His head must have been injured in the wreck. Yes, that was it. He was hallucinating. He would see a doctor as soon as he arrived in St. James.

Harvey was in the kitchen continuing his story. Sean listened even more intently. "In about 1893 a Rock Island friend, a physician, Dr. Benhardi, prompted him to book passage on a freighter for a leisurely trip to Northern Michigan. And like so many chance encounters that turn the destiny of a man's life, a violent storm forced the ship to take refuge in Paradise Bay. Can you believe it-a castaway on the shores of Beaver Island?"

"Can I believe it?" Sean murmured. "What irony!" The arrival of Protar seemed like the ordinary mode of transport for intellectuals arriving on the island. Just dump them on the beach in a storm, Sean thought.

The double entendre of Sean's response passed over Harvey as he continued the Protar story unimpeded, as if he were rehearsing for the next meeting of the Michigan Historical Association. It was a story he had obviously told before, yet he recited it with the passion of a painter who was restoring an ancient lost triptych to splendor for display in a Russian Orthodox cathedral.

"Protar never told the islanders his story, except for Johnny Green, a close island friend. He went about buying this old cabin, built with Mormon cut logs, gardening and ministering to any islander in medical or spiritual need on an old carriage pulled by his horse, Harry. After 25 years of service old Harry was buried with full honors out back there with a brand new bit and bridle. Protar delivered more babies on snowy nights, sewed up more wounds, and nursed more islanders with fever back to health than any island physician since. He even took in unmanageable children and taught them the meaning of a disciplined and thoughtful life. And when he died, despite his wish to be buried at sea, the islanders carefully built a tomb from the rocks of the lake. They laid him to rest in a birch forest, and at the tomb's head they placed a bronze relief of the old man."

Sean suddenly interrupted. "That bronze relief of Protar. Does it depict a man with a long flowing white beard?" Sean described the figure in the bowl.

"Yes, yes, you've described him to a tee. In the last years, he never used a razor. Here." Harvey pointed to a picture behind the door. It was the image in the bowl.

"Harvey, come over here. Look in the bowl. What do you see?"

Harvey walked over to bowl. "I see a bowl." He lifted it, and turned it over. Sean lunged to avoid a spill. "See, Chicago pottery, 1891, inscribed right here on the bottom. Common piece. They made thousands of them." Sean cringed. Grabbing the bowl from Harvey, he turned it over and over, pondering its dry contours.

Harvey continued his lecture. "And so Sean, that's how you become an islander, you love them. That's how you become a saint." Harvey ended his historical soliloquy in uncharacteristic reverence, pausing and looking toward the tomb to the west as if it were Mecca.

Sean tried vainly to dismiss the image and the broken stone. "Harvey, with all due respect, don't you think this Protar stuff has grown to mythic proportions over the years. You know it makes for good reading for the tourists."

"Sounds like you got an overdose of that highfalutin' eastern snob school education to me, Sean. Protar was a Mother Teresa to these people, and you'd be hard pressed to find a better example of the American spirit." Harvey walked briskly back to the car.

"Harvey, I just meant that the Irish do tend to exaggerate and . . . well, I didn't mean to offend."

"Forget it! When you've been around the island awhile, you'll feel Protar's spirit in the midst of a forest of other spirits, . . . and you'll understand."

"I think I do understand, Harvey," Sean said as he climbed into the Rover, "You remind me of a teacher I once had. He would have said the same thing. So, you see, maybe the eastern universities aren't full of snobs after all."

"Hey, you know what Protar said to Governor Osborn when he made a special trip to the island to honor him? A island driver came to get him, and yelled excitedly to him in the garden, 'Governor Osborn is here to see you, sir. He has heard of you and wishes to meet you.' 'I am here,' said Feodor as he continued to hoe. 'He can see me from where he is.' Feodor had balls." Harvey looked at Sean and they laughed. "Big balls!"

The Land Rover sped around a corner, raising the dust over fields of wildflowers and past long stands of apple trees planted almost 140 years ago by the Mormons. Down Sloptown Road to the Kings Highway and onto the short stretch of worn blacktop that led into the village of St. James. They sped past the Christian Brothers retreat, the island school, and Holy Cross Church to a stop sign at the hill overlooking the village. There, the old truck stalled as Sean surveyed the view before him.

He gasped . . . spellbound. The words jumped from his lips. "Holy Mother of God, it's Inishmore!"

Harvey was lifting the bonnet of the Rover, swearing under his breath. Sean jumped out and stood frozen by the scene. Except for the absence of rocky outcroppings, it mirrored the curvature and size of the harbor at Kilronan. The shipping wharf in the middle faced the bay entrance. The shops and houses lined the road around the harbor, with clumps of homes positioned on the rise above the shops below. The small village stretched around the harbor to an isthmus. There stood a magnificent whitewashed lighthouse, gazing out at the great blue inland sea. I've been here before, he thought. No, it was not Inishmore, he thought. It just resembled it.

The rush of Ireland spread through Sean. The mingling of moist cottage peat smoke, whiskey, and wind off the Atlantic filled his senses. Was it really the Mormons who drew him here, or was it Rose speaking to him again? Infernal imagination. A Yeats verse rolled through his head.

Here, travellor, scholar, poet, take your stand.
When all those rooms and passages are gone,
When nettles wave upon a shapeless mound
And saplings root among the broken stone.

Travellor, scholar, poet. Protar of the broken stone. Protar of the room and passage gone. He must see that doctor, Sean thought, as he walked down the hill to the harbor.

Chapter XV
Kate

The Shamrock Saloon buzzed with island chatter. The lunch crowd filled every table, including the pool room in the back. Sean passed through a haze of cigarette smoke, past the pinball machine to the far end of the heavy oak bar. Above its gleaming surface hung rack after rack of mugs adorned with coats of arms and the names of island families—Kelly, Gillespie, Lyons, Molloy, O'Mooney, McCafferty, and O'Byrne, names reaching back to Arranmore and County Donegal. Some were noted in the Donegal style of naming people with the family history recited. There were the Paddy Bawn Boyles and the Liam Hughdie Boyles, the Eamonawn Gallaghers and the Paudeen Eoin Gallagers, the Condy Neddy Molloys and Illion Molloys. Empty spaces indicated the presence someplace in the bar of a family member. The back wall displayed a strange mixture of relics. A mounted deer head with rack graced an old Guinness sign. Faded ribbons from county fairs, both Ireland and Charlevoix, fluttered beside shelves of baseball trophies where miniature bronze batters swung away. A string of perch dangled over a model of a Great Lakes fishing trawler. The memorabilia of Erin joined the rustic cacophony of North woods plunder. Curling photographs of lumbermen, Indians, and Irish pipers adorned rough-hewn cedar walls.

Sean surveyed the sprawling mix of patrons. Two realtors with an Island map spread before them extolled the beauty of various plats of lake shore property to a tourist couple whose children fidgeted with boredom. A group of cyclists from the mainland lifted their Perrier in a toast to their encirclement of the island in record speed. Two elderly men with white shirts and suspenders, concentrated on a checkers game, their cohorts egging them on. A meandering group of teenagers slammed the pinball machine as bing after bing rattled over the din of conversation and laughter. Several Indians sat hunched over a back table, heads bent close in rapt conversation over beer, each with a filleting knife strapped to their worn and oily jeans.

What a group, Sean mused. And not a vestige of Mormonism to be seen, not even a clean cut missionary in traditional white shirt and black tie with his bike parked in front. Of course not. What a foolish thought. Sean's library research had so enmeshed him in the past that he had expected to see a few Mormons wearing 19th century garb strolling the streets of St. James.

"Well, stranger things have happened today. Why not?" he muttered. A feminine voice from behind the bar interrupted Sean's rumination.

"So, what will it be traveler?" The voice sang out.

Sean turned around and encountered a face that drew him back to Inishmore with a jolt. Was it the reincarnation of Maude Gonne? Teal eyes sparkled like the silver gleam of a late afternoon sun. A silky shock of thick auburn hair swept along one shoulder and across a tanned line skimming her breasts, a line below which Sean did not dare gaze.

Embarrassed, he muddled a hasty, "What? I mean . . . ." He surprised himself with the naturalness of his next response. "You're a beautiful rose." What a corny line, Sean thought. God! I can't believe I said that.

"Yeah, the rose of Trelee. Maybe, you ought not to be drinking after all, traveler." The beautiful stranger turned away to serve another patron.

"Wait!" Sean called. "I was referring to that bottle up there. Ah! Five Roses . . . right . . . yes, that's what I'll have, Five Roses." Quite a recovery Seanaghan. Maybe, your Irish isn't so bad after all.

"Okay, not what I pegged you for, but it's your stomach."

The girl reached for the bottle. Sean examined her long, sinewy legs. This was not his style. Gawking at a barmaid was not his style at all.

"My name is Sean Connaghan, what's yours?" he spoke awkwardly.

"Kate . . . Kate Fox."

"Kate of the B & B Kate Fox, I presume." His balance had returned. "Leah Greenbach recommended your place. Do you have an available room for a tired student weary of life on the high seas?" Charm came hard for him, but he was determined to engage this enchanting woman.

"Oh yes, Leah told me that you'd be showing up. I've prepared a bedroom for you. But if you want a ride, you'll have to wait until I get off at five. Of course there's always Kerry's Jeep Rental up the street. You can rent Dartangan for a song. You look like the Dartangan type. Or there's Archemedies and Galileo."

"Jeeps with names. Do they have Jung or Freud? Such a jeep could run on dreams."

"Some people around here think they do, or at least on hope. They're in constant need of repair." She paused, scrutinizing Sean in a keen gaze. "So you're a student. Look a little old for the books."

"You're never too old for books. Actually, I'm working on my dissertation." He hesitated to say more. The Dartangan illusion suited him well, he thought, for this occasion.

"He's modest, Kate." A voice interjected. "This one's a Yaley chasing Mormon ghosts. Wants to appoint Strang king of the Mormons again. How would that play back in Salt Lake?" Harvey appeared from behind the bar, strapping a white apron to his waist.

"Not well, Harv. Afraid he'd need your shotgun for protection."

Kate moved down the bar to serve another customer.

"Harvey, is she from Salt Lake? I could have sworn she was an islander," Sean probed.

"Can't help you there, champ. All I know is that she graduated from Brigham Young in fine arts. Arrived here about a year ago. Some relative left her a place near Donegal Bay. She keeps pretty much to herself, 'cept if you talk about her sculpture. Strange stuff. She displays it around her house. Everyone has trouble understanding it. Modern motif, you know, geometric shapes mostly. Some say it looks like Calder, others Moore. That is, until she set out a piece called *The Bondage of the Virgin Mary*. All hell broke lose! Father O'Toole nearly had a heart attack when he saw it. Wrote the Pope about it, some say. Women's circle of the church condemned it in the *Beacon*. Some outraged locals even tried to enforce the zoning regulations to stop it. They argued that it violated some restriction on junkyards. Good

God, half the property on the island has abandoned junkers in the back yard. Hurt my business for awhile, Kate working here and all. But saints alive, strange things happened when the locals took it to the township board meeting on that bogus zoning claim. Every Indian on the island showed up, even the Kennabawasi band, and without saying a word, voted against it and went home. You should have been here. Nobody said a word about it the next day, 'cept Father Leo. She's a strange bird, that Kate, a beautiful, wild, strange bird. Throughout it all, she didn't say a word about it. Just went about her business." Harvey gazed across the room toward the door. "Excuse me Sean, that's Deputy McCulloch, the island law around here. I better go see what he wants." A tall, paunchy man wearing a brown and green uniform approached the other end of the bar. He beckoned to Harvey.

Sean yearned to ask Harvey more about Kate. The bartender's description had only confirmed that sparkle of spirited independence and intrigue which he had seen in her eyes. He waved to Kate for another round. Jesus, another round of rock gut, Five Roses.

Kate poured him another round.

"Kate, this isn't Five Roses, it's . . . ."

"Its Irish Mist, dope. You drink anymore of that Five Roses and I'll be cleaning up the john. Besides, we know it's not your drink . . . never was. In fact I've got this feeling that you don't drink much anyway."

Sean blushed. "Is it that obvious?"

"Yeah, Dartangnan. After that one it's Pepsi if you're going home with me." There was a protective note in her voice. He liked it.

"Heard about your sculpture, Kate. I'd like to see it. I hear that your plowing new ground in the art world." He had framed the entree upon Harvey's suggestion, and it fell flat. "I didn't mean that, Kate. Actually, I don't know much about sculpture, but I find the presence of a sculptor in the northern bush quite intriguing."

"No, Sean, you're right about plowing new ground. I damn near cut myself out of the small piece of this planet that I can call my own. Ah, the sacrifices one makes for the arts." She laughed softly. The laugh, touched with a poignant Irish lilt, reminded him of Lily's.

Harvey returned, slipping onto the stool neighboring Sean's. "Happened again, Kate. Damnedest thing for this island. The little

O'Donnell girl disappeared last night. Her clothes washed up on the shore of Whiskey Point. She'd been missing since dinner. Second one this summer. How do you figure it? Kids have been swimming off this island for decades, and we haven't had two accidents so close together! I better take one of my pot roasts to the O'Donnells tonight. God, they must be distraught—their only daughter. Seamus loved her more than life itself." Harvey turned his back, slamming his palm against the counter.

"Go on, Harv." Kate urged. "You get that pot roast. I'll take care of things here." Kate placed her hand on his shoulder, gently pushing him toward the door.

"Okay. Thanks, Kate. I'll make it up to you. Oh, Sean . . . our gumshoe deputy, Judd McCulloch, wants to talk with you. Said it was standard procedure. Until they determine the cause of death he'll be talking to everyone leaving the island. I told him that you'd be staying for several days. Ole Judd's going to be one busy beaver interviewing everybody." Harvey winked with one eye and leaned toward Sean whispering, "Boy, is he in his element. He's been looking for the big break to get back to the mainland for years. The man's macabre!" He took off his apron, handed it to Kate, and headed toward the door.

Sean looked up at Kate. "Have you ever felt you've been living a bad dream before, and you couldn't wake up? Ever since I left the mainland, I've felt like an alien visiting some distant star. Now I'm the subject of a police investigation."

Kate giggled. "Judd would love to hear that. He's been waiting for years to hone in on a deviant serial killer from Yale. Yep, you've been found out by the Columbo of the North woods. You're history, Sean Connaghan, history!"

Sean was startled by her humor. "Good grief, Kate, how can you tease me at a time like this? A little girl died last night. While we were sleeping soundly in our beds, she may have been thrashing about in that god-awful black lake. It's deep tragedy we're talking about here." He could not help but recall his narrow escape from Missipishu. The O'Donnell girl's death hit close to home.

"Tragedy, Sean, is what these people have lived with for years. It followed them from Ireland. You should know that. This island has seen more grief than you can imagine. If you don't believe me, take a close look at the *Northern Islander* tomorrow when you visit the Mormon Print Shop. If you haven't already discovered it today, you need to know that it's not tragedy that drives this island . . . it's survival. These people have been setting tragedy aside, dealing with it for years, refusing to address grief and pain. They'll hold a mass at Holy Cross, and have a wake and then go about their business. Then they'll forget. They'll just forget."

Sean was struck with the intensity of Kate's reaction. Beyond that, he sensed in her lecture a closeness to him, a knowledge of his work and destiny which transcended his own.

Sean passed the remainder of the afternoon wandering about the little village on Paradise Bay. He ruminated about the furious pace of the last few days. The tug of Inishmore pulled at him more than his research. He strolled the docks, examining the fishing vessels. One old fisherman, marooned by the treaty settlement with the Indians, reminisced that at the turn of the century more than a hundred vessels had sailed out of the harbor at dawn every day. Fishery brokers from Chicago and New York occupied permanent offices on Beaver and telegraphed the catch totals every day to the markets.

"It was the heyday of the island," he explained to Sean. "As a boy I worked from dusk to midnight packing fish for markets across the country. The island loved the lake for her bounty. It was a decent living, a time when our families depended on nothing but the sea and our hands."

Shading his eyes, Sean scanned the harbor. The docks had changed. Now there were more yachts than trawlers. An old Great Lakes schooner, the Manitou, once the fastest freighter on the lakes, lay moored at the municipal dock for tours. It once broke the record for passage to Chicago. It had been gracefully and lovingly restored by a foundation which depended on summer tours and donations. Crewed by teachers off in the summer, the vessel dropped anchor at all the vacation watering holes, trailing a bit of lake history in its wake.

Sean gazed up at smoothly varnished masts and hemp rigging. He imagined a dozen of these sleek craft at anchor in Paradise Bay. Schooners such as the Manitou had arrived early one morning to load hundreds of captured Mormon families for their final trip to Voree, Wisconsin. Such ships had participated in one of the most violent upheavals of a community in American history. He imagined the families huddled along the sandy shore of the bay in the early morning light, shivering in the crisp air, and gazing at the full sailed ships on the horizon. Some had walked miles that night with their children on their backs, down the Kings Highway that bore the name of their assassinated leader, into the village, and onto the cold beaches. Some had witnessed their homes burned, their belongings looted, resistors hunted down in the forest and shot, and now they had been herded to the shore, taunted by their captors. "Polygamists, heathen, thieves!" The invaders screamed. The refugees looked back at the orchards they planted, their homes ablaze, their livestock lost, and they wondered why their God had forsaken them.

What was it that moved the ancestors of these proud Irish islanders to dispossess these pioneers? Of all people, they understood the harsh realities of survival in a harsh land. Fresh from the oppression of English landlords and the starvation and plague of famine, how could they turn so quickly from exploited to exploiter? Was it religion, land lust, or jealousy that moved them? There was no class war here. The poor fought the poor. Where was justice on the frontier?

The assassins of Strang were taken to Mackinac for trial and released hours later. The surviving Mormons never attempted to reclaim their island home, and the new owners never looked back. They built their churches and shops, moved into the remaining Mormon homes . . . and forgot. Maybe Kate understood them all too well. They would say a mass, hold a wake, and forget. But historians remember. They force remembrance. Perhaps, his trip was more about remembrance than it was a letter of appointment. Tomorrow he would begin the journey toward that question at the Mormon Print Shop.

Sean waited for Kate at twilight on the deck of the Shamrock. The new deck was a recent addition to accommodate the upscale tastes of the Perrier swilling cyclists and summer residents. There was a kind of sensible segregation to this arrangement. Some of the tourists veered away from the saloon's shabby interior, and the islanders were preserved their inner sanctum. Harvey had recently added patio furniture with large 'nouveau European' umbrellas from Paris. The scene created an odd flavor, consistent with the contradictions of an island in transition from a working fishing village to a popular watering hole listed in the tourist guidebooks. Harvey said that it had all began when an executive from one of those upscale mail order catalogue firms had been forced to weather over in the harbor during the Chicago to Mackinac regatta. Struck by the natural beauty of the harbor and its quaint fishing village, he immediately built a wharf for his yacht, bought up a dozen large parcels of prime lakefront property, and lengthened the airport for his Lear jet. In exchange, the islanders received a generous gift of a new library. But with its discovery as a retreat for the wealthy, the demise of the very qualities which attracted the executive began. The island was evolving into the very thing that he was trying to escape. Boutiques appeared. A new car rental firm had contracted to offer late models to the burgeoning clientele. Creative writing seminars were available to tired city housewives eager to write Great Lakes romances. The grocery store had expanded into a new modern building. It featured a video counter and deli bar. Yes, the island was dying of modern progress. The executive and his pilgrims led the charge in the assault on island ways. In the battle, charm would have to yield to creature comforts. Suburban culture would eventually absorb the island.

"Deep in thought of the way things were, traveler?" Kate pulled up a chair beside him.

"How did you know?"

"This island reeks of pastness. If you're sensitive, as I believe you are, you can't avoid it."

"And do you avoid it , Kate?"

"Don't want to. I derive strength from it. It's why I'm here," she paused and turned her lovely blue eyes toward the harbor. A regatta of sailboats was heeling in a brisk wind off the point. "So, traveler," she broke the respite, "you ready to head home?"

"I'm always ready to head home, if I only knew where it was."

"That's what I like about academics, always stretching for a universal thought. In this case, however, the answer is simple, my house. That's home for now, be it ever so humble."

Sean smiled. He sensed that Kate's answer implied an intimacy for which he yearned.

"That's the best offer I've had all day. But no detours. Okay?"

"Agreed."

Kate's jeep rolled leisurely down the Font Lake road toward Donegal Bay. The late evening sun cast leafy shadows on the road, as they moved from mottled shade through shafts of golden light. When they approached the boat site at Font Lake, Kate brought the jeep to a grinding halt. An otter splashed from the shore. It swam a few yards out, diving under the clear green water which sparkled gold in the slanting light.

"Enchanting isn't it? It's as if that otter knows I pass here everyday at this time. He waits to greet me." Kate gazed across the reeds to the distant shore. Sean sensed that Kate knew this place in a way he could not. He waited for her next words, afraid to interrupt her reverent silence.

She finally broke the stillness. "Yes, Sean, I am praying. It is a prayerful place."

A bullfrog croaked in the distance, across a stretch of marshy grass. "How did you know what I was thinking?" Sean replied, astonished at her intuition.

"Simpatico, I guess. This place is a holy place, Sean. It's where the Mormons conducted their baptisms. Thousands of souls were baptized in Font Lake. If you listen, you can hear the rites whispering across the water . . . 'in the name of the Father, Son, and Holy Spirit' . . . Listen!" She urged. "You can hear the saints slide into the water and emerge washed in goodness."

"So, what was your prayer, Kate?" Sean hesitated, waiting patiently for the response.

"Redemption, Sean, redemption from pain, injustice, and grief. I pray it for everyone on this God forsaken island." With the blessing she jerked the shift knob into first gear and accelerated down the road toward Donegal Bay.

Chapter XVI
A Letter of Appointment

Sean arrived at the Mormon Print Shop Museum early the next morning. It was an unimposing white clapboard house which had been the second location of Strang's newspaper, *The Northern Islander.* He hesitated on the small veranda to examine bookshelves wedged between the windows which housed row after row of dime store novels. A sign hung over one shelf, *Take one, Leave one, and Enjoy!* He chuckled under his breath. This is where I find the Rosetta Stone of Strangite Mormonism? He began to think that this long, arduous ordeal was all for naught. Still, hadn't historians over time found the greatest treasures in the most unlikely places—attics, garages, and rare book shops? He comforted himself with this hope as he opened the creaky screen door.

A single desk faced the door. An ornate frame picture of King Strang with beard and stern black eyes commanded the small room. A kindly matron was engaged in animated conversation with a middle-aged man dressed in blue jeans and a black shirt. As the man turned, he noticed his clerical collar. He bore a striking resemblance to Sean Connery.

"Yes, it's a sad thing, Molly . . . but the good Lord knows best when he calls his children home," the man spoke softly.

"But, Father, she was only eleven, surely the good Lord could have waited a few years," the matron replied.

"Molly Burke! You know better than to question the will of the Almighty. That's my job. And if you ask Father Leo, he'll tell you that I take the job all too seriously," the cleric advised impishly with a wink. "It's better that only one of us be in trouble with Father Leo. The good Lord I can handle!"

Molly giggled. Sean seized the opportunity to interrupt them.

"Ma'am, . . . my name is Sean Connaghan, I believe that I wrote you about the Strang collection." Sean spoke with an official air.

"Oh, yes, Mr. Connaghan, we've been expecting you. Not too often that we get someone from Yale here, not since Doyle Fitzpatrick was researching the collection for his book, *The King Strang Story.* Ironic isn't it? His research led him in the opposite direction, to Yale. I'm afraid Fitzpatrick has tilled this ground already," Molly spoke authoritatively. "I've always wondered why he didn't consult church archives in Salt Lake."

Sean answered in a matter of fact tone, as if he were lecturing a class of undergraduates.

"The Mormon church purged every reference to Strang in its histories. After the death of Joseph Smith the elders apparently decided to assure the succession of Brigham Young and the Council of Twelve by eliminating the history of anyone who claimed prophetic succession."

"Well, it doesn't surprise me. Does it you, Father Andre?" She glanced at the cleric as if to confirm her witness to the true and only church. "The Mormons don't like contradictions in their history, and they've got a lot of them to reconcile."

"Now, Molly," Father Andre chided, "the Mormons are still children of God, and based on their experience here on the island, they deserve a place in whatever heaven they have divined for themselves."

"That's how you irritate Father Leo. You've been reading too much of the *Northern Islander.* I think it's gone to your head!"

Father Andre turned to Sean.

"Looks like it's gone to your head too, young man. Well, there's plenty of madness in this place for both of us. Let me welcome you into the company of saints and sinners. My name is LaFrenier, Andre LaFrenier, recovering Christian Brother, set adrift on this island of paradise to work out my salvation. The French have always loved to put their prisoners on islands. This one is the Catholic equivalent of Devil's Island for priests in need of reconciliation with papal authority. I am doomed to read Mormon theology and history until I can demonstrate the folly of its doctrines. Fact is, I'm gettin' to like the buggers."

"Father, you're a trip!" Molly exclaimed. "Wait here, Sean, I'll get your first installment of the collection. In the meantime don't let this friar tempt you with his charms. He may be from Quebec, but I assure you that he's kissed the Blarney Stone." Molly chuckled as she placed her reading glasses on the desk and climbed the rickety stairs to the attic.

"Quebec, eh? Do a dare ask how you migrated to the island, or should I heed Molly's warning?" Sean asked.

"Molly's right. I'm full of crap. Fact is that I never understood the meaning of my vows. I asked too many of the wrong questions or gave too many of the wrong answers. You know . . . abortion, celibacy, liberation theology. Problem is, I had this nasty habit of making it the subject of my sermons. So off to the Christian Brothers Retreat here for R & R. Strange thing, I find it strengthening to step from one orthodoxy into another. Still, I'm afraid that this reading is raising those old wrong questions again." Father Andre shrugged his shoulders and closed the book he was reading.

"There are no wrong questions, Andre," Sean replied, invoking the tired teaching adage. He liked the prisoner priest. He would have made a good academic, Sean thought.

"Spoken like a true professor, *ami*. I think we'll make good cell mates in our Mormon paradise." Father Andre stretched out his hand, and Sean shook it heartily.

Molly returned from the attic and deposited several sturdy boxes on the table in a small room next to the entry. "This will get you started. It covers the period from 1846 to 1856, the assassination year. It contains Strangs' diaries and letters, although most have been microfilmed for the Coe collection. Well, I guess you know that. Oh, I almost forgot, we'd appreciate you using these surgical gloves to handle the documents. Most have been encased in plastic, but we may have missed some."

"Yes, *mon ami*, you won't want some of that Mormonism to rub off on you," Father Andre intoned gravely in a mock reverential voice.

Sean dove into his work hungrily. It seemed like ages since his departure from New Haven. He regretted the loss of his computer. It possessed a deep vein of golden research which he now needed. With every sentence he read, the loss of it frustrated him. Fortunately, he had made backup discs before the departure. He must have them sent with a new computer from the mainland, he thought. He must remember to make an insurance claim. What was it about this island that encouraged the avoidance of practical necessity?

Sean chuckled as he reviewed Strang's diary and letters to his second wife, Elvira Fields. He had taken Elvira as his personal secretary, dressed her in men's clothing like Princess Regan in *King Lear*, eager to conceal her identity from the prying public. Their affair had begun on Strang's various missionary journeys to New York and Wisconsin. Another contradiction. Strang insisted upon traditional wifely obedience, but accommodated, even enjoyed, the independent, self-sufficient air of Elvira. One could argue that she was the first and only feminist recognized by the church. In fact, prior to her "marriage," Strang had not promoted polygamy among the islanders. Elvira had provided a reason, some said an all too convenient reason, for sanctioning the practice. In many ways, Elvira became the "Eve" of "Adam" Strang's demise. With the official endorsement of polygamy, the mainland Irish, seething from their dispossession, found the pretext for attack that they had eagerly sought. Ancient Catholic values had been assaulted and must be defended. The devil was loose on Beaver Island. He had declared himself King. The declaration constituted a heresy against the Constitution. Both church and state sovereignty had been challenged.

Sean found solace in paging through the old records. He greeted them as old friends who had invited him to stay at their summer house. Surrounded by the memorabilia of an earlier day, the experiences of the Strangite Mormons emerged from the shadow of dusty library shelves. The Strangites were an industrious people with a dream. They had tried desperately to carve out a godly lifestyle from the frontier wilderness, only to fall prey to the folly of a man consumed by the passion of overlordship. It was an old story, as old as Sodom and Gomorra, yet so characteristic of the religious fervor that attached itself to Western expansion. New land inspires novel experiments in living. The harsh but splendid isolation of the island kingdom offered a pine and birch canopied sanctuary for worship apart from secular intrusions. The work of man became the work of God. Until, of course, one man saw another benefit from his misfortune, greed, or shrewd artifice. Strang had coveted power. And power over others rubbed against the rugged individualism of the American frontier. It finally frayed the edges of the patchwork quilt of island community. Whether from without or within, the island experiment was probably doomed from the beginning in the sin of pride and the will to power of this strangely inspired prophet of the New World.

Sean longed to discover the reasons for Strang's obsession with power. It was so alien to the ascetic monasticism of Inishmore. Strang's brazen visions were meant for broadcast to the multitude of nonbelievers, to attract converts to the cause. The monks retired to the islands to search for divine guidance through humble prayer and supplication. Their visions were of a very different sort. Their supplications were turned inward, arrows piercing the doubting soul, not like the Strang missives in the *Gospel Herald.* They were designed to attack the errant ways of the faithless. If Strang were proselytizing in the twentieth century, he would have become a televangelist working the crowds with a microphone in hand and inspiring his viewers to mail in their redemption coupons.

Perhaps, Sean thought, his indictment of Strang was too harsh. His eyes settled upon a description of the island written by Strang. It had a familiar ring, poetic in nature.

> *Come away to the floods and the fields, the flower banks and the forest—out here, in open space and free air, where sea and earth and sky mingle in mutual embraces, like the greeting of youthful lovers! Listen to the pine-songs which are chants of praise, and the wind-warbles which are hymns of hallelujah! Look up yonder on the fire-dance of innumerable rolling worlds, and then answer me before the sun and all the stars—"Is there no God?"*
>
> James J. Strang
> *Gospel Herald*
> April 26, 1849

Such discoveries always upset Sean. Strang's love for the island seemed so genuine. Strang was a troubling paradox. Sean usually dismissed his preaching as hucksterism, but this segment echoed the strains of Yeats' poem, *The Stolen Child,* which had become one of the last memories of his father. They all seemed tied together . . . his father,

Yeats, Inishmore, and now Strang. He felt like a stolen child himself, transported from one island to another by the curious pull of a past which eluded capture. His own history seemed entangled in a net of Irish and Mormon intrigue. He began to think that the net was now being pulled into the boat, and he was the catch.

"Mormons got you down, Sean?" Father Andre interrupted his contemplation. "They'll grab you. Just when you think you have them figured out, another curve ball will hurl right past you. Say, its almost quitting time. How 'bout a little cocktail at the retreat?"

"Thought you were off the sauce, Father? Wouldn't I be undermining a holy mission? Besides, where are you going to find a brew at your retreat . . . raid the sacramental wine cellar?"

"My scholarly friend, have you forgotten that this is a Christian Brothers retreat. The Order has a long tradition of distilling liquid bliss. Com'on, nothing like a brandy, good conversation, and the evening air off the lake."

At the Damnon Lodge Sean feasted on a filling supper of whitefish and garden sweet corn prepared by Brother Kevin McCarthy. Brother Kevin ran the retreat center for the last thirty-five years, but it had seen better days. In the fifties the summer would bring hundreds of Brothers from throughout the country for respite and contemplation. But now Brother Kevin opined that recent New York visitors left complaining that there just wasn't enough action on the island to suit their tastes. The modern generation had grown tired of nature walks. The sixties saw the center's resurgence. It briefly served as a youth retreat for inner city children from Detroit and Chicago. But now the Order was graying with age, and there were fewer brothers willing to devote a summer to camp counseling. There were even fewer brothers who could teach fishing, archery, canoeing, and swimming.

Brother Kevin had been relegated to spend his declining days caring for elderly brothers and the occasional exile priest like Father Andre. Lately, he occupied himself with preparing the retreat center to host a camera and production crew from *National Geographic* . The crew would attempt to find and photograph the remains of the *Carl Bradley*, a 660 ft. freighter sunk off Gull Island in the November gales of 1971. The project had reinvigorated the old monk. He regaled Sean and Andre with the story of the *Bradley's* sinking and the rescue of her four crew at sea. Nautical charts and journals about the disaster were scattered about dining room tables. Brother Kevin was determined to find the *Bradley* before the camera crew arrived. It would be his last hurrah. The aging retreat center was scheduled to close permanently at the end of the summer, but Brother Kevin held out hope that the *Geographic* stay would highlight its plight and attract renewed financial support. The retreat had been his life, and he believed that so many people had found God in their stays at the center that the Lord would allow the place to survive through the grace of the National Geographic Society. As Sean listened to the aging cleric, he thought of all the monks on Inishmore who had seen their "centers" wither and die. As sturdy as the faith, these brothers could not sustain their remote outposts of contemplation and worship. Brother Kevin was the captain of a sinking ship. He would most likely go down with it, like the captain of the *Bradley*.

The long veranda of the Christian Brothers Retreat was almost vacant as Sean and his new found friend settled comfortably into two immense oak rockers. Father Andre pulled up the skirt of his cassock and produced two small glasses and a bottle of brandy. Sean thought it was unusual that Andre still wore the outdated uniform, but Andre had explained that it was part comfort, part rebellion. The juxtaposition of his modern views on the church was best hidden in the trappings of the past, he said. To the island world he was a devout monk. To islanders who had been taught by nuns in habits, the ancient dress inspired confidence in Father Andre's faithful devotion, while to Father Leo it was a perpetual reminder of Andre's devious deception of the community. It irritated him to think that Andre's outward appearance evoked reverence. Andre too was a paradox, Sean thought, charming but purposeful.

The two were engaged in casual chat when the Sheriff's patrol car circled the driveway in front of the lodge and came to a stop in front of the steps. A deputy emerged from the car, donned his hat, and approached them with an official step.

"Well, if it isn't the village gendarme! So, Judd, what brings you to this *sanctum sanctorum*. Someone steal the altar wine again?" Father

Andre chuckled. He could not resist the urge to gently heckle authority. "Let me guess, the teenage Boyles said they were simply practicing for the priesthood?"

"I wish it were that simple," Deputy McCulloch responded in a crisp formal tone, removing his hat and placing it under his arm. "I need to ask this young man some questions."

"Be careful, Judd. He's a budding professor. You might just learn enough to finally earn that high school equivalency degree, " Father Andre offered boldly.

"Hitting the bottle again, Father? I'm sure Father Leo would be interested." The tone of Judd's voice threatened retaliation.

"That would be a low blow, even for you, Judd."

The deputy flipped open his notebook and looked Sean squarely in the eyes. He began to read in a monotone.

"Sean Connaghan, 25 years, blonde hair, blue eyes, resides at 431 East Lincoln, New Haven Connecticut, student, Yale University, formerly of Winston-Salem and Asheville, North Carolina. Researching Mormon history on the Island. Am I correct, so far?"

"You seem to know many of the answers, already, officer. What about the questions?" Sean pressed curtly.

"How long have you been on the island, Mr. Connaghan?"

"Two days."

"I understand that you were involved in the wreck of the *Amikwa*. Is that accurate?"

"Involved? Well if you mean was I on board at the time she went down, yes. Look, officer, where are you heading with this?" Sean was growing noticeably agitated.

"Calm down, camper. Maybe nowhere. Maybe somewhere. It's routine . . . just routine."

Father Andre steeped between them as Sean rose from his chair.

"Routine? Good grief, Judd! You're fishing in the wrong stream. You know as well as I do that another girl disappeared off Iron Ore Bay three days ago. Why don't you just tell him? It's not a secret. The whole island knows. Now, do you want to get to the point?"

"Well, it's an awkward coincidence, Mr. Connaghan, you arriving at the same time and place of the drowning, if you know what I mean?"

Sean stiffened.

"No, I don't know what you mean. And I can't remember a damn thing about the wreck. Why don't you ask Whitesides? He captained the old scow!"

"When he shows, I will. But for now, you're here, and he's not. "You sure that's all you know?"

"Yeah . . . damn straight! That's all I know, or care to know."

"You heard him, Judd. It appears to me that you need to talk to Whitesides," Father Andre interjected.

"I will, Father. I will," the deputy said resolutely as he pointed his finger at Sean. "Meanwhile, you stay available. If you intend to leave the island, I want to know. Got it?"

"Oh . . . I've got it! Thanks for the hospitable welcome to paradise, deputy."

Deputy McCulloch doffed his hat as he slipped it over his brow. "Think nothing of it, Mr. Connaghan. Evening, Father Andre. Sure hope Father Leo doesn't inventory the wine cellar tonight."

As the deputy descended the steps to his patrol car, Father Andre whispered an obscenity under his breath in Latin.

"Why Father Andre, I'm shocked," Sean said sardonically, "What about rendering onto Caesar a little respect? Weren't you a little harsh on him?"

"Harsh? His family has a long history of thinking it can rule this island from Charlevoix. I'm surprised you don't recognize the name."

"McCulloch . . . McCulloch," Sean strained his memory as he repeated the name. "Wasn't there a McCulloch in the party of sixteen that led the attack on the kingdom?"

"Not bad, Sean. His great, great grandfather led the attack. Some say he burned more farm houses and raped more Mormon women than the entire gang. After the whole grizzly affair was over, he cashed in old revolutionary land warrants, collected on Mackinac Island for a pittance, and became one of the island land barons. Later, he lost most of it to old Black John Bonner in a poker game. That game left him bitter to his dying days in Charlevoix. I suspect that's why his great grandson resents being here. Everyone knows the history. Some of these families can date there beginning on this island to a purchase of land from the ole' man. I suspect that bitterness still runs in his veins."

"But history doesn't explain your reaction, Andre," Sean replied, "Does it?"

"Oh . . . I guess not. He's just dense . . . dense and wooden as that tree." Father Andre pointed at the large oak at the edge of the veranda. "That intermeddler can't see the forest for the trees, because he is one! If he'd study the records of these occurrences, he'd begin to understand what he's up against. Right now he's just playing in the sandbox. Of course, he'd never believe it if I told him. No one would."

"Tell him what? Don't tell me you know something about these deaths?"

"Not anything that would appear sensible or comprehensible right now. And certainly not to Judd. He'd ship me off to the loony bin if I told him. But someday . . . ," Andre reached for the bottle again and spoke distantly into the night air, "someday, he'll learn."

Sean took the bottle from him and emptied it into his glass. "You know something you're not telling, Andre. What is it?"

"*Santé, mon ami*," Andre replied as he clinked his glass with Sean's. "It's a tale as long as yours, but unfortunately not as verifiable, especially if it were advanced by a fucked up North Woods friar. They'd burn me at the stake after the diocesan inquisition . . . with Father Leo leading the pack. He's just itching for me to get involved in local politics as a pretext to send me packing on the next ferry." Andre paused and stroked his goatee. "But if you . . . if you could find the evidence. Maybe . . . "

"Spit it out, man! Nothing on this island is going distress me. In fact, trouble seems to latch onto me whenever I travel out of the library. Hell, I'm already the subject of an investigation. I think I'm entitled to know."

"All right, but mind you . . . I wouldn't blame you if you threw me into the lake after hearing it."

"Apparently, I've already been accused of that. Get on with it!"

Father Andre spoke quickly but tentatively.

"It began about six months ago. I was culling through old Traverse City *Record Eagle's* for Father Leo, collecting obituaries for church records. There was a fire in the rectory a few years back and many of the parishioner records had been lost. Leo thought he'd confine me to a useful and harmless task . . . to get me out from under foot. It was about that time that the O'Hannahan girl, Colleen, I believe, disappeared and her clothes washed up near McCauley's Point. She was the second of three, now four as you know, that have drowned in the last year."

Father Andre lifted his skirt again, this time withdrawing a long Havana cigar and lighting it. He puffed smoke rings into the cold evening air.

"Strange . . . as I think about it, I still get chilled. I had just finished researching the entire genealogy of the O'Birne family. They had lost two young girls, one in 1975 at the age of ten, and another in 1985 on the same date! So I began to concentrate my research on obituaries for 1975 and 1985."

Andre rose from his chair, walked over to the railing and flicked some ashes into the bushes. A chipmunk scampered from the undergrowth. When Andre turned around, his eyes were red and blurry. A tear rolled down his cheek. His voice quivered.

"If you wish, we can talk about this tomorrow. It can wait, you know," Sean spoke softly, sensing Father Andre's pain. He rose from his chair. "I need to be getting home anyway. I'll just . . . "

"No. Stay. I'm fine." Andre sighed, bracing his back against the veranda post and looking up into the star speckled night sky. "I need to tell someone this story. It's preyed upon my mind for months now, prying its way into my dreams as I lay awake listening to the waves lap against the shore. And . . . well . . . you're that someone, Sean. I guess I knew that when you walked into the museum today."

"You sure. I've been told that I'm a cynic by nature."

"Perhaps, but you're also a fellow voyager. Like me, and the French voyagers before us. We come only to discover what's already been here for ages. We come . . . and we go. Pere Marquette came to deliver a message. He gave names to the places he visited, and then he left the settling to others. We're revealers, Sean. Discoverers and revealers. Some people are destined simply to bring messages and disrupt the order of things."

"Sounds pretty lofty to me. Frankly, Father, that's pretty heady stuff for a graduate student. I'll settle for discovering one simple letter of appointment, and I'm out of here."

"I once thought that way too. But the island has a way of pulling you into the vortex of its swirling past. I suspect you know that Sean, or you and I wouldn't be sitting here."

Andre returned to his chair and began slowly rocking as he continued his story.

"I had initially dismissed the drownings as coincidence. These things happen on islands. They've happened for centuries. The sea claims even the youngest . . . the most innocent. But one day while leafing through the *Northern Islander* I came across an article which painted a poignant portrait of a disaster at sea which claimed two twin girls on their family's voyage from Charlevoix to the Island. The year was 1860. The family was Irish, fresh from County Donegal and in hope of establishing a new life. After suffering the depredation of the famine, crossing an inland sea must have seemed a modest last leg in their long journey. They miscalculated. Daughters lost, they eventually returned to Chicago. The daughters were ten years old. I began to study all the news of drownings on or in route to the Island. That's what I was doing today. It's what I've been doing every day for the last six months, either at the museum or the public library. I've even had copies of old newspapers sent from the university in Ann Arbor."

"And I thought only graduate students were obsessed," Sean interjected.

"It <u>has</u> become an obsession . . . a desperate race against time," Andre replied abruptly. "Sean . . . children, island girls, usually the age of ten to twelve as far as I can tell, have been drowning and washing up on the beaches every ten years like clockwork since the Mormons left this island in the 1850's. It's not coincidence. Every tenth year Sean, it happens again! And it's happening now . . . right now!" Father Andre's eyes widened now and sparked with intensity. "Good Lord, you'd think these people would have put it together. Whole generations have been through this thing. It's a small island. You'd think they would have sensed the cycle of disaster as they sense the passing of seasons. And it's the season again, Sean, the season for death. And I'm powerless to do anything about it. We all may be."

Sean shuttered as he gazed up at the night sky. Why did he attract these people, he thought? Did they lay in wait for him at each destination in life?

Father Andre waited patiently for a reply. He had said his piece and felt comforted by the telling. The old rockers creaked as they swayed in unison back and forth. The story deserved pondering. Several minutes passed before Sean spoke.

"It's been a pleasant evening, Andre. Thanks for the meal and the brandy."

"You're most welcome. I suppose you'll be needing a ride," Father Andre replied casually. "I'll let you borrow my bike for the ride home. There's a full moon, and it'll be a quick trip."

Father Andre disappeared briefly and returned with an old Huffy with large balloon tires.

"These antiques were built for dirt roads. I think you'll find it more than satisfactory."

Sean swung his leg over the center bar and then grasped the handle bars.

"Sean, you believe me, don't you . . . as one fellow voyager to another?"

"Father Andre, if I learned one thing in the last few years, it's suspended disbelief. Yes, I believe you. Until someone proves otherwise, I believe you. Maybe, I'll believe you then too."

Sean peddled down the lane and turned onto the King's highway. There was a full moon. The French voyagers must have longed for the full moon to speed them to new destinations.

Chapter XVII
West to Donegal Bay

Sean had forgotten the exhilaration of riding a bicycle through the cool night air. He stopped on the rise near the church as he approached St. James. The full moon cast a river of silver across the bay, illuminating the deck of the *Emerald Isle* as she lay moored to the wharf, groaning as if she longed for the summer voyages to end. The Shamrock was closing, and the voices of the last departing drunkards echoed across the bay as they staggered in song, arm and arm, back to the King Strang Hotel or their yachts. In the distance the St. James Light's red beacon crossed the path of the silver moonlight in vain attempt to match its brilliance. A dense fog was moving in from the lake. The moonlight would soon be obscured in favor of the red warning light. Later tonight, the lighthouse would provide more guidance to the mariner than the moon.

Sean thought momentarily of gliding down to the Shamrock and asking Harvey for a ride home, but the moist night air beckoned him on. He pushed off the pavement with his foot and made a long sweeping turn onto the gravel of Donegal Bay Road, past the lights of the public library and into the darkness of the forest. The old Huffy with its balloon tires cushioned the shock of the washboard ripples of loose stone as its spring seat chattered with each bounce. Sean marveled at the marketing acumen of the Madison Avenue folks who had converted the old fifties flyers into the mountain bike craze of the nineties. He smiled to himself. They had just slimmed down and souped up the old model. Packaging was everything in this age. The yuppies bought the big sticker price without batting an eye. They had not rode the old flyers in their youth.

The fog followed him as he descended the hill toward Font Lake. It was beginning to seep under his feet as he approached the bottom land. He could still hear the long, low bellow of the harbor fog horn in the distance. The sound was ominous, forbidding. He felt the urge to peddle faster, but as he accelerated at the bottom of the hill, he hit soft sand. The bike slipped out from underneath him as he skidded sideways to the ground.

"Damn," he muttered to himself as he arose, dusting his jeans off. "What a fool you are Sean Connaghan! You're always trying to push things too fast, too soon!"

Beyond the shoreline birches the moon cast the lake in foggy iridescence. Lily pods dotted it with their waxen yellow flowers, floating just above the incoming fog. And in the distance, surrounded by the floating lilies stood a figure. Sean shuttered. The figure was naked. It was a woman . . . her full breasts clearly visible in the moonlight amid the lilies. Sean looked down instinctively, embarrassed for his intrusion, but then moved toward the shoreline, drawn by the enchanting beauty of the scene. As he edged forward, he noticed something familiar about the woman's figure. It was unmistakenly that of Kate's. Yes, it was Kate. He immediately thought of yelling to her, shouting some clever epithet, but the look on her face was blank, as if she were in a trance. He studied her body as she turned and walked slowly, purposefully into deeper water, her breasts floating with the lilies on the rising fog. She was captivating, he thought . . . a timeless vision. His eyes caressed her figure. He wanted her. He wanted to rush into the mist, plunge into the lake, and swim to her side. But such a moment would not permit such intrusion. He knew that. It was a private moment . . . even sacred, it seemed. The scene mesmerized him. He didn't want to leave. He longed to capture the moment forever.

Such moments are elusive, and Kate slipped under the water among the lilies, lost to his view. He searched for her to emerge, to renew the vision. But minutes passed, and he became worried. Where was she? Had she become entangled in the lilies? He began to take off his shoes. Still no Kate. He removed his shirt. Panic began to overtake him when the figure surfaced and glided through the water toward him. She was carrying something in her arms. Sean strained to make out her burden. What he saw shook his soul.

"Holy Mother of Jesus!" He whispered frantically. "It's a girl . . . a young girl!"

Sean covered his face momentarily, hoping to blot the scene from his consciousness. But it would not go away. Kate had stopped waist-deep in the water and was raising the child toward the heavens. She lifted her limp head as she sung a somber, moaning chant. The chant was repeated several times as Kate faced each direction with the limp uplifted body. Then, lowering the body to the surface of the water, she immersed its head once . . . twice . . . three times, each time whispering words in the most kind and solemn tones. Then, she waded into the deeper water and released the body. It sank amid a sea of lilies. Kate dove after it, disappearing into the fog once again.

This time Sean did not wait. He plunged into the water, breaking the spell with shouts to Kate which reverberated in the night air and echoed against the dunes of the opposite shore. He swam furiously out to the middle of the lake, becoming entangled in the lily pods. Their beauty now seemed to subvert any attempt at rescue. They pulled at his ankles as he tried to kick them lose. When he finally broke their grasp, he found himself at the drop-off where Kate had slipped beneath the surface. He cried out several times to her, then dove successively in a vain search to grasp her in the dark water. He dove deeper and deeper into the lake, surfacing only to gasp and catch another breath. He dove until he could feel his hands and legs go numb. His breath became fast and short. Only then did he swim through the lilies to the shore where he collapsed, prostrate. His eyes gazing through the mist at the stars, gasping for breath, tears running down his eyes, . . . crying and choking with the pain of loss.

"Kind of late for a swim, don't you think, baby prof?"

Sean pushed himself to his knees and looked up at White Fox. He was a welcome sight. His outstretched hand pulled him quickly to his feet.

"You're soaked, *chemokmon*," Whitesides said as he wiped his hands across his jeans.

Sean spoke hurriedly, desperately trying to enlist his help between coughs.

"I'm fine . . . but Kate . . . she's drowned. I saw her go under . . . out there . . . beyond the lilies! We must find . . . ," his words stopped as he coughed convulsively.

"Hold on there," Whitesides replied, rubbing his back, "nobody's out there except a few otter."

Sean turned and grabbed his collar, twisting it tight against his neck with all his strength.

"Bull shit, asshole! I know goddamn well you saw her and the girl. Any jerk that believes in manitous certainly saw it. You did, didn't you? Didn't you! Besides, what are you doing here if you aren't connected with all this? Christ, I haven't seen you since South Head, and now you fuckin' pop up at Font Lake in the middle of the night."

Whitesides clutched Sean's wrist and twisted it hard until he yelped.

"You really want to know?"

"Yes!" Sean spoke emphatically as he faced him, "Yes, I do!"

White Fox paced across the road, turned and motioned him to follow.

"Honest Injun' . . . so you want an honest Injun', huh, Chemokmon?" White Fox taunted, as he started to stride purposely down the road to Donegal Bay, his filleting knife swinging from his belt. Then he broke into a run.

"If you can keep up, I may tell you. Let's find out how much you really want to know!"

Sean thought about picking up the Huffy for the chase, but Whitesides was fast disappearing into the foggy marshland. There was no time. He raced across the road, slipping and sliding on the loose gravel as he tried to keep his focus on the shadowy figure in flight.

The fog rolled in off the lake as they rounded the bend in the road along the bay. Sean increased his pace, fearing that the elusive figure would escape his view. Sean had run "the mile" in high school and knew that he had the stamina to keep up if only he weren't so sopping wet. As he started the rise toward Mt. Pisgah, the island's highest captured sand dune, the fog began to lift. Whitesides was less than twenty feet away now, and he could hear his labored breath as they rose the hill, struggling to keep balance in the soft sand underfoot.

Both Sean and Whitesides had caught their wind now and seemed to glide together step for step in unison, like runners pacing themselves in the middle of a marathon. At the end of Donegal Bay road they ran onto a fire lane and then a trail circling Barney's Lake to the left, past Protar's Tomb and inland to the runway lights of the airport. When they emerged onto Mrs. Reddings trail, Sean estimated that they had traveled more than four miles. The last year of sedentary days in the library were taking their toll. He was flagging. Try as he might, Whitesides was gaining the edge. His feet were beginning to feel rubbery, and the inside of his legs were chaffed raw. He was weary. Perhaps, Whitesides had just contrived a convenient exercise to save face, he thought. Yes, that was it. He would run him into the ground and then berate him for not being spirited enough to discover the secret which he held before him. But Sean was determined to find the answer to the happenings at Font Lake, and he trusted Whitesides to reveal it, if he could only stay on his track. This last thought prompted a sudden burst of energy as he sprinted to meet the sand flying up from Whitesides' heels.

White Fox was flagging too as he turned off Redding trail, over Angeline's Bluff and into a clearing, where he raced to a large boulder and dropped in exhaustion. Sean fainted in a heap next to him as they both gasped for air. A startled crow fluttered from behind the rock and flew into the woods, cawing at the sudden appearance of the two swift night runners.

"First time a Yale man could keep up with me," he panted. "You know I ran track at Harvard."

"Oh, really," Sean replied between breaths. "I just thought it was the Indian blood . . . you know how you people can run!"

They both laughed. It was the first time. The run had bred a kinship of flight between the two runners.

"*Kah-wam-da-meh*," Whitesides said grasping Sean's inside forearm, "*Kah-wam-da-meh*, fog runner!"

Sean returned the grasp. "*Kah-wam-da-meh*, White Fox," he repeated the phrase hesitating, "what does it mean?"

"In Chippewa it means: 'We see each other.'"

The early glow of sunrise spread across the field. Wild daisies glistened in the dew as the fog began to lift. Sean sat up and placed the arch of his back against the huge boulder as he surveyed the clearing. Other boulders of lesser stature but of similar size and character sat in a gentle arc about fifty paces from the main boulder. Following the arc as he stood, one could see it circle the mother stone and meet. The mother stone formed the axis of a giant wheel. Imaginary spokes emanated to each satellite stone. The perfect placement of each piece evoked a sense of harmony with the forest and the sky. Sean felt dizzy as he spun his head and body around again and again trying to capture the unity of the wheel. White Fox broke his whirling dance with his laughter.

"I may have been wrong after all, Sean," he spoke. "There may not be as much of the *chemokmon* in you as I thought. Feel dizzy, don't you?"

"Yes, I don't know what got into me. It's just that it's so perfect in its symmetry. I wish I could see it from the sky!"

"They did."

"What? Who?"

"Our spirit mothers and fathers . . . they saw it from the sky. They could locate us and we them through a communion with the sun, moon, stars, and planets. This is sacred earth, Sean. It is our tether to the spirit world. And it could help perform great medicine. Our 'shamans' would come here to show love and respect for Mother Earth, prevent war, heal our band, travel safely on the great waters, or assure a bountiful harvest. "

"In many ways it reminds me of Druid ruins I saw in Ireland. Sean surveyed the clearing again. He pulled a long stem of grass from the earth and began chewing it. But it is the work of ancient peoples, John, unschooled in the knowledge of astronomy, weather patterns, and modern sociology. It's fascinating, and it does remind us of our ancient roots, but it's nothing more—just the pull of the past, an attraction I might enjoy studying. No more. No less."

White Fox repeated the words in a high nasal drone. "No more. No less." He stopped and snatched a daisy from the grass. He could not reveal the true meaning as confided by his ancestors. It was meant only for the ears of Indian people. He could not reveal the secrets of the Ceremony of Unity celebrated periodically by his people here. He could not reveal that one of its purposes was to seek a vision for the benefit of the whole Tribe. His voice returned to normal as he began to pluck each petal from the center. As he plucked the last petal, he presented it to Sean.

"Doesn't look like a daisy anymore, does it, Sean? In fact without the petals, you might not be able to recognize it, could you?" He rubbed the large boulder, caressing a carved out indentation at its center. "So too this great rock. Without its satellite stones it's just another big stone set randomly by nature in a field." Whitesides paused again to rub the great cold mass.

"Sorry, John, but your metaphor escapes me."

"Okay, Sean, you ever heard of Carl Jung?"

"The Swiss shrink who studied dreams. Yeah . . . sure. But what does he have to do with rocks and flowers?"

"Not much. But Jung's theories about the significance of dreams crystallized after his encounters with Native Americans in the Southwest. He began to see that through our dreams we experience the tug of an ancient consciousness, perhaps even an earlier life, but most certainly the pull of past experiences in the unconscious which influenced, and through our dreams continues, to influence the course of our lives." White Fox swept his hand in a circular motion as if to embrace the entire medicine wheel. "This is the manifestation of one of those ancient dreams. A mantra of our past and our future. It still holds secrets for us."

Sean looked puzzled. "Crap! I've heard it before . . . in another land . . . across an ocean, and it hasn't influenced me. You can't tell me it could move the earth for your ancestors either."

"You are a pedantic sonofabitch after all! Well, consider this little piece of evidence, professor. In 1811 an Odawa chief of the Little Traverse Band, just across the waters, Kekoonshartha by name, came to this place and predicted a great earthquake which would shake the world. He conveyed his vision . . . or dream . . . to the great Shawnee warrior, Tecumseh, through his prophet brother, Tenskwatawa. When Tenskwatawa told the vision to Tecumseh, he sent messages to tribes throughout the country to rendezvous for a last battle to prevent the white man's settlement across the Mississippi river. The signal was to be a great shaking of the earth. And on the day predicted, the greatest earthquake in American history occurred along the New Madrid fault. It reversed the course of the Mississippi for a time, felled forests in Alabama, rang church bells in Charleston, South Carolina, knocked down buffalo herds on the plains, and caused huge tidal waves to dash upon the shores of this island. Check it out, professor, the next time you're at one of those big university libraries. It's true, and it may have begun with a vision right here."

"That's all very well, but I didn't bite your dust last night to hear a history lecture on the influence of ancient ruins on Tecumseh's battle plans. I followed you because you promised to tell me about Kate. You saw what I saw. I want to know what happened?"

"I can't say for sure. That's why we're here. I figured this place might help us."

"You mean that you saw what I saw, and you have no explanation!"

"That's it. It's a strange happening indeed."

"I'm sitting here exhausted after running a marathon with an Indian, and . . . "

Whitesides interrupted, "Native American, Sean."

"Okay, John Whitesides, White Fox, Chippewa, Native fuckin' American, I'm going to skin you alive! I'll lay you out on your Jungian altar here and send you to a dreamland you'll never forget. Now, tell me what you saw?"

"No need to ask me, Sean. Why not ask Kate?"

"Jesus, John, are we on the same planet here. There is no Kate. She disappeared!"

"No she didn't. I saw her crawl onto the shore as we began our run.

Chapter XVIII
Town Meeting

When Sean arrived at The Dove he found a note from Kate on the kitchen table.

> *Seanaghan, I suspect Father Andre shared too much 'Christian Brothers' brandy with you last night. He has a way about convincing strangers to support his habit (no pun intended!). I've left some bran muffins. Juice is in the 'fridge. Sleep it off. I'll be home before going to the township meeting tonight.*
> *Kate.*

Such a casual note from a woman who had murdered a child and committed suicide the night before, Sean thought. Maybe he had drunk too much brandy. Maybe it was some fantastic dream. No, he had seen Kate. He examined the note again, turning it over in his hands. Last night the thought of losing Kate was unbearable. He felt a oneness with her that he had never before encountered.

His thoughts turned to the young girl. He had not searched for her in the dark waters of Font Lake. He imagined her body surfacing among the lilies, tangled and muddy. It was a chilling thought. He must call Sheriff McCullough. They would have to drag the lake. He reached for the telephone, lifting it off the hook, then paused, and replaced it. He couldn't call McCullough. How would it sound after last night's conversation with him? "Hello, Sheriff McCullough. This is Sean Connaghan. I just thought I'd let you know that a young girl is dead at the bottom of Font Lake." Sean paced back and forth across the kitchen, pausing to pet Kate's black cat, Keats. The cat purred as she weaved her way between Sean's legs.

"Well, Keats, old girl, this is a fine fix I've gotten us into," Sean whispered to the old cat, "I can implicate myself or the woman I love."

Sean surprised himself with the words. Yes, he thought, I do love Kate. I love a woman whom I hardly know, yet I feel I've known her all my life.

The front screen door clattered open and shut, and Keats bounded out of the room.

"Miss Kate, are you here?" a sweet voice asked.

Sean moved into the front hall to see a young girl with a white cotton shift holding a bouquet of daisies and Indian paint brush. Silken, sun drenched blonde hair, tousled by the island wind, fell over one eye. She brushed it to one side.

"I'm afraid she's not here. She's probably at work."

"Oh . . . we were supposed to meet this morning to hunt for berries. Who are you?" the girl replied.

"One of Kate's borders . . . Sean Connaghan." Sean bent on one knee and gently offered his hand to the girl. "Pleasure to meet you. Do you live on the island?"

"Oh yes, always . . . I've never been over."

"Over?"

"Yes, you know . . . over to the mainland. My father says its not worth the trouble. But I know better. Someday Kate said she would take me to Chicago and tour the museums and shop at Marshall Fields. I ordered my dollhouse from there. I think my father just wants to keep me from learning about the mainland. Most of the children on the island grow up and leave. I think he's afraid I might leave him . . . especially since my mother died."

"I'm sorry about your mother."

"Me too. But Kate takes me everywhere with her. She's great! We take hikes, and she's teaching me how to crochet and we've got a great collection of snake skins. Bet you didn't know that she likes snakes. Yep, she's got a whole collection of 'em. 'Cept for water snakes. They're viscous."

"Does she keep them here?" Sean asked with a grimace. He hated snakes.

"Oh yes, would you like to see them?"

"No . . . I mean I think we should wait until Kate returns."

"Okay . . . but you don't know what you're missing. She's even got a Massasauga rattler. It's really something! But it's really mean . . . and you have to handle it real carefully." She petted her hand, imitating how she might handle the snake.

Sean cringed. He was thankful that their conversation was interrupted by an old Ford Bronco which had wheeled into the driveway.

"It's Leah!" the girl squealed in delight as she ran onto the front porch.

Leah waved as she jumped out of the Bronco and yelled to Sean, "So you've met the charm of Donegal Bay, Annie Daggett. Has she shown you the snake collection yet?"

"I've heard about it . . . and that's as close as I want to get to it," Sean shouted in return.

Leah bounded up the steps and tousled the little girl's hair in greeting.

"Did you tell him about the Massasauga rattler, Annie?"

Annie looked down at her feet and placed one toe on top of another.

"Well . . . I kinda wanted to . . . "

"Shame on you, Annie Daggett," Leah admonished, shaking her finger, as she whispered to Sean, "the last guest she tricked fainted when she pulled a snake from her dress."

"You don't have a snake up your dress, do you, Annie?" Sean asked tentatively.

"Nooo," Annie giggled in reply, "but I'll find one if you want . . . especially for you, Mr. Connaghan."

"Annie! That's enough!" Leah barked. "Sean, there are no Massasauga rattlers on Beaver Island . . . except of course in this little girl's cleaver little head." She turned to Annie. "And you . . . you rascal, Kate told me to tell you she couldn't make it today. But if you wait a few minutes in the truck, we'll go a looning . . . okay?"

"Okay. Bye Mr. Connaghan. Next time we meet I'll find you a nice little garden snake." Annie waved as she chased Keats to the truck.

Leah followed her figure as it danced around the old cat. "God knows Kate loves that little girl. I'm afraid she might even marry that fool of a father. Jack Daggett treats that lovely waif just like one of his land development projects . . . a lot of big talk about how beautiful it will be and no follow through. That man will promise you the moon!"

"Kate's really serious about this guy?" Sean anxiously inquired.

"Oh . . . it's on and off with Kate. You know she's the kind of woman who can't stand the thought of any permanent connection. But Annie is a powerful incentive. Who knows? So how's the research going? Are you ready for a press conference to announce that the whole Mormon Church hierarchy has been fraudulently appointed?"

"Dead end, Leah. Seems like every lead turns back onto old furrowed ground. A few more days like this, and I'll be headed south."

"Maybe you're looking in the wrong place. Rumor is that a lot of old records were stashed in the attic of Holy Cross when a state archivist came snooping around here in the sixties. He wanted to move the whole collection to Lansing."

"Jesus, Leah, why didn't you tell me that in the first place?"

"Didn't ask. Anyway, its just a rumor. This place abounds with them. Well, gotta run. There's a nest on Barney's Lake that I've got to mark before the tourists overrun it." Leah started for the truck, then turned, "I almost forgot. Kate said that she wouldn't make it home for dinner, but that if you wanted to meet her at the township planning meeting, you could have dinner at the Shamrock afterward."

"Anything of local interest happening at the meeting?" Sean casually asked.

"Anything of interest? It's just about the most important meeting we've had in these parts for years. Jack Daggett's corporation has petitioned to put a road through Angeline's Bluff to access Greene's Bay, right through the heart of sacred Indian ground. The easiest access cuts plumb through some ancient medicine wheel. Powerful stuff around here. The island needs the employment after the fishing treaty thing, but the Indian's believe that great harm will come to the island if the wheel is disturbed. Yeah . . . I guess you could say it's of interest if you believe that an island's destiny hangs in the balance." Leah spoke the last words with a mysterious lilt, . . . half cynical, half serious.

"And what do you think. Does it hang in the balance?"

"My friend, everything is tenuous around here. But I'll tell you one thing. If Kate thinks its significant, well . . . I do! Yep, if you like fireworks, you should go. Kate's something to behold when she's mad, and Daggett's as shrewd as a fox trying to get into the chicken coop. See you there!"

Sean was glad to see the dust of the Bronco fade into the distance. He longed for a long sleep to erase the memory of the previous night. As he ascended the stairs to his bedroom, he wondered where Kate kept the snakes.

Sean arrived late to the township board meeting that night. He stood in the back of the meeting room which had once served as a Coast Guard station near the lighthouse on Whiskey Point. He felt out of place at the meeting, like an uninvited guest at a family reunion. The room was crowded to capacity with faces he had seen about town. All of the historic families of the island seemed well represented, many of them sitting at the front table as members of the Board itself. Across the room he noticed Kate in the front row with notebook and pencil in hand. Harvey and Leah sat behind her. Deputy McCullough stood with an official air, arms crossed, near an open window on the opposite side of the room. Father Andre sat in the last row. Sean moved to a position behind him, sensing that he would be more comfortable near the friendly priest.

The meeting was chaired by the harbor master, Captain Walter Wajowski, a distinguished elderly gentleman who had retired as a Great Lakes freighter captain. The sound of his commanding voice was familiar to Sean. He had heard it frequently on the marine radios throughout the village. They were usually tuned to channel sixteen to monitor the traffic in the harbor. It was a common pastime to listen to the chatter of lake business on the open channel, as common as tuning into the baseball game on a Sunday afternoon. Captain Walt's voice was as familiar to the islanders as Ernie Harwell, the play by play announcer for the Detroit Tigers. It inspired confidence and deference.

Captain Walt was explaining the next order of business for the Board, a petition by Daggett Enterprises Inc. to dedicate a public road south of Bonner's Landing for the purpose of accessing a large new development. He recognized Mr. Jack Daggett to present the proposal.

A large handsome man with red hair approached the lectern which faced the assembled board. His dress was casual but bore an unmistakable resemblance to an L.L. Bean model Sean had seen in a recent catalogue. A young assistant briskly followed him with maps and blueprints which he placed on easels on each side of the long table where the township representatives sat patiently. Daggett spoke crisply but in a familiar, almost jocular way. After explaining the path of the road and the plan in meticulous detail, he proceeded to outline the many advantages that the development would offer to the island. A new golf course was planned along with nature trails and a wildlife conservation area. He extolled the benefits to the local economy of such a development. It would provide jobs for many of the island contractors and a growing market for island services. He ended his remarks by committing to pave all the roads in and leading to the development. This last commitment caused many in the audience to buzz in conversation. Only the King's Highway was paved on the island. The idea of a paved development, free of spring mud, was unheard of on the island. It was the *pièce de résistance* to his presentation.

Daggett's presentation was followed by the testimony of several contractors and business owners who supported the new project. The shore below Bonner's Landing was one of the last coastlines which could be developed on the island. The recent state legislation protecting sand dunes made it nearly impossible to plan such an ambitious development elsewhere on the land. It obviously would be an economic boom for island businesses, and a few of the otherwise stoic board members nodded in approval at many of the statements. It was a persuasive presentation. Daggett smiled broadly in self congratulation as he returned to his seat. He had already made a small fortune in his developments on the mainland, and now he would add a pristine wilderness pelt to stuff in his trapper's bag.

Captain Walt thanked Daggett for his presentation and opened the floor to discussion. A few hands immediately rose from the audience. Captain Walt recognized Leah. Sean cringed. Leah's tendency to wander across the landscape of a topic was notorious on the island, and there were a few groans from the back of the room. Her status as a relative newcomer to the island would not help.

Leah centered her remarks around the environmental impact of the development on island wildlife. Much of the area was flood plain that drew migratory flocks to the island. In her harsh Brooklyn accent she articulated the effects of run off, septic tanks, and roads on the delicate ecosystem. Then she proceeded to examine the possible effects on each species of island bird. It was dreadful, Sean thought. Even he knew that such arguments were a poor match for Daggett's economic sophistry.

As Leah took her seat, Captain Walt opened the floor to discussion. The ensuing debate seemed as chaotic as the brisk wind whipping the trees outside. An early evening thunderstorm was stirring across the lake, pushing breakers against the pylons upon which the building set. The waves washed beneath the floor boards creating the feeling of being adrift from land. But the islanders were accustomed to the rising surf, and their voices simply rose to accommodate the growing maelstrom outside. The lights flickered as lightening flashed in the warm night air. With the quickening wind, the debate grew more intense. Kate had jumped to her feet. Daggett was speaking again.

"We've got plenty of state land here to enjoy. What's a few rocks. Good God, they're strewn all over the island!"

"Not those, you ignorant ape," Kate yelled, "I suppose you'd agree to haul them to the town square and set them in place for the tourists to gawk at if it would sweeten the pot for the Board!"

"I would indeed, Kate, if they weren't already traipsing off to gawk at your profane sculpture!"

Dagget's last retort induced a gale of laughter as a mixed chorus of jeers and applause muffled the rising storm outside. As Captain Walt hammered his gavel to the table with staccato blows in a vain attempt to restore order, the two oak doors at the back of the room blew open. It sent a gust of wind sweeping down the aisle toward the front table. The gust turned over the easel, sending maps and documents aloft to float and spiral around the room in an eerie whirl.

"Dammit! Somebody, batten down those hatches!" Captain Walt ordered as he spread his arms across the table to secure his notes.

But the doors had already slammed shut as he uttered the command, and a tall, sinewy shape was striding purposefully down the aisle to face the Board. Sean smiled as he recognized the stride. It was not trailing a cloud of dust behind it this time.

Whitesides turned to face the assembly as he grasped a sheet of paper that descended to the floor. He held it crumpled tightly in his upraised fist before the hushed crowd. Only the sound of the rolling waves below now echoed through the silent chamber.

Whitesides stood silently, his legs spread, fist in the air. No one spoke. Slowly, he lowered the paper, and gazed upon it.

"Such papers have destroyed this island. Rocks do not blow in the wind. They are this island. Remove them, and you too shall be cast upon the wind and into the sea. Listen to the sea beneath you! Listen!" Whitesides paused and tore the paper in half. "Remove these stones and the dead shall rise out of the sea to claim your children and their children's children!"

With these last wards, Whitesides released the paper to flutter like tiny autumn leaves to the floor behind him as he retraced his steps to the oak doors. The wind subsided as he opened the doors. The waves ceased to roll beneath the planking. It was silent. The sea was calm now, calm like the eye of a hurricane.

Chapter XIX
The Sculptress

The sharp, hard strike of hammer on steel awakened Sean. The hammer's retort was strong and resolute. It echoed across the dunes in discordant contrast to the quiet dawn. Sean followed the steady beat outside The Dove and down the back stone path. The path turned near a clump of cedars to reveal an aged Mormon barn, its doors open wide to the morning sun's creeping rays. The banging had stopped now, giving way to the sparks of an arc welder. An incendiary spray illuminated the barn's darker recesses like a miniature Fourth of July celebration. Each shower of little stars revealed the strong figure of a woman in welder's helmet and gloves bending under a tangled mass of metal many times her size. Sean slipped inside the door and watched Kate for several minutes as she deftly wound her way inside a steel dinosaur, joining pieces together with a crackle of blinding light. She moved with purpose and direction, entranced by the unseen creative force that flowed within her.

Eventually, she crawled out of the beast and flipped up her helmet, dropping the long heavy welding cables. Sweat dripped down her face as she reached for a red bandanna stuck in a pocket of her jeans.

"So, what do you think of it?" Kate asked as she strode toward Sean. "Bet you can't even begin to figure it out!"

Sean leaned against a beam and crossed his arms, stroking his chin.

"Trojan Horse, Kate. It's your style." Sean probed as he began to circle the beast.

"It's too early to be coy, Sean . . . even for you. What do you mean, 'my style'?"

Sean climbed into the iron cage and peered at Kate between the bars. "You're a Mormon, aren't you Kate? A Mormon hiding in an Irish Horse. You know the Greeks waited ten years to make their assault on Troy. How long have you waited?"

Kate moved toward the sunlight of the open doors. "You have quite an imagination, Sean."

Sean leaped from the platform and strode toward Kate, grasping her hand and turning her to face him.

"I didn't imagine the other night. It was you at Font Lake. Weren't you?" His eyes flashed as he repeated the question emphatically and tightened his grip. "Were you there?"

Kate grabbed his hand and preyed it loose.

"I don't answer questions under duress." She walked outside into the morning sun and looked plaintively upward, then turned to meet his gaze again. "Yes, Sean, I was there . . . .I'm everywhere, you fool!"

"Shit . . . You're dodging, Kate. A young girl died the other night . . . ," he stammered, "or was dead already . . . and you were there . . . and I was there . . . and we better damn well talk about it."

"Spirits, Sean. Spirits!" Kate yelled as she paced up and down. "Don't you understand? You just got caught up in the island spirits."

"Yeah . . . do you mind telling that to Deputy Judd. Look Kate, I wasn't born yesterday. I know what I saw . . . and . . . "

Kate approached him, cupping his face in her hands. She kissed him gently and ran her fingers through his hair. Sean froze momentarily, then embraced her tightly. The embrace pulsated with imprisoned passion.

"I love you, Kate," he whispered.

"I know."

The rare moment Sean had longed for was broken by the approach of singing voices on the path to the barn. By the time Leah and Annie emerged into view, the embrace was broken. The magic of the moment had evaporated.

"Hope I'm not interrupting anything!" Leah shouted, "Just thought I'd check out the latest bold artistic assault on island conventions." Leah peered inside the barn with Annie. "Holy Moses, this one is guaranteed to set the tongues to chattering! Where did you get all this steel? Looks like a scene from one of those futuristic movies. Can you believe right here in the middle of paradise someone dropped an atomic bomb!"

"All right, Leah. I get the point," Kate complained as she seized Annie by the arms and twirled her around. "I bet you like it, my little island waif! What do you think it is?"

Kate swung her around and plopped her right in front of the platform. Annie walked around it, staring up into the tangled mass.

"It's a prison. But here . . . , " Annie pointed at a space that looked like an entrance to the inside of the structure, "here is the place where people can come out."

"Why would you ever want to go inside that thing?" Leah asked.

"Oh, they wouldn't, " Annie replied. "They were put there. It's a prison. They'd want to get out."

"Ahh . . . you see Leah. Out of the mouths of babes! She understands. It is a prison of sorts. And you, of all people, Leah, should understand." Kate gently stroked one of its steel cross members. "I call it 'Liberation of Dachau.' Do you know who liberated Dachau, Sean?"

"Can't say, I do."

Leah now circled the piece in a solemn fashion. She paused to inspect Annie's entrance.

"Arbeit macht frei," she whispered in a low tone. "You've started to spell it out here." Leah pointed above the entrance. "It's all tangled. Like its been shot through, and over here . . . here it looks as if . . . I see a twisted Star of David with a missing link, superimposed on a much larger Nazi cross."

Leah dropped to her knees slowly, and bowed her head in her hands, like a supplicant before an altar in a war torn cathedral. The rising rays of the sun through the barn doors illuminated her shiny black hair. Her chest heaved. She began singing, singing a Kaddish between sobs. Kate translated the ancient Hebrew in solemn whispers.

"May God's kingdom soon prevail, in our own days and lives and the life of all Israel." Kate's words followed Leah's in a harmony of mourning, rising and falling in grieving solace. "May the One who establishes peace in the heavens above let peace come to us, to all Israel, to all the world, and let us say, Amen."

Sean could now see what he had not seen before. The mass of steel now seemed recognizable as a horrible instrument of torture and war and devastation. Leah became a part of the scene, imparting meaning to the sculpture, a mournful pilgrim to a shrine of despair.

"It's scary," Annie whispered.

"Yes it is," Kate whispered in reply as she reached down to stroke Annie's hair. "It's even scarier inside. When I'm inside it, I feel like I might get trapped there forever." She leaned down and looked her in the eye playfully. "Sure glad you came along! I may have never gotten out!"

"Oh, we would have gotten you out!" Annie announced as she ran to Leah's side and comforted her. "Don't worry Leah, its just imaginary! It's Kate art. It comes from her mind. It's not real, you know."

Leah reached out for Annie's hand as she rose and faced Kate. "Tiger brigade. It was the Tiger brigade. My grandfather told me that the first face he saw was a tank commander, with tears running down his face. He first thought that the face was blackened by smoke, but he was a black American. Can you imagine the irony?" Leah sighed deeply between heaving sobs. "The oppressed freeing the oppressed under the banner of 'work makes you free!' Grandpa said that he saw the image of God in that face. He never forgot." Leah gazed up at the sculpture. "He never forgot that face."

Annie broke the momentary silence that followed. "You said we'd go for a walk on the beach this morning."

"So I did little one!" Kate replied. "How 'bout taking Sean with us? Maybe he can find some snakes along the beach."

"Okay!"

"I think I'll let you find those snakes, Annie," Sean interjected.

"Want to come along, Leah?"

Leah had recovered her composure and was brushing straw off her jeans. "You go ahead. I've brought a few groceries for Kate. I'll just put them in the kitchen and catch up later."

"Okay."

Annie had already run from the barn and disappeared over the dunes. Kate patted Leah on the shoulder and wiped a tear from her cheek. Sean heard her whisper, "Tomorrow in Jerusalem, sister." How was it, he thought, that he had not seen the Star of David?

The sand near the waterline on the beach had not yet warmed in the morning sun. As Sean removed his shoes, he watched as Kate grasped a dragonfly in mid-flight and revealed it to Annie. They inspected it carefully before she released it to flutter across the waves toward the distant misty image of High Island.

"How does a Mormon girl learn Hebrew?" Sean inquired of Kate as they began their walk down the broad expanse of beach. Annie had raced ahead in pursuit of another dragon fly.

"I don't. I guess I've just heard that prayer before. Leah and I have been friends for a long time." Kate replied as she veered near the rippling waves lapping onto the shore, following their edge to the high water mark, then flowing back with them.

"Did Leah also inspire your sculpture?"

"In a way, she did. But the island was more at fault."

"That's a strange way of explaining an artistic expression. Fault is not a common inspirational motive."

"On this island it may be. Paradise is often associated with fault. Ever heard of Adam?" Kate missed the curve of the last wave. "Good God, the water's cold!"

"Yeah. He's the guy who fell from grace for a woman's love." Sean replied coyly as he grasped Kate's hand and pulled her away from the next incoming wave.

"Not love you fool! It was an apple. Just a simple product of God's creation."

"Com'on, Kate. As a Mormon you should demonstrate a little more knowledge of theology than that."

"I was Mormon. I am no longer. I was raised in the Church. That's all."

"And now, Kate, what are you now?"

"Myself . . . Sean, just myself, part of the stream of life and history that we all are. Like that wave washing up and sinking back into the eternal sea. Just rolling over miles until that one moment of landfall, then gone."

"But why here? Why wash up here?"

"Originally, for missionary work. It was my assignment. I think the Church knew that the island would affect me far more than I would affect it. Others had come and gone without one convert. Strange isn't it, I feel more of a Mormon here than I ever felt in Salt Lake."

"I can't believe any one could believe that American millennial nonsense. Think about it. This guy named Joseph Smith from a notorious family of conjurers and clairvoyants ascends this hill in New York on his horse to find a stone box. When he opens it, he finds a toad guarding golden plates which assumes the appearance of man and tells him to come back in a few years because he just wants the gold and is not holy and pure enough to understand the meaning of his find. Four years later he finally retrieves the plates and uses two seer-stones to divine the history of an ancient lost Israelite tribe which found its way to the New World!"

Sean stopped to pick up a stone and hurl it into the lake. It skipped across the mirrored surface.

"Wow, did you see that? Five times! It must be a magical stone! Perhaps even a seer-stone, a modern day Urim or Thummim! Oh, if only I had used it to look at your sculpture, I would have been able to discern the meaning of our island history." Sean danced around Kate in a furious swirl, whooping like a crazed person. "Yes, we may have discovered that White Fox is the descendant of the lone Nephite survivor, Mormon himself! And it is he, White Fox, who seeks to protect the last Indian mound containing the secrets of the cosmos and lead the chosen people of America to their destiny of peace and prosperity through a divine series of revelations. And only the Irish Americans with their icons of the medieval past stand in the way. You, of course, will dispel the old ways with your magical modern metallurgy and drive them away, thus saving the island to establish it as the new Kingdom of the Latter Day Saints!"

Kate tripped Sean in mid-dance. He fell face down in the sand, laughing and rolling around wildly.

"You're hopeless, Sean Connaghan. What made you so cynical in the first place?"

Sean turned over and propped himself up by the elbows. He pulled Kate down onto the sand beside him.

"Education Kate. The enlightened mind does not play games with the soul. The whole history of the world is full of religious charlatans who have claimed that man can find a quick way to divine understanding . . . who claimed they alone knew the way to truth. Their lies have ruined our capacity to see ourselves as what we are, just like those waves that roll across the lake and evaporate on the shore."

"And I thought you had enough of the Irish in you to understand that we are in the process of refining ourselves, baptizing our natures by the fire of pain and grief and then refreshing ourselves by belief in a spirit of life greater than ourselves."

Sean jumped to his feet and pointed his finger at Kate. "Alchemy! Refine . . . purify . . . purge! You all want to be saints. Find Adam's secrets. Restore the garden before the fall. Human beings aren't pieces of metal for smelting by the Holy Spirit. We're meant to experience all that there is of this world, not try to make of ourselves something we're not."

Kate rose, dusting the sand off her jeans.

"Fool! Haven't you read the *Rosa Alchemica* ? It was given to you, wasn't it?"

Sean froze. How did Kate know this fragment of his life, the only fragment left of his history. He felt violated by the revelation, as if Kate had entered a room in his life which he had closed and locked to the outside world.

"Don't you remember reading it?" She began slowly quoting the Yeats' essay.

> *You must come to a great distance, for we were commanded to build our temple between the pure multitude by the waves and the impure multitude of men.*

"Shall I go on?"

Sean breathed hard and fast. It was Rose Malloy's last gift to him. The *Rosa Alchemica* was Yeats' nightmare of the soul. He wrote of a dreamy vision of finding the Temple of the Alchemical Rose and a secret society of apparitions who had discovered the key to immortality through a book found in a mysterious box. The book had disclosed that alchemy was the gradual distillation of the contents of the soul, until it was ready to shed its mortal coil and put on the immortal. The essay told the story of a gathering of the ancient mythical divinities who governed the lives of mortal men.

Kate approached Sean, gazing directly into his eyes and again quoted flawlessly from the text of the essay.

> *All things that had ever lived seemed to come and dwell in my heart, and I in theirs; and I had never again known mortality or tears, had I not suddenly fallen from the certainty of vision into the uncertainty of dream, and become a drop of molten gold falling with immense rapidity, through a night elaborate with stars, and all about me a melancholy exultant wailing.*

Sean wanted to run . . . run far away. But Kate's stare transfixed him.

"Stop! You are a devil! How did you know?"

Kate turned and strode down the beach with a purposeful air, her arms swinging back and forth like a speed walker. Sean raced in front of her.

"I'm goddamn tired of this cat and mouse chase. I'm not a pawn in some cosmic chess game."

"No, Sean, you're not. You have a free will. Use it. Figure it out! You're the enlightened man, full of logic. You figure it out! Or let it go! Just get out of my face!" Kate continued her stride, staring resolutely down the beach toward Annie. Annie had picked up a stone and was running toward them.

"Look, Kate, look at this beautiful stone!" Annie exclaimed with a lilting laugh as she approached them.

Kate leaned over to inspect the find. It was a Petoskey stone.

"Oh, Annie, do you know what you've found?" Kate asked as she took the stone and wet it in the surf.

"No. But isn't it divine!"

"It is indeed, little one. It's a Petoskey stone. Very rare to find one on an island beach. Let's show it to Sean. Maybe it will cheer him up."

Annie placed it in Sean's hand. "Look, Sean! When it's wet, it sparkles like a jewel!"

"Yes, Sean, examine it carefully," Kate directed. "Indian legend has it that such stones represent what remains of ancient animals which were lost when the glaciers created the inland seas. If you don't cast them back into the water, they may come alive and devour you." Kate placed the stone in his hand. "Keep it. Since you don't believe in such myths, it shouldn't come alive. But then again, it might be a wolverine and tear out your heart."

Kate grasped Annie's hand.

"Com'on, little elf, let's find another. See you later Sean."

Sean watched as the two disappeared down the beach and around a dune covered with sea oats. He turned the stone over in his hand, then stuck it in his pocket as he retraced his steps up the beach. As he came to the path leading back to the barn, he stopped, reached into his pocket to retrieve the stone and hurled it into the lake. The stone skipped across the surface several times before descending into the water near the blue line. Better to let the wolverine sleep for now, he thought, as he ascended the path to the barn.

Chapter XX
The Loon's Shadow

Sean's feet sunk ankle deep in the sand as he ascended the path across the dunes. He stopped at the barn to pour sand from his shoes. As he leaned against its door, he saw Leah, sitting with crossed legs in front of the sculpture. Her meditative pose seemed to convert the old barn into a temple, with the sculpture as its altar. Sean felt like an intruder. But as he turned to leave, Leah whispered, still staring straight ahead.

"Ever heard a loon wail, Sean?"

"Can't say I have, Leah," Sean replied softly.

Leah rose and turned around.

"You probably haven't been listening. It's a mournful cry. I've seen dogs stop in their tracks and howl when they heard it. It's not like their yodel or their tremolo. No, the wail is special. It's reserved to contact other loons flying overhead, or . . . maybe for contacting people as well."

"Doesn't sound like something I'd like to hear, Leah."

"Oh, but you're wrong. Most people find it entrancing. They're drawn to it. Remember when you were a kid, and you knew that those vampire horror movies would give you nightmares, but you still wanted to see them. That's the feeling you get when you hear a loon's wail, its sorrowful and blood-curdling . . . but . . . beautiful!"

"I once heard the keening of women at an Irish funeral," Sean replied, thinking of Inishmore.

"Yes, I imagine it's like that. Loons wail only at night. But this morning when I went to the nesting site, they were wailing. I've never heard a wail in the morning. But today, they mourned the death of their young. Today, it was keening." As Leah spoke these last words, a tear rolled down her cheek.

Sean brushed it away. Leah's own Brooklyn yodel had been silenced. He sensed the same pain he had seen earlier this morning.

"What happened to them?"

"I don't know. When I couldn't find them, I drove back here. I just couldn't stand the wailing." Leah cupped her hands over her ears, and shouted, "God, hasn't there been enough killing in this world for man? They were in the way! Don't you see? Daggett's damn road has to go right around the lake where they nest. No nest, no young, no reason for not permitting the road to go through. Me and my big Brooklyn mouth! Shit! Why did I ever feel compelled to speak at that meeting?"

"Leah, calm down. Get real. I hardly think that Daggett is some environmental terrorist engaged in loon snatching or worse."

Leah bristled. "He'd do anything to line his pocket. That's the trouble with that man. Why, the loon's ten times more humane than the human. It mates for life. It carries its young on its back. Both mates care for the nest. And they're more artful. Not even Da Vinci could master flying. But the loon . . . ahh! What bird can dive at torpedo speed one hundred feet underwater and fly at over a hundred miles an hour! Right now I'd like to see Jack Daggett about a hundred feet down for five minutes!"

"Get a grip, Leah! Daggett's not a beast. He's just a capitalist, and most capitalists know that loons are a draw to summer vacationers. It's against his best interests." Sean said the words to comfort Leah. He didn't believe them.

"Maybe you're right. But they're gone, and so is three years of work. You know it takes three years for a loon to mature enough to mate and lay eggs." She shook her fist. "Three years of waiting!"

"Look, Leah, you could have been mistaken. Let's go over to the lake and search again. Maybe, they just got separated." Sean looked her straight in the eyes as he grasped her tightly by the shoulders. "We can hope . . . right?"

Leah nodded.

Sean's hope was misplaced. As Leah's Bronco ground to a stop at the primitive boat launch at Fox Lake, the wailing of the loons had ceased. A solitary figure stood in the reeds near the shallows. Sean recognized Whitesides almost immediately. Leah jumped from the truck and ran to his side.

"Ahaa-ooo-oooo'ooo-ahhh," Whitesides sang through his cupped hands. Leah searched the surface of the waters as Whitesides repeated the call. They waited silently, patiently for a reply.

"A-a-whoo-queee'queee-wheoooo'-queee." Still no reply.

The calls echoed against the surrounding hills. The lake was still . . . silent . . . dead. Not a ripple moved across the black water. The insects had stopped their morning drone. Bullfrogs did not croak in the distance. Even the water lilies did not undulate to the motion of fish below.

The three figures stood together in vigil, waiting.

Several minutes passed before Whitesides turned to Leah.

Sean had not seen him so serious. His eyes expressed the sorrow of the lake.

"Mayne-go-taysee, Leah." Whitesides spoke the words as if he were expressing condolences at a wake. "In Odawa it means, 'thou art a loon-hearted one'."

"They're gone, aren't they?" Leah asked, hesitating.

"They will not sing again here. It is the beginning of the great shadow. The loon saved Anishinabe. But we cannot save them."

Whitesides grasped Leah's hands tightly before he walked up to a clearing and disappeared over a knoll.

Sean's dislike of the Indian softened. He had been there when Leah needed him. He knew to come.

"What did he mean, the great shadow?"

"It's an Odawa legend. And it's one I believe."

"Sounds melodramatic, even from Whitesides, who has a talent for the art."

"All legends are going to be melodramatic to you, Sean. But this one probably conforms to good science better than most. We'd be wise to listen," Leah advised. "It is an ancient legend about the origins of the Odawa. The loon was not just another bird in the legend, but the first act of creation. It is told that the very voice of the Creator sounded across the void, and the voice became a gray and black shadow, the spirit of the loon, now embodied in her song. Sun cast light on the shadow, giving the loon her vivid white markings. The loon loved Anishinabe, the first man, and saved him from drowning because of his love for him."

"And the shadow?"

"The shadow is the voice of God. When the loon disappears, the loon returns to the shadow."

"And we return to the void." Sean inserted.

"Yes. The loon is an ecological barometer. The legend tells us of our own demise. Maybe, we can't see it . . . not even on this island where we should know better, but these two birds have gone. The loon is over nine million years old. Perhaps, it was the first creation. And we're killing them."

Leah waded out into the water and began to sing a kaddish. The day had begun for Sean with this soulful wail. The kaddish echoed across the silent lake. It sounded like the call of a loon—ancient, lonely, mournful. The keening of Irish women, the kaddish, and the wail of the loon all merged together in one sorrowful plea. A cloud passed over the lake, casting a large shadow across the water lilies near the far bank.

Tomorrow, Whitesides would come to retrieve two dead loons in the reeds. They were riddled with buckshot. He would take them to Garden Island and bury them.

Chapter XXI
A Mormon Legacy

Several days past before Sean felt like returning to his work. The compulsion to finish it and depart had washed into the natural flow of island life. The island had captured him. One golden day faded into another. The island no longer appeared like its distant rock strewn cousin. Its deep forests and glens were abundant with wildlife. Each morning a fox appeared at the lake's edge. The twilight brought a family of white-tail deer to drink at a pond near the birch forest. Sean had taken to riding the old Huffy down to Barney's Lake to watch the beavers swim around their lodge in the early morning light. It was at these times that Sean felt most at peace with himself. The feeling would not last.

It was after one of his morning rides that he found the message from Father LaFreniere to meet him at Holy Cross. He had found some documents which might be of interest to him. Sean crumpled the message in his fist, resenting the return to reality.

The unpretentious white clapboard church perched on the knoll overlooking the harbor. It had seen better times. Paint peeled from harsh winter blasts off the lake. The bell tower needed a new roof. Untouched by the summer wealth that propped up the rest of the island economy, repairs waited like lost sinners in need of absolution. Summer vacationers usually left God behind during recreation. When the few dutiful summertime Catholics did attend, the offering plate clattered with loose change. "Church wind chimes," Father Andre called it, for such people floated on the summer breeze without caring what the winter of their soul might bring. It was an island church, as dependent on the fortunes of the islanders as they were on the summer traffic. The altar linen displayed an embroidered anchor, a symbol of hope. It was an appropriate symbol, Sean thought, as he entered the sanctuary and called softly for Father Andre.

"I'm up here, above the choir loft," he yelled back, oblivious to the chaste solemnity of the sanctuary. "Take the stairs to your left. And mind the last step, it's taller than the rest."

When he reached the loft, Sean saw Lafreniere's head peering down from a hole in the ceiling. A ladder was leaning against the loft rail. "Sure glad you arrived. I could have been stuck up here until the altar guild came tonight. Blasted old ladder never was quite long enough to reach up here."

Sean chuckled as he put the ladder in place.

"I thought all church's came with the standard issue Jacob's ladder, Father."

Father Andre laughed in reply as he steadied the ladder from above.

"Only in a rich diocese, *mon ami*. The poor rely on a nasty fall to find their way to heaven! Watch that last rung! It's a slippery devil."

The hatch opened into a large and musty smelling attic supported by rough hewn pine beams. Stacks of files and papers were piled randomly between bookshelves, filing cabinets, and cedar chests. Near the end of the room another fixed ladder rose to the bell tower. A solitary bell rope dangled through a small hole. Sun from above cast a laser shaft of light through the dusty air. An old wagon wheel hung from the peak. Light bulbs stuck in Christian Brothers brandy bottles were fixed to each spoke. The lights cast a yellow glow on the surface of a large ornate French provincial writing table in the center of the room. Two massive walnut high-backed chairs sat at each end.

"Welcome to the island mother load! That old fox, Father Leo, has kept this attic locked up tighter than a nun's habit for years. Holy Mother of Jesus, you'd have thought it was the Vatican Library! When he left for the mainland three days ago, I seized the opportunity to unlock the old fox's den. And *sacre bleu*, it's all here. Records of births, baptisms, deaths since the diaspora of the Mormons. And look here, an archive of Mormon letters and genealogies too." With obvious pride Father Andre pointed to several boxes behind the desk. "Can you imagine it, the Catholic Church consciously depriving the Mormons of genealogical history? Can't baptize ancestors you may not know about. It must violate some tenet of their faith!"

"But why?" Sean inquired, perplexed. "Why lock it up? Why not just deliver it to the Print Shop for cataloging and storage?"

"Exactly, my dear Perot. It makes no sense." Father Andre strode across the room, shaking his index finger dramatically in the dusty air. "So I took the liberty of making a few inquiries of some of our elderly parishioners. As far as I can tell, no one has been allowed up here except parish rectors who guarded it like the Palace of Versailles. Three years ago some teenagers were caught smoking up here and nearly got excommunicated. That's when Father Leo crafted this cock and bull story about it housing manuscripts from the Christian Brothers order. They were not to be disturbed according to the specific instructions of Father Damnon."

"So what tantalizing treasure have you found up here in this trash heap, you old iconoclast," Sean mused playfully.

Father Andre's grin turned sour, as he slumped into one of the high-backed chairs.

"Treasure? It is precious, . . . but precious only in its mysterious poignancy. Sometimes the exhilaration of discovering truth brings only momentary pride. Was it Job who wrote that greater knowledge delivers to us only greater sorrow? I wish I had never found what I have seen in the last few days."

Sean placed his hand on Andre's shoulder.

"An old Irish woman once told me that you must accept history for what it is, not what you wish it would be."

"If it were only history, I could accept it. But we're still living this nightmare. The past still haunts us."

"It always does, Andre. Sometimes we just can't discern its form. You've got to look in the right places. You've got to be prepared to accept the outrageous as well as the obvious."

"Spoken like a good little historian, Sean. But cast your eyes on this little piece of research."

Father Andre shoved a yellow legal pad across the table. Sean sat in the chair across from him, removed his glasses from his pocket and put them on. His eyes raced across the pages.

On the first page Andre had composed a chart from his research. Every ten years from the anniversary of Strang's death a list of children's deaths followed in chronological order. Two or three girls, sometimes as many as five, would appear on the list. All were victims of accidental drowning in summer, and all between the ages of ten and twelve. The pattern was unbroken except for the years 1896 to 1926. Then it resumed again. The names and family lineage of their parents followed on separate pages, a short genealogy for each victim. A second chart documented the original ancestors of each victim. The religion of each ancestor was noted in the margin. Each victim was descended from five originating ancestors. One was of Irish descent, the other Mormon. Sean examined the names of each until his eyes fixed on one. One that he knew. He shuttered. "Eliza Cropper Connaghan; birthplace unknown, immigrated from Inishmore, Ireland; date of death unknown. Married to John Connaghan of Pine River, Michigan in 1848. Elizabeth-Mormon. John-Catholic."

Sean scurried around the table to Father Andre's side, thrusting the chart in front of him.

"This one, Eliza Cropper Connaghan. Where did you find the record for her?" His voice trembled as he uttered her name.

"Well, let me think," Andre pondered. "Oh, . . . yes! Her vitals were found on the Mormon church rolls. That's an easy one. Say, . . . Connaghan . . . , why it never struck me. Is she some long lost relation?"

"I don't know who lost whom," Sean muttered under his breath.

"What did you say?"

"I think so," Sean replied tentatively as a draft of air swept down from the bell tower rafters and ruffled the papers on the table. "No, God damn it! I know so. Yes, she's my Great-Great-Grandmother!" The words sounded strange to Sean, like they had been locked inside him since the encounter with Rose at the hut on Inishmore. He repeated them slowly. "My Great-Great-Grandmother."

"Holy Mother of Jesus! Can you imagine it. You here . . . and . . . well, the good Lord works . . . "

"Yeah, I know," Sean chimed in, "in mysterious ways. Shit, Andre, he's done nothing else for the last few years with me! Spare me the priestly platitude!"

"But, I must verify this from the original record. It says here that she was Mormon."

"You screwed up, Andre. If she was my relation, she was Quaker, not Mormon."

"Unless, she converted," Father Andre queried as he knelt near a chest and began rummaging within. "I know it's here someplace."

"Shhh! Did you hear that?"

"What?" Andre stopped his furtive search, as they listened. Voices rose from the sanctuary below. "It's the altar guild. They're early. Mabel O'Donnel must have finished her cabin cleaning. Hurry! We've got to get down from here before we both get excommunicated."

Andre grabbed the yellow pad, and turned off the light before they descended quietly down the ladder, pausing in midstep as the ladder shook. Mabel and another woman had exited momentarily.

"Now's our chance, they're probably gathering the wafers for tomorrow's sacrament." Father Andre genuflected. "Saved by the body of Christ!"

Sean rolled his eyes in exasperation.

"Will anyone save me from this errant priest?" Sean mumbled as he stepped to the floor of the choir loft.

"I heard that," Andre whispered as he descended. "I'm touched, Sean. That's the first time anybody nominated me for sainthood. Beckett and LaFreniere . . . I like it! But if we don't get out of here before we're discovered, they'll be another murder in the cathedral!"

Father Andre stowed the ladder behind the curtain, and the two interlopers crept down the stairs and out of the church. Intuitively, they headed for the Shamrock. There was much to discuss.

The two trespassers found a table in the corner next to the pinball machine. Kate wiped the table and placed two water glasses and menus in front of them.

"You guys look like you just robbed the candy store. What have you been up to?"

"Are we that transparent?" Sean replied.

"Sean, you were born transparent."

"And you were born oblique. Guess that makes us made for each other. They say opposites attract, you know."

"Not these two opposites, friend. We come from different worlds," Kate bristled uncharacteristically.

Andre winked at Sean, as he examined the menu.

"Maybe, not as opposite as you think . . . . I'll have the western omelet and coffee. And ask Harv to touch it up with a little Irish whiskey, please."

"Same, here," Sean added.

"Pretty heavy brew for you, Sean. You've been hanging out with the friar too long," Kate chided as she snatched the menu from his hand.

Father Andre chuckled as she left. "You may not be as far apart as she thinks. It looks like you have a little Mormon in your background too."

Sean gazed at Kate.

"Hardly, we had a falling out on that subject a few days ago. This Mormon thing just keeps cropping up like a weed in the garden."

"Not bad, Sean. Cropped up, . . . Cropper. Get it?"

"Yeah, real cute. Didn't they teach you a little sensitivity in the seminary?" Sean chastised. "You know what I mean . . . sometimes, I think I'm living my research."

"Isn't that the way its supposed to be with a scholar?"

"Somehow, I don't think that's what Yale had in mind when they financed this island jaunt." Sean paused as he reflected on his original purpose. "My dissertation isn't any closer to reality than when I arrived."

"As I said, my cynic friend, maybe it's supposed to be that way. Life never unfolds the way you want it to. Consider what we just found. You're worried about your infernal dissertation, and we may have stumbled upon something significantly more important than a letter which will sit on the shelf of some library for a few scholars to ruminate about. Why not try making history instead of just observing it?"

Sean smiled. "You're a tough old bird, Andre. Okay, so tell me what else you've found up there!"

"Well, it's simple. All of the girls who died were descended from a Mormon parent and an Irish Catholic. Question is: how did these people get together in the first place, considering that they were mortal enemies?"

"Maybe, love conquers all."

"Naive, even for you, Sean!"

"No, I think they never were parents."

"You're not making sense. Children without parents?"

"Not these parents. You see, the official Holy Cross church records list the children as having Catholic parents. The fathers are the same, all Irish Catholic. But the Mormon records in the attic indicate births to Mormon women. The Mormons were obsessive about accuracy. Especially, when souls were at stake. But the Catholics prized respectability more. Their records note two Catholic parents, always a different mother, always Catholic."

"You mean that the Holy Cross records are a fraud."

"Exactly."

"And if the island knew?"

"Yes, if the island knew, inquiries would have to made. Maybe even a papal investigation."

"And what would it reveal?"

"I think . . . ," Father Andre paused. "I don't want to speculate now. I need to get back up in that attic."

Kate had returned to the table with the omelets. "Sean, this omelet may have to wait. Deputy 'Dawg', over there wants to talk with you. He's serious. There's been another drowning, I think."

It was too late. Judd McCulloch was towering over the table, looking very official. He threw a document on the table.

"Sean Connaghan. I am arresting you in connection with the death of Annie Daggett. Her clothes were found at Barney's Lake this morning. I think you better come with me."

Chapter XXII
Inquisition

Sean was not prepared for injustice. No innocent man is. His life had been one of solitary introspection. Over the years since his father's death he had learned not to trust others. He was proud of his ability to distance himself from crises. In fact he rarely had encountered them. When he did, they usually found resolution without his own intervention. Academic life had prepared him for observation and reflection, not action.

As he sat in the Sheriff's office waiting for interrogation, Sean felt frightened for the first time in his life. He realized that he was a drifter, alone and adrift by his own choice. Night had come to the island. As he looked out the window of the station house, the beam from the harbor lighthouse penetrated through an incoming fog. It reminded him again of that infernal question Graves had asked him so long ago in the tower.

"Connaghan, tell me," he queried, "a young man is sitting in a boat in the Irish Sea on a foggy night. He is poor, lonely, drunk, and Irish. He thinks he sees a lighthouse in the distance. What is the purpose of the lighthouse to this young man.?"

"I guess I'd need to know why he was there in the first place, Dr. Graves."

Smart ass, Sean thought. It was no longer an academic question. He didn't know why he was there, and the lighthouse offered him little hope of finding a safe harbor from the ordeal ahead.

The door to the room slammed shut. Sean turned from the window.

"You're in one heap of trouble young man," Deputy McCulloch declared in an angry voice. "Now, you can cooperate, and we can be done with this, or we can wait for the State Police to arrive from the mainland."

"I'm more than willing to cooperate. It's quite simple. I'm not a killer."

"Then perhaps you could explain why you were at Barney's Lake at the same time and in the same place that Annie Daggett's clothes were found on the beach."

"I've gone there for several days, and I've always gone alone. Except for an occasional truck I've seen no one."

"Four mornings ago you were seen on Donegal Bay with Annie Daggett."

"Yes. I was there with Kate and Annie. Kate can verify that."

"You were seen alone."

"Look, I was never alone with Annie! Ask Kate. She was there."

"I have. You may think I'm just some hill-jack, Yaley, but I've had you watched since you came to the island."

Sean detected resentment in McCulloch's voice.

"And what did she report?"

"She said you took a walk alone while she worked on her sculpture in her barn."

Sean was dumbfounded. Was McCulloch playing a deep game with him, or was Kate lying? Sean's thoughts raced. Worse, was Kate responsible for these deaths and protecting herself? Should he allow himself to trust Kate or should he reveal what he had seen her at Font Lake? He decided on attack.

"A walk on the beach does not establish murder, McCulloch. And where's the body? You said you found only her clothes."

Sean chanced the theory that if it was Kate, the body had disappeared, just like the night on Font Lake. If Sean could not trust Kate, he could trust his own intuition and logic.

McCulloch grabbed Sean tightly by the collar and pulled him toward him, almost lifting him off the floor.

"Listen, you little college shit, don't play games with me. I'm the law here, and I'm asking the questions." McCulloch pushed Sean into a chair as he released him.

"So, you haven't found a body." Sean sensed an advantage as he pressed forward. "I think, Deputy, that you're just wishing for a case against me. You're fishing. Since when does watching beavers in the early morning constitute a crime? I think it's time you get me an attorney. I'm not answering any more of your questions. Either get me an attorney or release me! You haven't got a case, and you know it."

McCulloch walked toward the door and turned.

"Maybe, I don't. But until that lake is dragged, you'll be staying here. And don't get too comfortable, son. When we do find that body, you'll be on your way to Charlevoix for trial. Then you'll get an attorney. And you'll need one. Until then," McCulloch pointed out the window toward the lighthouse, "that light is the only company you'll be seeing." The door slammed and locked.

The beam of the lighthouse circled the room. Sean had fended off McCulloch's awkward thrusts. The lighthouse would be comfort enough for now.

Several days passed in the station house room. Except for meals delivered to him, Sean was alone. He had hoped that Leah, Kate, or Father Andre would visit, but he surmised that McCulloch had held true to his word to keep him incommunicado. The splendid isolation of the island offered convenient excuses for detention. There were no attorneys, no bail bondsman, and no magistrates to question the authority of this one man who wrapped himself in the mantle of the law.

During his exile from island life Sean thought more of Kate than his own destiny. As a Mormon on the island, she too must be suspect. She had been close to Annie. Her unorthodox artistry had offended the islanders. Eventually, he thought, he would be compelled to tell the truth about what he had seen. It would doom her.

Lunch that day brought a visitor he had not expected.

"You're one lucky son-of-bitch," McCulloch shouted as he entered the room, "you've got a friend out there with a *habeas* order that says I can't keep your ass in here unless I've got cause. Well, I'll get cause. I'm releasing you in her custody. But you try to get off this island, and I'll throw your ass back in here as fast as you can say James Strang. Now get out of here."

Sean emerged into the bright light of day. A woman got out of a rental car and walked toward him. Her stride was unmistakable.

"Trouble just seems to follow the Irish, Seanaghan!"

It was Lily.

"Lily!" Sean hugged her. It seemed so natural. "More like the Irish following the Irish. How in hell did you find me here, you of all people?"

"Luck, I guess. Graves got a call from a priest here on the island who said you had been arrested and needed help."

"Father Andre?"

"Yes, he was trying to locate a relative. I was in New York at the time, working on some papers at Columbia, and well, . . . Graves contacted an attorney he knew in Traverse City, and this guy shoved a document in my hand before I made the flight over. So, here I am, Lily to the rescue!"

"You're a welcome sight! But why come all this way?"

"I guess Graves just took pity on your miserable, benighted soul."

"Graves doesn't believe in souls."

"You haven't changed much, Sean. Still the cynic."

"At least when it comes to Graves."

"Say, where can a traveler rest her weary body?"

"It will have to wait, Lily. First, I've got some business with a few of my island friends. We'll start with Andre."

Lily and Sean found Father Andre at work in the shop behind the Christian Brother's retreat. He was repairing a screen door, swearing uncharacteristically and asking forgiveness after each epithet.

"Saint's alive!" Andre exclaimed as he rushed to embrace Sean.

"You've escaped the clutches of the *gendarmerie*. And who's *la petite mademoiselle*?" Andre took Lily's hand and kissed it.

Lily smiled. "You could learn something from this one, Sean."

"I've learned too much from him, already. But I believe I could teach him a little about craftsmanship." Sean grimaced in reply as he inspected the door. "This screen is supposed to keep out the insects, Andre. You've put a hole in it big enough for a bomber to fly through."

"It's never been my forte. The Order was founded to teach trades. Just my luck to get stuck here with a bunch of carpenters! They think they can teach an old dog new tricks."

"Seems that I recollect one carpenter who taught some new tricks a long time ago," Lily interjected, as she winked at Andre.

"I've always believed that's why he got out of the business." Andre winked back. "I like this one Sean. She's a keeper!"

"So why have they got you on the fix-up detail anyway? I thought you'd be pouring over records in the attic of Holy Cross."

"That's just it, Sean. Things started to heat up when you were arrested. When Father Leo got back from the mainland, that busy body, Mabel O'Donnell, fingered me for foraging in the attic. She found the ladder and put two and two together. Father Leo hasn't accused me of anything yet, but there's a new lock on the attic, and I've been confined to the retreat center for the past week. Said he'd send me to an alcohol rehab center in Chicago if I took one step past the gate. Leo's crony, Brother Kevin, has been watching me like a hawk. Don't you think I would have gone after you myself if that ole' jackal would have let me? Had to rely on the phone to get it done. I can't wait until he gets the telephone bill! Winston-Salem, New Haven, and Dublin. It'll drive him crazy."

Sean walked over to door and closed it.

"Tell me, Andre, is there any news of Annie Daggett?"

Andre lowered his head and shook it.

"She just vanished. Not a trace. They've dragged Barney's Lake from shore to shore, but she's gone."

"How's Kate taking it?"

"Well, I haven't seen her since our lunch at the Shamrock. Funny, now that you mention it, she didn't express any shock at all. And her being so close to Annie, you'd kinda expect it. Wouldn't you?"

"Yeah," Sean puzzled, "Then again, maybe not."

"Lily, you must have been sent by Dr. Graves. I had a devil of a time getting his address from that college of yours, Sean. From their reluctance I sensed that he was as popular as I am with the authorities. Fine fellow, that Graves. We really hit it off. Told me all about you, Sean."

Lily scuffled her feet and walked toward the door. She was obviously uncomfortable with the drift of the conversation.

"I've traveled half-way around this continent, missed a night of sleep, and I still haven't had a meal since my plane flight. Can we spare the talk about my boss?"

"Your boss?" Andre replied. "Then you'll be interested in this conversation."

"Not now," Lily grabbed Sean by the arm and hustled him to the door.

"Hold on, Lily," Sean complained as he wrenched his arm free. "I know you well enough to sense intrigue. Go on, Andre, I'm listening."

Lily crossed her arms and leaned against the door frame.

"Well, Sean, we starting discussing the fact that you had no known relatives, and I offered our latest discovery. He was most interested in my discovery of Cropper. Said that she was active in lending financial support to some of the indigenous Irish authors."

Sean stared at Lily as Andre continued. Lily stared at the floor, avoiding his gaze.

"I think we've heard enough. Right, Lily?" Sean struck his fist on the door jam near Lily's face. "Poor, Sean," he intoned sarcastically. "Imprisoned on Beaver Island. I'll just hop on a plane and free him! Same old Lily. Dedicated to Graves and the cause! Let's dig up some archival dirt to upset the cause of peace. You're as manipulative as you ever were."

Andre intervened just as Sean bolted out the door, yelling after him.

"Sean! That's enough. She just did you a big favor. We can be thankful for that. She did what I couldn't."

"It's not just Eliza," Lily called, as Sean strode toward the bicycle rack near the lodge. "It was you, too!"

Sean had jerked a bike from the rack, and was swinging his leg over the seat.

"Yeah, Lily, that's the story of my life. I've always been a second thought."

Sean peddled down the sandy lane toward the entrance. Rounding the bend he confronted a solitary figure in the middle of the lane. He hit the brakes, skidding in the soft sand.

"Tasted a little white man's justice, huh chemokmon?" Whitesides stood above him with his hands on his hips. "I've been looking for you. There's a rumor circulating that McCulloch's found a body. He'll be after yours next." Whitesides turned and started walking down a trail to the right.

"Ever been to Garden Island, Sean?"

Sean dusted off his jeans and rushed to catch up.

"No. Do I have to race you across the water?"

Whitesides smiled broadly. Sean had not seen it before.

"It's time I taught you to paddle a canoe."

Chapter XXIII
Spirit Burial

The two island outcasts waited until twilight before pushing an old wooden canoe into the still waters north of the harbor. It was a quiet, sultry summer night. Fires crackled on the beach as children begged for marshmallows to roast. Yachters, relaxing in the afterglow of afternoon racing, uncorked champagne bottles as they chattered and laughed about the days miscues. The satisfied summer reverie of days end in Paradise Bay concealed an island in covert bereavement. The islanders would not broadcast the death of Annie Daggett. It was bad for business.

Whiteside's powerful stroke propelled the sleek craft silently past the anchored yachts glistening in the pink glow of sunset. Sean reclined on his back in the canoe's midsection as he watched the scarlet tinged clouds move across the sky. It was on such an evening that a howling drunken mob had descended upon the island and wiped out every last vestige of the Mormon presence. No one would hear about the killing , rape, looting of houses and stores, or setting fire to the Mormon tabernacle. Books and pamphlets from the royal press had burned in large bonfires where children now roasted marshmallows. Sean pondered how this history had been so conveniently forgotten, or repressed. No one could verify what actually happened. No one cared. The Strangite Mormons were troublemakers, even to their brethren in Salt Lake. As he gazed up at the clouds, he remembered reading a Mormon account of that last night on the island.

> *Shortly before sunset the beleaguered flock, huddling near the beach saw in the west a spindle-shaped cloud of a beautiful golden color which formed the letters Z I O N in iridescent hues of gold and red and purple.*

The cloud was a last benediction to a terrible revenge. Sean wondered if Liza had seen the vision.

The waves quickened as the canoe rounded Whiskey Point. They rippled along the underside. The lighthouse beacon swept over the stern every four seconds, illuminating Whitesides sinewy frame as he labored at the paddle. The small canoe headed resolutely into the open waters.

"We've cleared the harbor. I could use another paddle up here, Seanaghan."

Sean steadied himself, placing his hands on the gunwale as he positioned himself in the front seat. Canoeing had been a familiar sport growing up in the mountains of North Carolina, and he was anxious to show Whitesides his proficiency.

"You know, that's the first time you've called me, 'Seanaghan'." Sean turned toward the stern. "Why so familiar all of a sudden?"

"Common bond, I guess," Whitesides motioned ahead with his paddle. "Watch that next swell."

"Common bond?" Sean queried, wrinkling his forehead and paddling hard into the swell. "I thought I would always be a chemokmon."

"And you always will be. But you've now joined the hunted. I should have said 'common bondage'. I've seen the inside of that station house more than a few times. How did it feel?"

"Lonely."

"Yes." Whitesides replied firmly, his teeth gritted.

Sean laughed.

"Did anyone ever teach that Deputy any grammar? I would have thought the nuns would have at least hammered a little education into that small brain!"

"He got his schooling on the mainland, . . . what precious little he may have retained. He surely didn't learn his history."

"None of us has, John."

"Say, you paddle pretty well."

"For a chemokmon!"

"No, for a Chippewa."

They both smiled.

A full moon rose and cast a broad reflection across the waters. It lit a silvery pathway to Garden Island.

Sean slept soundly in Whitesides' cabin. He awoke to the sound of wood chopping outside. The cabin was modest but neatly furnished. Two bedrooms below a loft opened into a great room and kitchen with massive oak beams. It was apparent that Whitesides was a craftsman. The kitchen furniture was hewed from white pine. A large overstuffed chair and couch upholstered in red, white, and yellow Traverse Bay wool sat in front of a French provincial harpsichord. Reed baskets hung from the rafters, along with dried herbs. A magnificent field stone fireplace occupied one corner. Bookshelves covered every available wall. Charts of the Great Lakes were neatly rolled up and stuck in a large brass drum near a secretary which held a sextant and compass next to photos of Harvard crewing teams. Sean inspected the photographs.

"He rowed eights, you know," a voice spoke from the kitchen.

Sean turned to see a woman in a long flowered dress. Her flowing gray hair framed a strong wrinkled face. She carried a basket of greens which she placed in the sink.

"He was proud of their performance that year. They were Ivy League champions in eights."

The front door opened to reveal Whitesides carrying a load of wood.

"I see you've met Loon Feather."

"Not quite, we were just getting acquainted."

He placed the wood near the fireplace, and heaved a sigh of relief.

"She's not much on formalities. Sean Connaghan, meet my Aunt Grace Whitesides, Loon Feather, island medicine woman. Grace, . . .

"I know who he is," Grace interjected abruptly, "an Irishman . . . it's been foretold." She spit the words out as she strode out the back door.

"Loon feather's distraught this morning. She's usually not this way. She received news from the big island this morning that Daggett has begun bulldozing through the medicine wheel. It's a powerful omen."

Sean looked out the window toward a circular bay below. Beyond, he could see the clear trace of Donegal Bay with Mt. Pisgah rising above it. From a distance it looked so pristine, untouched by man, waiting for the voyagers to make landfall. He thought of Annie Daggett chasing sea gulls on that beach.

"His daughter understood the beauty of the island. I wonder why he doesn't."

"It's his nature."

"Bullshit! It's greed."

"That's his nature. It's the nature of your ecosystem."

"Not mine," Sean replied self-righteously.

"It's all the same. Part of the same cycle of western civilization."

"Cycle? You talk of history as if it were a weather pattern."

"When you live on this island you see cycles in all living things. Why not history?"

"Because there are too many variables. So much of what happens is just that, happenstance."

"Happenstance . . . the nature of things, Sean. It's all the same, isn't it? Loons migrate every winter. They return every spring."

"It's not the same with people."

"Yes, people are arrogant enough to rationalize difference." Whitesides stepped over to the fireplace and began setting a fire. "It's called free will. We want to believe in it. Take your Mormons and Irish, for example. They were caught up in a cycle, . . . a virtual whirlwind of one."

"How so?"

"They believed in manifest destiny. It all starts with religion. At first it reflects the order of nature. Then man wants more, a deity who will bless man's journey, then justify his depredations. The sky and the sea and the grass are not enough for this man. The Mormons created a tribe and endowed it with a mission to find the promised land. When they found it, they dispossessed the Irish fishermen who in turn felt it was their destiny to reclaim it from the heathen Mormons who had blasphemed the institution of marriage. Each tribe engaged in a holy crusade. The oppressed, fresh from exile in Navoo, oppress the Irish, fresh from the oppression of English domination, who in turn oppress the Mormons. See, a cycle! All done in the name of God. Create a God of a man and you can expect things to be done for man in the name of God. At least Moses saw God as a burning bush or a voice from the sky!"

"I tend to think it was greed, simple greed," Sean asserted.

"And lust for power. It's an old story, but God is always evoked at the source."

"Daggett has not evoked God."

"Oh, no? It's the force of your God that dismisses ours. That medicine wheel has served our people for centuries. It's our link to the mysterious forces of the universe. It's our connection to the world of dreams—God's way of talking with us. It is Bethlehem and Jerusalem and Mecca and Lahsa. Yet, to Daggett and the island, it's just a rune of primitive man. The context of your history won't let you acknowledge its worth."

"And if the Chippewa possessed the power to stop it, wouldn't they throw the chemokmon off the island?"

"Now, . . . no. We're part of your cycle now. We've adopted your ways. We run casino's on the mainland now. It's survival. It took us a while to learn how to fight with your tools, I'm ashamed to say."

Sean walked over to the harpsichord and struck a key nonchalantly. "I've heard it all before. Everyone seems to claim to be a victim of some oppression. It's a tired saw. It's just another misuse of power."

"Agreed. Why not? It's part of the cycle. If I can claim moral superiority for my tribe resulting from past injustice, I can claim the right to rectify it. Today, it is the law which has become our God. It's all the same, a way of justifying the taking of property from another."

"Careful, Whitesides, you're beginning to sound like a Marxist."

"Marxism was just a way to justify victimization ideology or liberation theology or whatever you want to call it. As soon as man thinks he's oppressed by another, he begins to blame others for his own problems, and before you know it, he actually believes that he is entitled to oppress in return. Strang began as a pacifist and ended as a warmonger, all in the name of reclaiming paradise on these islands. Stalin, Hitler, Napoleon, they all began by invoking ideology, even creating there own to justify oppression in the name of the oppressed."

"Okay . . . so how do we end this cycle?"

"Maybe, we don't. The Christians got one thing right. Man is inherently sinful. It's in our nature."

"I thought the noble savage didn't believe in sin. Didn't even know about it."

"Sin is your European creation. We believe in evil spirits and good spirits. The idea of the noble savage was your invention. We were neither noble nor savage. Some of us were, just like some of you were."

"So what can you offer to break this cycle? It seems an inevitable consequence of history, according to your theory."

"Come over to the window." Whitesides pointed to Loon Feather, kneeling on the beach, chanting and raising her hands across the lake. "She believes in the force of her dreams. In those dreams she is reminded of her faults, her hopes, her ancestors, her oneness with nature, and most of all, our need to live in harmony with one another. It is her confession. It teaches humility and grace to see yourself honestly through your dreams. She looks within for her wisdom."

"We call it prayer," Sean said.

"You use prayer to ask for divine guidance or mercy or something you want. We use it to discover meaning."

Sean smiled. "Maybe, she could tell me my purpose for being here."

"She already has. She believes you're here to break the cycle."

"What? Me?" Sean laughed uproariously. "I can't even figure out how to get off these damnable islands!"

"Maybe, you're not supposed to."

Chapter XXIV
The Wolfe Tone Society

It was the marching season in Ulster. July twelfth would bring swarms of Protestant loyalists into the streets of Belfast and Londonderry to commemorate the victory of Protestant King William of Orange over Catholic James II at the Battle of the Boyne in 1690. The Orangemen would sing anti-papist songs as they marched in time with fife and drums, banners and flags waving past Catholic neighborhoods. The Catholics understood the exercise. The huge Lambeg drums beat out a defiant pulse of domination. The words of one song echoed in his mind.

Slaughter, slaughter, holy water,
Slaughter the Papists one by one.
We will tear them asunder
And make them lie under
The Protestant boys who follow the drum.

The beat of the drums would not be heard by the man who traveled from the Boyne across the big lake to Beaver Island by trawler. But he remembered the day. It was the source of a seething historical grievance which burned in his heart. It was his very reason for making the long journey from Northern Ireland. The Orange ritual would merit no more than a mention in the *Detroit Free Press*. The "Irish Troubles" were a stagnant cesspool of hatred and recrimination which held little interest for Americans. Only an IRA bomb at Harrods or 10 Downing Street might raise an eyebrow over the morning coffee. And that day was presumably over after the peace accords. Americans liked their crises neat and tidy. Good versus evil. High Noon at the O.K. Corral. Americans were frustrated by the complicated confusion of sectarian conflict. They did not hear the beat of the Lambeg drums. They did not care about the "Irish Troubles." Besides, it was over. The "War on Terrorism" and economic crisis occupied their thoughts.

The man derived comfort from the lack of American consciousness about the "troubles". The island had served as a perfect cover for his activities for almost three decades. The distant outpost in the heart of the continent provided the perfect ingredients for covert action, sympathy, and isolation. Although he had traveled infrequently to the outpost, he had established this branch of the Wolfe Tone Society in the late 1960's. As the trawler slowed its engines at the harbor entrance, the man reflected upon his original motives for joining the Sinn Fein.

He remembered his innocent embrace of Irish republicanism during his classes with Anthony Coughlan at Trinity College. Coughlan had written an article proposing a civil rights movement patterned after the leadership of Ghandi and King to wrest concessions from the Stormont government of the North. Coughlan had reinvigorated the old Wolfe Tone Society, originally formed in 1798 to resist British rule. The man was young then, young and full of that lust for adventure and an idealist cause which fuels crusades. He remembered the formation of the Northern Ireland Civil Rights Association and his attendance at the first banned meeting in Belfast in 1967. It had been a bust. The small audience sat and muttered in a chilly hall while an IRA group from Dublin was captured on the way to the meeting by the Royal Ulster Constabulary. While civil disobedience in America had ignited an explosion of massive sit-ins and rallies, the movement for social justice in Northern Ireland sputtered like a wet firecracker. Undaunted by this failure the man had joined Conn and Patricia McCluskey in their Campaign for Social Justice in Dungannon "to collect data on all injustices done against all creeds and political opinions." They prepared to present a grievance case to the Commission for Human Rights at Strasbourg and the United Nations. No one paid attention.

The man could not remember when he relinquished his faith in non-violence for the IRA. It may have been Bloody Sunday in Derry, 1972, when he saw more than a dozen Catholic marchers gunned down by British Paras who allegedly had come under fire from snipers. It did not matter now. He had long ago surrendered himself to a destiny which he did not fully understand. He had been sucked into the eye of the terrorist hurricane, an accomplice to acts he abhorred, but which he justified as a necessary evil of any revolution. Once, he tried to distance himself from the bombings. He was, after all, only involved in protection of those innocently accused. But he knew better now. The IRA was a renegade organization with too many splinter groups to control. He was as blood soaked as Macbeth.

The man stepped onto the short dock near the Marine Museum and walked purposefully toward the light emanating from the two small windows of a World War II corrugated metal Quonset hut. Ostensibly, the hut was a storage building for commercial fishing gear. During the long bleak winter months island fishermen had huddled near its Franklin stove to repair their nets. It was a natural gathering place for the descendants of Arranmore to puff on their pipes and recount stories of storms and disaster on the sweetwater sea. Few would ever indulge the thought that it would harbor a secret branch of the Wolfe Tone Society.

The man knocked at the door and was ushered into a dimly lit back room where several men sat around a large old oak kitchen table surrounded by old packing crates. Others, younger men, sat on the crates, smoking cigarettes and playing cards. When the man entered the room, the group at the table rose in somber unison. One, Jack Daggett, stuck out his hand in greeting as the man approached.

"I'm sorry you had to come, Graves," Daggett declared, "We've been reluctant to call, but when your associate, Lily, arrived. Well, she made no attempt to contact us. We became worried that she and this Connaghan fellow were onto our trail."

"Rest easy, Jack, she knows just enough to believe anything that I tell her. I sent her to retrieve Sean. When she called two nights ago to report that Sean had escaped, I realized the risk of disclosure. So, I'm here, and we need to find our young intermeddler."

"I'll find him," a voice interjected from a corner crate in the shadows. "There's no safe house on this island 'cept the ones we created for our own. He'll have to surface soon, and then we'll nab him." The face attached to the voice emerged from the shadows. It was scarred severely on the left side, the hideous consequence of a bomb which had discharged prematurely.

"You'll not get involved in this business, Padraig O'Donnell. It's an internal matter," Daggett rebuked, "It's for islanders to handle."

"You best make him disappear. That's the only way to insure our safety," O'Donnell spit back. "You'll blow it, if I know how islanders handle these things."

"Like you blew half your head off in Belfast!" Judd McCollough interjected.

O'Donnell lunged at McCollough only to be restrained by Daggett. "At least the RUC knew how to interrogate and incarcerate. You let him slip right through your hands, fool!"

"Gentlemen!" Graves spoke authoritatively, "You are about to confirm my faith in the impetuous nature of the Irish. I've come here to handle this matter myself, and I will brook no interference from any of you!"

Graves exercised a commanding influence over the group. As he spoke an elderly man stepped forward from the group and tapped his pipe in an ashtray on the table. It was Tommy Gallagher. Tommy had come to the island as a boy from Arranmore in the 1950's. Tommy had been Graves first contact on the island in the sixties. He had helped to arrange the relocation of some of the first IRA bombing suspects. In the secret war of the IRA Beaver Island had become a sanctuary for those who had become targets of suspicion by the British SAS or the RUC. Graves, a product of an Irish mother and American father, had chosen American citizenship at the request of Ruairi O Bradaigh, the chief of staff of the Army Council. Having secured a position at an American university he was in an ideal position to find paths of flight and distant American safe houses for those accused of terrorism. After several abortive failures to hide refugees in New York and Chicago, Graves had discovered Tommy Gallagher through his Chicago network. Until the mid-eighties the Beaver connection had served to provide an initial hiding place for many suspects. Tommy's "relatives" from the old country would appear every so often on fishing boats from Chicago or Toronto. Sometimes they would stay for a year or two, then return to Ireland or disappear into the Canadian wilderness across Georgian Bay.

"Graves is right. Our job for these many years has been to protect, no questions asked," he paused and stared at O'Donnell, "Sometimes I've questioned whether we've done the right thing by helping out, but I'll not bring any treachery to this island. If we're to be discovered by this young man, so be it. I'll not have his blood on my hands."

"Nor I, Tommy," Graves responded as he grabbed Tommy's shoulder in fond embrace, "We've protected many an Irish soul to sing another day, and we'll not change our compact now."

Tommy smiled. "We have indeed, my friend."

Graves shuttered to think how he had failed Tommy. He had promised him that he would send him only innocent IRA members who had been falsely accused or whose lives were in imminent danger. It was a half truth, and as the years went by, he suspected that Tommy and the small circle of friends on the island knew that there was more to the history of each of the visitors from the old country.

When the meeting broke up, Tommy and Daggett stayed to question Graves about his next step.

"I'm afraid I can't obey your order, Graves," Daggett spoke resolutely, "You see, there's more at stake here than a few old romantic Irish dreams of a united state. As long as your occasional visitors kept to themselves and moved along in time, this little society helped to keep the island in the hands of a few of us who knew our secret. It bound us in a kind of brotherhood that assured that the island developed at a, shall we say, gentle and orderly pace, but now . . ."

"You mean, Jack, that things are beginning to unravel and you're scared," Tommy interrupted. "You're running scared that some one's going to discover that you spirited your daughter off to the mainland in a desperate effort to set Sean up and get him off the island. Except, how are you going to explain Annie's reappearance? Your blunder may have been as stupid as Padraig's aborted bomb!"

"Listen, Tommy, this Sean guy may be young and unsophisticated, but his senses are highly refined, and he is principled enough to set economic development on this island back to the depression." We must dispose of him—- permanently."

"I don't know, Jack, the idea of an IRA cell on the island may be just what the Chamber of Commerce ordered," Graves said sardonically. "Imagine the tour bus pointing out the secret American underground railroad for the IRA in a Quonset hut on Beaver Island!"

"You sound like Connaghan, Graves!"

"He was my student," Graves smirked, "He understands the irony of the Irish! Have you lost your sense of humor?"

"Yeah, I guess I have. I don't appreciate outsiders playing around with my destiny."

"Oh? Your destiny?" Graves raised his eyebrow quizzically, "And what might that destiny be?"

"It damn well wouldn't be playing army for a bunch of demented bombers with historic grudges against the winners. Besides, your living in the past. Ireland has resolved its problems. It's over, Graves. You need to go play your game somewhere else!"

"I think, maybe, you better go, Jack," Tommy interjected.

"Wait a minute, Tommy! I think Mr. Daggett has a point here to make," Graves paused. "History doesn't make much of difference to you, does it Jack?"

"Not on this island. We've had to fight for everything we have."

"And now you have a chance to cash in, right?"

"Yeah. You might say that!"

"And history stands in the way. It stands in the way because of one young man who might be able to rewrite a little of that history and embarrass you." Graves stroked his chin. "You know, Jack, I'm tempted to let him do it. Tommy and I have lived enough of life for a cause to know that people like you aren't interested in equal chances for success or prosperity or hope to escape oppression. No, my friend, I think you'd be quite at home with the government in Ulster. In fact there's a parade in Belfast you might want to march in. Com'on Tommy, it's getting stuffy in here."

Graves picked up his bag and headed for the door.

"Turn out the lights, when you leave," Tommy told Daggett as he shut the door.

It was a short walk in the cool breeze coming off the harbor to Tommy's cottage on Whiskey Point. The cottage occupied a commanding position near the lighthouse from which Tommy could spot all the incoming traffic into Paradise Bay. From his kitchen table Graves observed an old two masted schooner glide past the old Coast Guard station and lower its aft sail in the full moonlight.

"She's the Manitou, in from Grand Traverse," Tommy said as he poured a scotch on the rocks, "You do still drink scotch?"

"Too much of it for my own good," Graves replied. "She's arriving a little late, don't you think?"

"Probably holed up on High Island for a squall to pass. You know I once placed Liam O'Neill on board her for the summer season. Captain Harry said he never had a better seaman."

"Liam O'Neill . . . " Graves raised his scotch glass and looked through it with one eye at the Manitou. "Liam almost landed in a Derry jail. Got caught in an SAS ambush after a car bombing. So where do you think he is now, Tommy?"

"Running a sport fishing service up on Lake Nipigon. He's one who didn't return. Now he's Leonard Neil"

The Manitou had dropped her anchor in the middle of the harbor and was discharging her crew on little dingys. The dingys looked like a late night raiding parade.

Tommy joined Graves at the table with a bottle of Johnny Walker. "She's here for Museum Week. She's an artifact now, something for the tourists to enjoy and romanticize."

"Just like us, Tommy. Artifacts. The world seems to be passing us by."

"Passed me by a long time ago, professor."

The lights of cottages around the bay twinkled and cast slender golden trails across the still water. The two old conspirators sat there together in silence, transfixed by the beauty of the harbor asleep in the moonlight.

"They weren't all innocent, were they, Ed?" Tommy asked casually, his eyes still set straight ahead into the harbor night.

"No, Tommy. But I think you knew that."

"I didn't really want to think about it. Most of the boys seemed like such gentle folk, not driven by rage."

"Yes, but it's not the same here. They lived in a state of rage there. You know, when you don't feel free, your heart hardens to hope. It's a dangerous thing, Tommy, for a young person to lose his hope."

"Strange. I came to view my job as giving hope here rather than helping out the troubles over there. More like running an orphanage. You know, only the ones that couldn't spend that rage returned."

"Yes. And they usually ended their lives caught dead in the rage that consumed them."

"Padraig?"

"Yes, he'll go home. He'll go home to die."

"I hope not. He's a good lad. What do you think makes the difference in them?"

Graves rose from his chair and stepped over to the door facing the harbor. He opened it, and breathed deeply of the cool mist coming in off the lake.

"I expect that they want every Irishman to have what you have here. Those that return want to carry the breath of the new world with them, but of course they can't. History won't them.

Chapter XXV
Rendezvous in Paradise

Whitesides woke Sean early with news that he had a visitor. It was a visitor Sean had longed to see. As he dressed, Vivaldi's Four Seasons enveloped the cabin. The sharp staccato strikes of the harpsichord rose and fell against an orchestral background of surf and wind. Vivaldi had surely captured the song of summer, Sean thought.

Sparkling prisms of sunlight reflecting from the water below the cabin danced across the ceiling as deftly as Kate Fox's fingers moved across the keyboard. Whitesides sat transfixed on the woolen- clad couch with his eyes closed tightly, nodding in time with the quick allegro, his eyebrows furrowed in the trance of a timeless motif of nature's changing moods. Sean leaned against the door frame and shared the moment. He envied Kate's passion for life. He felt deep pleasure in hearing music so at one with the island. It was timeless. She was timeless.

When Kate finished, she paused and lowered her head over the keyboard, breathing deeply as if she had just made love. Whitesides broke the silence with a standing ovation.

"That was divine, simply divine," Whitesides exclaimed, "You should visit more often. That old box hasn't seen that much action since it entertained colonials at Mackinac Island."

"It sounds like it hasn't been tuned since then either," Kate replied, smiling.

Whitesides shrugged. "I do the best I can. I really should play it more often."

"Yes, it deserves it. You do too!"

"What I deserve is a shower and a good meal. Care to join me for breakfast?"

"I came on business." Kate's voice turned serious as she looked at Sean, "Thought the professor could use some advice."

"Got plenty of that Kate," Sean replied with indifference, "I'd prefer breakfast."

"I brought a picnic lunch. Grab a cup of coffee, and we'll take a hike."

"That's an offer I wouldn't turn down, brother," Whitesides interjected, "Kate's not known as an easy catch around here."

"I'll thank you not to refer to me as a catch, John Whitesides. I'm not one of your smoked whitefish! Now, how 'bout it, Sean?"

"Madam, I am always at your disposal," Sean replied, bowing genteelly. "It's the least I can offer for your music."

Sean had yet to enjoy a more lovely day than that planned by Kate. They hiked inland past small lakes and streams and through magnificent meadows ablaze with wildflowers. Kate moved through the tall meadow grass as gracefully as the rippling breeze. Occasionally, she would stop to pick wild daisies and Queen Anne's Lace or explain the legend of Indian Paint Brush. Together, they gorged themselves on ripened blackberries.

Sean had rarely experienced such joy any day of his life. He was loose in paradise with his love. The image of Kate, her eyes, her flowing skirt, her auburn hair blowing in the wind, conspired to set his spirit free from the bondage of an uncertain future. Time seemed to stop, caught in a rapture of midsummer enchantment. By the time they had reached a deserted beach on the far side of the island, Sean was drunk on a rhapsody of sun, wildflowers, and Kate. He chased her down a steep dune and into the teal green surf. As he gently placed his hands around her slender waist, the waves floated and swirled her indigo skirt around them. He pulled her to him in a tight embrace. Kate ran her fingers through his hair. The two lovers stood glistening in the surf as the waves splashed between them.

"The color of your eyes matches the beauty of the lake."

"Which part?" Kate asked playfully, stroking her fingers slowly over Sean's lower lip.

"The part just before the drop off," Sean replied smiling.

"And are we about to step off the blue line into the deep?"

"Only if you can swim."

"Or drowned together?" Kate teased.

"If you wish. Maybe we'll be reincarnated as fish."

"I think I'd prefer a cottage by the sea to pass my days with you," Sean said as he lifted Kate out of the water and carried her to the beach. He laid her near a large boulder, cradling her in his arms.

The sun was beginning to make its slow descent to the horizon. The great inland sea was giving up its turbulence, exchanging whitecaps for the liquid gold of setting sun. It illuminated Kate's face. It was as if Kate was the lake—shimmering, stormy, sunlit with each changing mood. Sean wanted to swim those moods. He gently caressed her face. His hands moved down her neck to her breasts. He could feel her heart pulsating.

"I want you," Sean whispered into her ear.

"And I you," she replied as she gently brushed his hands away, "but it cannot be."

Sean was perplexed.

"Don't you feel as I do?"

"In a way. But not as you might think," Kate pulled her knees to her chest and gazed out over the water, "Oh, look . . . two loons!"

The loons circled in a broad arc over the golden water and then descended in a long glide to the bay.

"You know they mate for life," Kate mused, "something we can never even think about"

"Have you?"

"Of course."

"Then, why?"

"Sean, how many times in your life have you felt unconnected with the people that you were around?"

"Always, I guess. It's just me. It's who I am."

"Yes, it is. But what you are is a missionary in the greatest sense of that term."

"And what is my mission, Kate? This is getting a little strange. I share one of the most beautiful days in paradise with a woman who enchants me, and she calls me a missionary." Sean sighed. "Don't you think I deserve a simple answer to my question?"

"You do. I am Eliza Cropper Connaghan."

Sean rose and circled the large boulder several times, pausing to throw his hands in the air and alternatively laugh or shake his head.

Kate continued. "I was hoping that I wouldn't have to be this direct. We had hoped that it would come naturally. It does to some of us, you know."

"No, Kate, I don't know. Just *what* comes naturally?"

"Listen . . . shhh . . . what do you hear?"

Sean paused and looked up at the sky.

Both remained silent for several moments.

"The clouds," Sean shook his head, "Did I say I hear the clouds?"

"Yes, Sean, look at them billowing on the horizon. You hear what humans cannot, and you've been blotting it out for years. Listen.."

Sean stared at the rosy puffs grouped to the west. He stood there for several minutes and listened . . . listened to the sounds he had never experienced consciously before. How could he have missed this wonderful sense, he thought?

"Just like you've missed the point of Graves question about the lighthouse, or Rose's message. Or Yeats for that matter. He was one of us."

"How do you know these things?"

"I've listened. Sometimes across continents. It's not hard. You'll catch on."

"You mean, we're ghosts," Sean stuttered.

Kate laughed as she grasped Sean's hand and kissed it.

"Don't be silly, Sean. We're real people. See." She kissed him again.

"But you said that you were Liza . How do you explain that."

"I am her conscience, her memory, her dreams . . . but I have my own as well. I have been sent here to make right what was wrong. She wanted it so much when she died that I am the shadow left here, born here to see it done."

"And what is that which you must do?"

"I don't know exactly. But I do know that you are a critical part of what will happen, and happen it will . . . soon. And now we best be heading back to Beaver. I sense that it is unfolding as we speak."

"Wait. What do you call us? I mean, as I stand here, I can hear Loon Feather chanting on the beach across the island. She's praying to save the wheel. It is a powerful prayer. It moves me."

"Yes, there is pain to these heightened senses. You'll now sense the full range of emotions and those of others as well. You will be able to see auras not seen by others, and you will come to know things, past and future."

"Kate," Sean hesitated. "Are we immortal?"

"That sounds like a question that Eve might have asked Adam."

"I think I know the answer."

"You're using your new senses well. We bleed just like everyone else."

"Kate. Graves has returned to the island, hasn't he?"

"Yes. And you know that he's been here before."

"It's time to pay him a visit, don't you think."

"It is, indeed."

The two sojourners in paradise plunged onto the path toward Whitesides cabin. It was pitch dark, but they would easily find the way home.

Chapter XXVI
The Sermon

The Shamrock was packed with islanders for Sunday dinner after the eleven o'clock service at Holy Cross. The subject of conversation was the same at each table. Father Leo was in attendance at the annual Diocesan meeting downstate and Father LaFreniere had been tasked to substitute for him. Father Leo had taken great pains to arrange every detail of the service. He didn't trust LaFreniere. Brother Kevin was to deliver the homily, and Father Andre was to administer the sacrament. But as fate would have it, Brother Kevin took ill on Saturday, and the responsibility of delivering the sermon fell to LaFreniere. It was a moment Father Leo had feared and for which Father Andre had prayed. The islanders had anticipated this day, for they had come to know Father Andre as a rascal who spoke his mind without deference to convention. Most islanders respected honesty, especially if it was laced with a bit of humor. But this day there would be no humor. Andre LaFreniere had an important message to deliver.

"I'm telling you Tommy Gallagher," Molly Burke said as she pulled up a chair at his table, "I haven't heard anything as outrageous since Father Hennessy cast a curse on the Clancy woman at the turn of the century. And he said he had the Pope's blessing. But this, . . . well . . . I like Father Andre, but I'm afraid there'll be hell to pay when Father Leo returns."

"Calm down, Molly, and have a seat with us," Tommy coaxed. "Meet my friend here, Dr. Edwin Graves. He's here studying Irish immigrant history, you might say."

"Pleasure to meet you, Dr. Graves. And I sure hope you don't take serious anything I'm about to tell you about Father Andre's sermon, because the man has lost his mind."

Graves nodded and shook Molly's hand. "I suspect it should be entertaining none the less."

"You could say that . . . but entertainment is for the theatre, and this was the church, bless my soul," Molly asserted, genuflecting, "Tommy, I be telling you, they'll be talkin' about this day for decades to come."

"Now, Molly, you know that legend starts on this island as soon as a good story gets passed around in the winter. Why last year they had old John O'Hara married to a movie star because he took a trip to Hollywood."

"Tommy, I'm not talkin' harmless gossip. We're talkin' strange stuff."

"Okay, Molly, spit it out. I guess I ought to know the first version before January, so I'll know how tall this story will grow."

"It doesn't need any growing room . . . "

"Molly!"

"Okay. Well, Father Andre began with a verse about the sins of the fathers being visited on the sons of the next generation, and every body expected Father Andre to make a joke about how Art McDonald's son, Michael, made the same error in the ninth inning of the McDonough Softball Classic finals as Art had made last year. You know, he threw to second for the out instead of home. Art never lived that down, and Michael never will either."

"That's not a joke around these parts, Molly," Tommy chided playfully.

"It would have been a far sight better than what he began to tell us, Tommy Gallagher! He started talking about the missing children like we was responsible for their loss." Molly genuflected. "Bless their sweet departed souls. I can tell you there was a lot of mumbling and shuffling and coughing in the congregation. Maude Flaraghty raised herself from the front pew and walked straight for the door."

"Now, Molly," Tommy chided, "Maude's known for her theatrics."

"Well, she wasn't the only one. Andre started in on Father Damnon concealing records of marriages between Mormons and Catholics after the Mormons' passing."

Graves interrupted, "Passing? You mean when the Irish kicked them off the island."

"That's a harsh interpretation, Dr. Graves," Molly whispered, "We prefer the passing."

"Interesting bit of history, Molly, but it's been a long time. What's it got to do with missing children."

"That's just it, Tommy, Father Andre said the disappearances were divine retribution for the depredations of the Mormons by our ancestors."

"I can understand why Maude walked out," Tommy retorted.

"But wasn't that almost 150 years ago?" Graves inquired.

"Ed, you of all people should know that time does not soften the memory of the Irish," Tommy interjected, "Go on Molly."

"Well . . . Father Andre was on a roll. He started naming the children and describing their family histories. Went all the back to the Hanrahan girl. Traced lineage of the O'Boyles and the Riley's and the Kilkenney's. Sweet Mother of Mary! It was awful. People crying and wailing at the mention of those children. And he didn't stop at describing the marriages. He talked about rape and the children born of the rape of Mormon women that were adopted secretly by island families. About that time, Brother Kevin tried to coax him down from the pulpit. But he just keep railing about the injustices done to the Mormons in the name of Christianity, and how no proper confession had been offered for these sins. 'As long as this island continued to live a lie', he said, 'we could not longer expect the favor of God's grace and absolution.' Then he started to read from the Book of Revelation. "These words are trustworthy and true", he read. "And the Lord, the God of the spirits of the prophets, has sent his angel to show his servants what must soon take place."

Molly slumped into the chair next to Tommy, placing her face into her hands. "It was a horrible moment. The congregation just sat there. They sat in silence as Andre took off his vestments, dropped them in front of the alter, and walked out, straight down the center aisle. Nobody said a word. It was as if a tomb had been opened, and we were all staring into a dark hole."

Graves looked at Tommy across the table. Their thoughts were the same. The sermon was an unexpected complication.

Lily arrived at the table just as Molly departed. "From the way you two look, you've heard the news, no doubt." Their eyes exchanged the silent, knowing greeting of old friends with deep secrets.

"Molly leaves no stone unturned," Tommy whispered under his breath. "Before nightfall, even the campers on the South end will be telling the story around the campfire."

Graves reached across the table and patted Lily's hand. "It's good to see you. Any news from our erstwhile scholar?"

"I'm afraid I made somewhat of a mess of things, " Lily replied as she gazed down at the table. "He saw right through me. Sorry you had to come."

"Not at all, lass. Besides, it's always good to see this old salt." Graves slapped Tommy on the back. "Now, tell me. What do you think he knows?"

"Hard to figure. He hasn't let on to Kate, at least. Seems it could all be a coincidence."

"Coincidence? Lily, you're smarter than that," Graves retorted. "One just doesn't find this place by happenstance. Good God, it's in the middle of nowhere. The odds are infinitesimal."

"He's got to be a deep plant," Tommy interjected as he stoked his pipe, "I'll bet he was recruited early on. After all, his father did serve in the army."

"Rubbish. That's about as absurd as it being a coincidence," Graves responded, "No…there's something else going on here. Who has he met, Lily, since he's been on the island."

"Well, there's Kate and Harvey and of course Deputy Judd . . . ," Lily hesitated looking into the distance across the room, "And then there's . . . Father Andre."

"You mean, the priest who delivered that cockamamie sermon?"

Graves stoked his chin. "Maybe . . . just maybe he doesn't know."

"You mean to suggest that he's as innocent as a new born lamb!" Tommy exclaimed. "Now there's a stretch, if I ever heard one!"

"No, Tommy," Lily offered, "He's conducting research on the Strangite Mormons, and Andre . . . well . . . we know from his sermon that.."

"Shit," Tommy interrupted, "Those rumors have been traveling the gossip airwaves for years. It's a cover, I tell you."

"Maybe, Tommy," Graves replied, "But linking it with the deaths of the children will bring the police down on this island like a herd of banshees, and that's bound to bring attention to our operation. Especially, if they discover that Daggett's daughter is alive and well at her Aunt's house in Pellston."

"They'll be a lot of questions for Daggett."

"Yes, Tommy. And I don't trust Daggett. He'll protect his island interests and spill his guts before he'd lift a finger to save our boys. And when the police discover the presence of bombers and murders on this island retreat, it's natural that they'll suspect . . . "

"Our boys," Lily added.

"Lily, you've got to find Sean. We've got to talk. I've got to know what he knows. Take Tommy and Padraig with you. Have you got any idea where he might be hiding?"

"Garden Island, I believe. At least that's where Kate went to find him."

"Bring him to Protar's Tomb at midnight. It's time for a little seance with our Mormon scholar."

Chapter XXVII
Message from the Tomb

Sean and Kate expected the arrival of Tommy Gallagher and Padriag O'Donnell on Garden Island. They also knew their destination. Tommy and Padraig were mystified by Sean's acceptance of the invitation to return. They had planned a forcible kidnapping, but instead found the two waiting on the beach. Tommy was troubled by the calm reception. It was too easy. Neither Kate nor Sean spoke on the return voyage. It was a moonless night, perfect cover for a covert docking at the Quonset hut in the harbor. The drive to the tomb would take little time. They would arrive early.

Tommy's old Chevy spun in the sand as it rounded the curve of Sloptown Road and onto the trail to the tomb. The beam of the headlights briefly captured the old narrow gauge railway line which ran the length of the trail. The old track had once carried loggers to their death in an accident which was commemorated by a plaque near the roads edge. Tommy always grew edgy as he drove alongside the track toward the tomb. His grandfather had died in the accident, and he remembered the gruesome scene of tangled steel and scattered logs enveloped in a cloud of hot steam pouring from the overturned engine. The line had been closed after the accident. No one knew how it happened, but some on the island believed that it was the ghost of Dr. Protar who had caused it. Some said he was angered by the sound of the iron horse, chugging through the virgin wilderness. Others speculated that he was upset by the destruction of the forest and the homes of its animals. Still others thought that the old ghost had tried to ride the train to the coast on account of the fact that the islanders had not obeyed his wish to be buried at sea. Tommy discounted such explanations, but even at his seasoned age, he was not able to shake the anxiety which overtook him as the image of the tomb approached in his headlights. His silent passengers only added to his anxiety. He would leave the headlights on for this visit.

The tomb was an unimposing structure. Dwarfed by a huge boulder the size of a clochan, it appeared like an small enclosed courtyard of field stone. A bronze relief of the old doctor was embedded in the center stone. As the passengers exited the old Chevy, Graves and group of figures emerged from behind the boulder and approached. Graves lit a cigarette and exhaled smoke upward into the cool night air.

"You're not surprised to see me, Sean?" he inquired cocking his head to catch Sean's down turned eyes.

"Can't say that I am, Professor Graves," Sean replied, "You have a habit of cropping up in out of the way places."

"You do too, my scholarly friend," Graves said as he moved closer, "We seem to travel in the same circles."

"I've stopped traveling in circles, Graves. It's straight lines now."

"I see you haven't lost your penchant for the pun, Sean."

"Some things don't change," Sean paused, "others change immensely. You know what they say, nothing's new except the history you don't know'."

"Harry Truman, right? And I hope you don't know some of our recent history."

"I'm afraid I do. It's my job now, you know."

Another figure stepped from behind the boulder and into the glare of the headlights. Sean recognized the voice as Jack Daggett's.

"Enough of this bullshit, Graves. Let's get on with it."

"Like you want to get on with desecrating Indian spirits, Jack?" Kate interjected.

Daggett laughed and spit on the ground before the tomb. "The only spirits I'd be desecrating tonight are the two of you."

"Maybe, you're right about that, Daggett," Sean whispered calmly as he stepped close enough to Graves to make out the whites of his eyes amid the glow of his cigarette. "Since when did you start keeping the company of robber barons, Mister Chips?"

"Unfortunately, he came with the package. But we're wasting time here, Sean. I want to know what you know."

"I know that your friend Daggett here doesn't deserve to grace the ground upon which we stand," Sean spoke resolutely as he turned toward

Daggett, "You're a rapist, Daggett. Born of rapists and bred by them. You're that little seed of greed that impregnated this island with evil."

"You little bastard, I'll kill you for that insolence."

Daggett dove at Sean in a furious rage, pushing him to the ground and hammering him with his large fists. Padraig and Tommy pulled him from the prostrate Sean as Graves yelled for Daggett to stop.

"You little fart!" Daggett screamed as Tommy and Padraig tried to restrain him. "You have no idea what we built here!"

"You built a glass house," Sean replied getting up as Kate began to nurse a bloody face. "And I'm here to shatter it with my sling shot!"

Daggett broke away and disappeared down the trail yelling, "Graves, you better keep that asshole away from me. He's a dead man. You hear . . . a dead man."

Tommy moved toward Graves and whispered in his ear. "He may be more dangerous than Sean, Ed."

"I know," Graves whispered back, then turned to Sean and Kate, "Look, Sean, I need you off this island, and I need you off it now! It's in your best interests, you know. "

"You mean, it's in your best interests, Graves," Sean retorted, as he wiped his bloody lip. "But why should you worry, professor? I have no intention of blowing the cover of your pathetic little group. They're just symptomatic of a larger virus on this island." Sean pointed toward Protar's tomb, " He knew it. He ministered to the people who had contracted it. He knew the truth of this place, and hoped that his example would make a difference . . . eventually reveal the truth. Do you know the last thing that he wrote in his journal? He wrote the words of Jesus, . . . 'from the days of John the Baptist until now, the kingdom of heaven suffereth violence, and the violent bear it away.' Your little group found this island because it was the perfect place to hide your dirty little secrets. But actually, the island found you, just like it found my great, great grandmother." Sean sighed and grabbed the collar of Graves shirt. "You old fool . . . don't you understand. It found me!"

"Does it really matter who found whom? What matters is that it has been a refuge for many a young Irish lad who was courageous enough to hear the clarion call of freedom."

"Freedom?" Sean scoffed, "What do they know of freedom? Most of them work for Daggett."

"It's a small place. They've got to have work. With the fishing gone . . . "

"Doesn't it strike you as ironic that they work for a guy who owns half the island and plans on turning it into a golf course."

"It's a small corner of the world. It will survive. Golf courses aren't bad. In fact, they're a damn site better than the poverty of Ulster."

"Ulster is the old world, Graves. This is the new. Have you forgotten that America is also about new beginnings, a faith that we could breath a new life free from the misery wrought by the old orthodoxies."

"You've been reading too much Thoreau, Sean. Wake up! It was the old that settled the new. They brought their greed with them. It was Germans and Scotch-Irish that decimated the buffalo herds. The world may be different. Man is not."

Sean pointed at Protar's tomb. "He didn't think so. When he died, the islanders discovered that he was Baron Parrot, born of German aristocracy, university educated, and sent to an isolated prison camp in Siberia at age 21 because he resisted Russian domination of his native land. He was a rebel, Graves, just like your little band, . . . except that he chose to work out his salvation here, ministering to the needs of island poor and living a simple life."

"I fail to discern a difference. He's just like my lads."

"The difference is that he wasn't a killer! He escaped to find a new life, and he lived it nobly. Like the Mormons who settled here before him, they just wanted peace and an opportunity to live in harmony with the world."

"Oh, you are just as naïve as the first time I met you. Have you learned nothing, Seanaghan? All men say that they want to live in such harmony, but the world plays a harsh joke on them. They really just want to survive. And they'll take what they need to do it."

"They'll take more than they need and in the process they'll lose the one thing that moved them to find peace in the first place."

"And what's that?"

"Their soul, Graves."

"Their soul?" Graves laughed uproariously. "You've been hanging around that priest, Andre, too long. Mankind doesn't think or act on the impulses of the soul. That's the line that slaughtered armies from the dawn of the crusades to the . . . "

"To the bombings in Ulster. Yes, you're right. But that's not the soul acting, Graves. That's man pretending to act as God. It's man-made god. You should know that. Yeats knew it. Protar knew it. St. Patrick knew it."

"And I suppose you know it."

"I do." Sean placed his hands on Graves shoulders. "And you know it too."

The two gazed deep into each others eyes. Then Graves slumped down upon a boulder near the tomb, and gazed through its wrought iron gate. "What am I to do?"

Sean's words echoed inside the tomb's enclosure. "A man is sitting in a boat in the Irish Sea on a foggy night. He is poor, lonely, drunk, and Irish. He thinks he sees a lighthouse in the distance. What is the purpose of the lighthouse to this man.?"

"I thought I once knew, Sean," Graves replied softly, "Now I may be too old to figure it out."

Sean crouched near Graves and grasped his hands. "The lighthouse means we have a way home, if we can but keep it in view. You may have lost sight somewhere along the way." Sean patted Graves on the leg, and whispered gently, "I'm not here to expose your group. I'm here to correct an injustice."

Sean turned to Kate. "Com'on Kate. It's a long walk home."

Tommy watched as the two shadows disappeared into headlights of the Chevy. He heard a train whistle in the distance. It chilled him. He couldn't help but think that it would stop to pick them up.

Kate decided to take refuge at Leah's house. It was safer for them. They found Leah at the kitchen table, wide awake and as talkative as ever.

"It's about time," Leah declared as she rose from the table, "Where have you been? I've been waiting half the night."

"We were delayed."

"Graves, eh?"

"You know?"

"Half the village knows. They're not dumb. They just play dumb."

"You mean, they've known about Graves and his group?" Sean questioned.

"Just one of those island secrets that they've lived with for years. Unspoken is unseen here. And that which is unseen does not exist."

"How do they keep such a thing under cover for so long?"

"They don't anymore, Sean," Leah replied. Her voice cracked as she got up from the table and walked over to the stove. "Like some tea? You must be cold. It'll warm you. Tea's always comforting when..," Leah started to cry. Kate hugged her.

"What is it, Leah?"

"I thought you'd have sensed it . . . he's gone!"

Kate placed her head on Leah's shoulder and whispered, "Father Andre."

"Yes."

Sean rose and put is arms around the two sobbing women.

"Daggett's men?"

"I think so," Leah replied between sobs, "They said it was an accident. I told him where you were. After he delivered his sermon today about the 'passing', he rented a small boat to find you on Garden. First, they said that the boat foundered upon on a reef and capsized. But the seas were calm, and there's no reef that could shatter a boat with such a shallow draft into a hundred pieces. Now the Coast Guard has attributed the accident to a faulty gas tank which exploded."

"Who did he rent the boat from?" Sean queried.

"Padraig . . . Padraig O'Donnell."

Sean paced to the window overlooking the dunes and down to the black lake. Padraig, the Ulster bomber, had not lost his touch, he thought. Andre had violated the island code of silence. Now he was permanently silenced. He had found the resting place for which Protar had so longed been denied. Sean pressed his tear soaked face against the glass. Andre had been a true friend. He had told the truth.

Kate gently pulled Sean from the window and whispered to him softly.

"He'll be back. He delivered the sermon. He set the stage for us. Now we need to make sure that it happens."

"What happens? I can't see that far ahead. Can you?"

"Not ahead, no. But you need to trust that you'll know what to do. The table has been set for our visitors."

Sean rose and paced the floor in front of the window, open to the wide black lake. He heard the call of loons in the distance. The sound grew closer. He had never heard so many plaintive cries at one time.

"Leah, I haven't heard that wail before. Have you?"

Leah opened the front door and listened. "Nor have I. Strange. And so many. There must dozens of them out there. It's magnificent . . . simply divine!"

"But the wail, Leah," Sean asked anxiously, "What does it mean?"

"You don't have to ask, Sean," Kate spoke impassively, "Listen to your heart."

Sean gazed upward into the star studded sky. Occasionally, he could see flickers of white darting among the stars. Loons dancing with stars. He closed his eyes and listened intently for several minutes. He sensed that he was flying on the wings of loons.

"Leah," Sean finally spoke, "Can Harv get you into Holy Cross Church?"

"Why, I guess so. He's got the keys for the historical society meetings. Why?"

"I want him to ring the bells one hour before dawn. I want every one on the island to hear them. I want them down at the docks to see the loons."

"How do you know they'll come?"

"The loons. They'll come to see God's gift to them. They'll come to see the loons." Sean raised his arms toward the horizon where black lake met black sky, where the flash of white waves met the flash of the stars. The loons kept coming.

Chapter XXVIII
The Reckoning

The bells of Holy Cross rang clear and strong through the crisp early morning air. They could be heard across the length and breadth of the island. They roused islanders from their sleep as far away as the South Head Light along Iron Ore Bay. But only islanders heard the alarm. While yachters rocked silently in their berths and campers rested soundly in their down sleeping bags, the islanders from Arranmore awoke to the resounding ringing of Holy Cross. The great bells, cast in Dublin, had only been rung this early in the morning but once before. The occasion had been Protar's death. And they kept ringing, their sound reverberating in the deep birch forests, across the bogs, along the dune ridges and beyond into the blackness of the big lake. They beckoned the fisherman near Hog Island to raise anchor and head for home. The descendants of Arranmore, responding to some ancient pull, understood the call. They arose from their beds, left their homes and traveled to the village to gather along the wharves and sidewalks and beaches of St. James.

Sean, Lily, and Leah had already arrived at the ferry dock to watch as dusty trucks, jeeps, and cars poured into the village, headlights streaming like the fires of St. John's Eve. They rolled down past Holy Cross and onto Main Street until the traffic snarled in gridlock. Passengers emerged in animated chatter. Questions abounded amid the chaos. Deputy McCullough's Jeep with its flashing lights could be seen near Whiskey Point trying to make its way through the gridlock. Sean caught sight of Captain Walt. He was dressed in an old Mackinac, open to pajamas underneath. He weaved his way through the crowd from the Mormon Print Shop. People were shouting at him. Questions abounded. Had a freighter run aground? Why had the electricity gone out? Who was ringing the bells? Captain Walt was trying to calm them down, but he had no answers to offer. Speculation ran rampant.

At the boat launch near the municipal wharf Sean could see Tommy Gallagher and Graves gathered with their Irish exiles, huddled together in rapt conversation. Several families had gathered on the public beach as children began to play on the swings and monkeybars. A small group of elderly Christian Brothers, led by Brother Kevin, threaded their way silently through the crowds. It was pandemonium.

A solitary loon had landed in the middle of the harbor. It was flapping its wings and shrieking at the stars. Soon, another landed, sliding across the still surface, taking up the wail. Then, flocks streamed across the sky, circled, and cried to the pair below. The circle of loons in flight grew larger and larger with flock after flock arriving to join the swirling vortex overhead. It seemed a tornado of loons. Their wails crescendoed as group after group joined the throng. The flapping of their wings silenced the chatter of the crowds below. Children stopped playing at the public beach. The crowds ceased their aimless roaming. They moved in mass toward the edges of the bay and poured out onto the docks, transfixed by the wonder of so many loons. The white necks of the birds flashed by the hundreds in the sky as the beam of the harbor light turned to illuminate them on each sweep across the bay. The entire bay was now encircled by the loons. Nothing could be heard above their cry. Even the bells of Holy Cross were silenced.

As the first glow of morning sun spread across the horizon of the lake, the loons began to descend and splash down on the glassy bay. The sky rained loons. Wave after wave landed until the harbor rippled with their bobbing heads. The flotillas merged near the center of the bay and then spread in a broad arc from one side of the harbor to another. Then, their wailing stopped, almost in unison. A dense fog bank in the distance rolled toward the entrance to the harbor. The rising sun illuminated the fog with a sparkling iridescence.

Leah clutched Sean's hand and gasped in disbelief, "There can't be this many loons in all of God's creation!"

"Yes," Sean replied calmly. He gazed out over the phalanx of loons. "They've been gathering for weeks now."

"Look!" Kate pointed toward Whiskey Point. A large Indian war canoe with a solitary figure emerged from the edge of the fog bank. "It's White Fox!"

"He comes on the breath of God," Sean whispered as he placed his arms around the two women.

As the mist enveloped the harbor, the crowd drew restless. The dark blue sky above them finally disappeared. A fog horn sounded. The fog hovered like a golden cloud just above the water. The crowd strained to see three large shadows in the distance. They could hear the harbor buoys clang as the shadows moved ponderously around the Point.

"Seems like we're all marooned now, Connaghan," a voice from behind Sean said.

Sean did not turn to meet the voice. "We've always been marooned, Graves."

The shadows began to emerge into view. A bow sprint split the mist. A graceful wooden dolphin adorned her. Soon the full view of a huge Schooner appeared. She moved forward without a breath of air in her limp sails. Her hull creaked and groaned. Two other similar ships followed in her wake. When they neared the phalanx of loons, each dropped anchor.

Sean boarded the Beaver Islander with Kate, ascended the stairs to the wheelhouse and switched on its loudspeaker. His voice boomed across the Bay.

"The words of Saint Patrick are yours this early morn.

I see his blood upon the rose
And in the stars the glory of his eyes,
His body gleams amid eternal snows,
His tears fall from the skies.
I see his face in every flower:
The thunder and the singing of the birds
Are but his voice—and carven by his power
Rocks are his written words.
All pathways by his feet are worn,
His strong heart stirs the ever-beating sea,
His crown of thorns is twined with every thorn,
His cross is every tree."

Sean stepped from the wheelhouse and walked purposefully along the starboard deck to the stern of the old ferry. He could see Whitesides. But he was now Waugoosh, the Fox, sitting erect in his canoe with a long paddle resting across his legs. The canoe was stationed between the phalanx of loons and the three ghostly ships. His hair was drawn tightly back revealing a strong, stern face. It was streaked with red and blue paint. A red cross cut across his forehead and a silver ring hung from his nose. Two loon feathers crowned his head. As their eyes made contact, Sean lowered his head. Waugoosh rose from his seat and stood tall, clutching his paddle in one raised hand.

"Kewaygeshick! Kewaygeshick ishpiming!"

Waugoosh lowered his paddle and swept it in a slow broad arc across the water.

"Gitchi Manitou! Jibam!"

Kate and Sean whispered the words together as a prayer. "Homeward bound to the spirit land in the West. Great Spirit awake."

Sean placed his arm around Kate's shoulder. "Ettawageshik."

"Yes," she replied, "Both sides of the sky are now one."

Near the shallows, along the length of the shore, steam erupted in small geysers. One. Two. Then dozens. Near the public beach. Between the wharves. At the boat landing. Each geyser encircled a small form. As the steam rose and dissipated in the cool air, the forms were revealed as children. Boys and girls dressed in clothes from the past and present. The faces of the children were smiling as if they had just dove off the docks on a summer afternoon. They turned toward the shore and gazed upon the huddled masses straining to recognize them.

"Oh, sweet Jesus," Mary O'Donnell screamed, "It's Shannon . . . my baby . . . she's alive! My baby's out there. Shannon!" Mary cupped her hands and called out, "Over here!"

But Mary's voice was muffled by the shouts of a hundred others. Grandfathers, grandmothers, fathers and mothers, uncles and aunts, cousins and friends yelled and sobbed and screamed in a strange cacophony of joy and desperation. Some rushed into the water toward the children, splashing in a vain effort to get their attention. But the children only waved, smiled, and then turned to walk or swim toward the ships in the harbor. They were met by flocks of loons who surrounded them. The loons cooed softly as they buoyed each young body through the water on a feathery cushion to their destination.

Near the boat landing Sean observed Jack Daggett screaming at the small band of Irish exiles as he and Padraig waded into the shallows. Kate nudged Sean and pointed to a place several boat lengths in front of Daggett. It was Annie! She was swimming toward the loons. Daggett jumped into the water and launched into powerful strokes. He shouted at Annie as he swam. Padraig followed close behind. As Annie was lifted by the loons to float gently toward the waiting ships, Daggett hesitated in the water as the wall of loons closed behind the retreating flotilla. He yelled one last time toward Annie. She did not hear him. Then he swam furiously toward the loon wall. The loons retreated, cawing furiously at him as he splashed toward them. But Daggett did not heed the warning as he sped forward. The loons encircled him. He spun around in the water and lashed out, grabbing one loon and breaking her neck with a powerful twist. Padraig joined in, lunging to grasp and kill. They exhausted themselves in a frenzy of killing until Daggett felt his legs go limp as he was being pulled under. He screamed for Padraig. But Padraig had disappeared beneath the surface. Bubbles gurgled up from the depths around the floating carcasses of dead loons. Daggett struggled to keep his head above the surface, gasping for air. But the loons carried him downward, downward into the murky depths. It was a message to those in the shallows not to follow.

The children climbed the nets which draped the hulls of the schooners. They laughed and sang as they climbed. It was a reunion of kindred spirits. Aboard they lingered near the rails and waved to the crowds on the beach. The people gathered together with arms around each other, tears in their eyes, and waved back. Sorrow gave way to a quiet reconciliation. They sensed that the loss was not really a loss at all, but a resolution which brought peace in the heart.

Sean looked down from the stern. Whiteside's canoe had paddled alongside. Kate was climbing in it from the wharf ladder.

"Kate!" he shouted down. "Why now?"

"It's Eliza now. The time has come to leave."

"But we haven't had time to share...we haven't even..."

"Yes, we have Sean," she said as she blew a kiss and pointed to the ships, "We've shared all there is to know. Keep it in your heart, along with my love."

"Kah-wam-da-meh, Seanaghan!" Whitesides shouted.

"Kah-wam-da-meh, Waugoosh!" Sean replied.

"What does it mean?" a voice from behind asked.

Sean turned to meet Lily's gaze, as Kate yelled from the canoe. "And take care of Lily. She's one of us."

Sean smiled at Lily and grasped her hand. "It means 'we see each other'. Just as I see you now as a friend who I really understand for the first time."

"And I you." Lily replied as she kissed him on the cheek.

The fog was beginning to lift as the three ships lifted anchor. Sean thought he caught sight of Father Andre waving to him from the stern of one vessel. A favorable breeze began to blow from the West. It filled the sails as they rounded Whiskey Point. The flutter of loon wings filled the harbor as flocks followed in the wakes of the schooners, soaring above their masts toward the horizon.

"Where do you think they're going, Sean?"

"Home."

"And where's that?"

"Wherever the loons lead them."

"Maybe to Hy Brazil?"

Sean smiled at Lily as he pulled a Petoskey stone from his pocket. "I believe so."

He turned it over several times before he hurled it into the water. It skipped across the surface several times. "Do you know what Petoskey means in Chippewa?"

"No."

"It means 'Light Coming at You'."

The ships with their precious cargo were now a faint glimmer against the rising sun. They disappeared into the golden orb in a flash of consuming light.

Postscript

Every year on a midsummer's eve during Museum Week an audience gathers with their lawn chairs in front of the old Mormon Print Shop for a traditional island "house party". "Music on the Porch" features island musicians, songsters, homespun poets, dancing, and the community choir. If one occasions a visit, choose this event. It is a celebration of the Island spirit and of a camaraderie that still binds old and new to the heritage of this "Brigadoon of the Lake." As the sun sets over the harbor, it has become traditional for the mistress of ceremonies to ask the audience to rise, face the harbor, and give a round of applause for Paradise Bay. It is homage to beauty and nature and the people who seek to preserve a way of life that is quickly vanishing throughout America. One can only hope that the Great Manitou hears the applause echoing across the Lake and smiles.

Author's Note

West to Donegal Bay is a work of the imagination inspired by historical events. As with all works of fiction, I have taken license to embellish, exaggerate, and modify. Many of the Irish settlers of Beaver Island came from Arranmore Island off the coast of County Donegal, not the Aran Islands in Galway Bay. Many Beaver Islanders still maintain strong bonds with their "cousins" in Arranmore, exchanging visits in an effort to revive the kinship of years ago. Although many island surnames are reflected in this novel, the characters are fictional and do not represent actual individuals.

The Mormon experience on Beaver Island has been the subject of differing historical interpretations by writers for the last 150 years. Those interested in this history are advised to consult the many histories written on the subject. Many consider the work of Milo M. Quaife, *The Kingdom of Saint James: A Narrative of the Mormons* (New Haven, 1930) to be an authoritative source because Quaife interviewed several original Strangites. O.W. Riegel's *Crown of Glory* (New Haven: Yale University Press, 1935) has been criticized by Strangite Mormons for unfair characterizations of James Strang, invented statements, and anti-Mormon sentiment. Doyle Fitzpatrick's *The King James Story* (Lansing, Michigan: National Heritage, 1970) treats Strang and his followers as historical figures, avoiding religious characterizations. Roger Van Noord's *King of Beaver Island: The Life and Assassination of James Jesse Strang* (Chicago: University of Illinois Press, 1941) also contributes to this body of knowledge. Vickie Cleverley Speek's account *"God Has Made Us a Kingdom": James Strang and the Midwest Mormons* (Signature Books: Salt Lake City, 2006) represents in this author's view the most comprehensive and conscientious effort to capture original source material and portray the Strang period in an objective, albeit sympathetic, light. I am indebted to these authors for their scholarship and insights into a fascinating period of American history.

No rendering of Beaver Island history would be complete without reference to the contributions, traditions, and spirit of the Odawa and Chippewa, the people of the Little Traverse Band. Their ancestors probably occupied island land extending back thousands of years. They survived the coming of the French, British, and Americans without surrendering their culture. The sacred pipe and drum remains on the Island. Their spirit pervades tribal legends, language, and the burial places on Garden Island. George "Skip" Duhamel continues to fish the waters surrounding the archipelago. He crafts exquisite totem poles of island wood. Andrew J. Blackbird, Ray Kiogima, and Constance Cappel's book, *Odawa Language and Legend* (Xlibris, 2006), provides an excellent introduction to the rich Odawa tradition. George Cleland's work, *Rites of Conquest: the History and Culture of Michigan's Native Americans* (University of Michigan Press: Ann Arbor, 1992), applies an ethnohistorical perspective to chronicling Native American history in the Great Lakes region. I am particularly indebted to the Honorable George A. Anthony, Appellate Court Justice, Little Traverse Band, for his instructive book on the history of the Beaver Island Native Americans, *The Elders Speak: Reflections on Native American Life Centering on Beaver Island, Michigan, in the Nineteenth and Twentieth Centuries* (Beaver Island Historical Society: Beaver Island, 2009). Anyone interested in an accurate report of the history and traditions of the original Beaver Island peoples should consult this remarkable work, which represents over forty years of recorded interviews with tribal leaders knowledgeable about Native American culture on the islands. I apologize if any license taken with characterizations of this ancient culture may be inaccurate or unfounded. I have endeavored to honor this heritage, as all Americans should. May the ancient spirit of the Odawa & Chippewa endure on Beaver Island and inform our understanding and preservation of its beauty and meaning.

I am most grateful for the continuing devotion of the Beaver Island Historical Society in preserving Island history. I first became acquainted with this history over twenty five years ago when I read one of the many volumes of *The Journal of Beaver Island History*. The authors of the journals' essays (archeologists, historians, educators, poets, artists, musicians, biologists, and Island sages) have given unselfishly of their time and talent to preserve a rich history for future generations. William Cashman, the journal's original project director and present director of the Beaver Island Historical Society, deserves considerable credit for sustaining this initiative and founding the Society for Strang Studies. As an outstanding writer, he provided invaluable editorial advice in reading my first draft.

In ways that they may not fully realize, many islanders and summer residents have provided valuable insights into island culture over the years. Their kindness and hospitality, is a source of solace, humor, and inspiration in the happy and the trying times. Special thanks to the Lamers, Neihauses, McDonoughs, Carys, Martins, Specks, Wojans, Olneys, Cashmans, Mestelles, Olsons, LaFrenieres, Gillespies, Duhamels, Lounsberrys, Cains, and Mary Stewert Rose. So many more deserve my thanks.

Our mainland home is Wake Forest University in Winston-Salem, North Carolina. It too is a mystical place of discovery and imagination whose faculty, staff, and students form a close and unique community of higher education. It has preserved its religious heritage while advancing academic freedom in ways that few private universities have. Several friends there have endured my ramblings about Beaver Island and reviewed my drafts with patience and good humor. I am especially grateful to Drs. Edwin Wilson, Mary Gerardy, Michael Hyde, Reid Morgan, Leon Corbett and novelist Julie Zimmerman. My exceptionally able and congenial assistant, Ms. Marie Teague, labored over successive drafts with a buoyant and forgiving spirit. Students over the years have also touched me in ways that inform the character of Sean Connaghan. Jessica Cannon, a talented Ph.D. candidate in American History at Rice University helped immeasurably in that regard.

Most importantly, there is my family. My mother, Dorothy Fox Zick cultivated the love of literature and history that lives within me to this day. My beloved wife, Pamela, the true artist in the family, has been the source of trust and inspiration that has moved this project forward. A former English teacher, her editing skills were invaluable. The idea for this book began as romanticized stories for our children, David and Leigh, while the family summered on the island. Their enthusiasm and encouragement, as each chapter unfolded, assured its completion.

Finally, there is the haunting mystery of Beaver Island and the fragile nature of its future. Islands have always stimulated the imagination. They are places which exist apart from the mainland. They are defined by their apartness. One must face the broad horizon of sea and sky to reach them. Islands arise out of the mist as a dream or apparition. People who live on islands often define themselves in terms of this difference. Crossing to the mainland is referred to as "going over," as if the crossing were an unnatural act or a betrayal of a way of life. Island visitors go to escape, to reflect upon their destiny, or simply forget. Islands pull one inward to self and away from the incessant race of modern turmoil.

Because island cultures often elude a visitor's understanding, we are drawn to them. Beaver Island is a place where past, present, and future mingle in a strange and mystical embrace. If we are to save our islands as places of spiritual renewal, apart from the ravages of modern life, we must understand the power of their splendid isolation. We must learn to appreciate their magnificent capacity to inspire thought about who we are, were, and hope to be.

Made in the USA
Charleston, SC
29 March 2010